Praise for

'A writer who has created a world of her own – a world claustrophobic and irrational which we enter each time with a sense of personal danger … Miss Highsmith is the poet of apprehension' **GRAHAM GREENE**

'Highsmith is a giant of the genre. The original, the best, the gloriously twisted Queen of Suspense' **MARK BILLINGHAM**

'One thinks of comparing Miss Highsmith only with herself; by any other standard of comparison, one must simply cheer' **AUBERON WAUGH**

'Highsmith was every bit as deviant and quirky as her mischievous heroes, and didn't seem to mind if everyone knew it' **J. G. BALLARD**, *DAILY TELEGRAPH*

'My suspicion is that when the dust has settled and when the chronicle of twentieth-century American literature comes to be written, history will place Highsmith at the top of the pyramid, as we should place Dostoevsky at the top of the Russian hierarchy of novelists' **A. N. WILSON**, *DAILY TELEGRAPH*

'One of the greatest modernist writers' **GORE VIDAL**

'One closes most of her books with a feeling that the world is more dangerous than one had ever imagined' **JULIAN SYMONS**, *NEW YORK TIMES BOOK REVIEW*

'For eliciting the menace that lurks in familiar surroundings, there's no one like Patricia Highsmith' *TIME*

VIRAGO
MODERN CLASSICS
626

© Jerry Bauer

Patricia Highsmith (1921–1995) was born in Fort Worth, Texas, and moved to New York when she was six, where she attended the Julia Richman High School and Barnard College. In her senior year she edited the college magazine, having decided at the age of sixteen to become a writer. Her first novel, *Strangers on a Train*, was made into a classic film by Alfred Hitchcock in 1951. *The Talented Mr Ripley*, published in 1955, introduced the fascinating anti-hero Tom Ripley, and was made into an Oscar-winning film in 1999 by Anthony Minghella. Graham Greene called Patricia Highsmith 'the poet of apprehension', saying that she 'created a world of her own – a world claustrophobic and irrational which we enter each time with a sense of personal danger', and *The Times* named her no.1 in their list of the greatest ever crime writers. Patricia Highsmith died in Locarno, Switzerland, in February 1995. Her last novel, *Small g: A Summer Idyll*, was published posthumously, the same year.

THOSE WHO
WALK AWAY

Patricia Highsmith

Introduced by Joan Schenkar

virago

VIRAGO

This paperback edition published in 2014 by Virago Press
First published in Great Britain in 1967 by William Heinemann Ltd

Copyright © Patricia Highsmith, 1967
Introduction copyright © Joan Schenkar, 2014

The moral right of the author has been asserted

A CIP catalogue record for this book
is available from the British Library.

ISBN 978-0-349-00486-0

Typeset in Goudy by M Rules
Printed and bound in Great Britain by
Clays Ltd, St Ives plc

Papers used by Virago are from well-managed forests
and other responsible sources.

MIX
Paper from
responsible sources
FSC® C104740
www.fsc.org

Virago Press
An imprint of
Little, Brown Book Group
100 Victoria Embankment
London EC4Y 0DY

An Hachette UK Company
www.hachette.co.uk

www.virago.co.uk

To Lil Picard, painter and writer, and
one of my more inspiring friends

INTRODUCTION

2.30 A.M. My New Year's Toast: to all the devils, lusts, passions, greeds, envies, loves, hates, strange desires, enemies ghostly and real, the army of memories, with which I do battle – may they never give me peace.

Patricia Highsmith, 1947

Well, she's back.

Just when we thought she'd settled down to a quiet Afterlife, too.

But here she comes, The Dark Lady of American Letters, frowning and smiling and blowing her smoke rings of misdirection at us through the slow, insidious pull of her novels on the gravitational field of modern fiction.

She's back and she's putting the frighteners on again.

Oh, it's Patricia Highsmith all right. I'd know those cloven hoofprints anywhere. She sidles into your sentences, hacks your *aperçus*, drunk-dials your dreams. Scatters her props and propensities all over your imagination, then shatters your sense of self with her secret plans for sharing: 'What I predicted I would once do, I am already doing[;] that is, showing the unequivocal triumph of evil over good, and rejoicing in it. I shall make my readers rejoice in it, too.'

Here are her maps, her charts, her obsessive little lists. Her art-loving psychopaths and lovesick stalkers. The minds marred by murder, the ambitions cleft by failure. The ice-cold blondes, the amnesiac alter egos. The beer-stained, tear-stained love notes on napkins. The traces of blood at the corner of her smile.

An outsider artist of gravelled gifts, savage talents and obsessional interests, Mary Patricia Highsmith (1921–1995) wrote some of the darkest, most delinquently original novels of the twentieth century. She is responsible for inserting an adjective ('Highsmithian'), a proper name ('Tom Ripley'), and a phrase ('strangers on a train') into the language, but her best books are still corralled in categories which cannot account for their depth, their dazzle or their direct attack on her readers.

'Crime' and 'suspense' are the classifications to which her work is most often relegated, but her novels and short stories splay across genres, interrogate genders, disrupt the idea of character and offer the most thorough anatomy of guilt in modern literature. Patricia Highsmith isn't a crime writer, she's a *punishment* writer.

Born in her grandmother's boarding house in Fort Worth, Texas, rooted in her family's unreconstructed Confederate past, raised in Greenwich Village when it was 'the freest four square miles on earth', Pat Highsmith was a paradox from birth. She was both 'legitimate' and 'born out of wedlock' nine days after her artist mother divorced her illustrator father. She grew into her contradictions.

High art was always her goal, but in the 1940s she had a secret seven-year career as the only woman scriptwriter for Superhero comics.* Proustian in her innumerable love affairs and desired by many, she brought a headsman's axe to all her relationships. She

* It was Pat's anonymous writing for comic-book superheroes and their mild-mannered second selves that gave her an early (and unacknowledged) opportunity to explore her affinity with alter egos and double identities. 'My obsession with duality saves me from a great many other obsessions,' is how she put it.

'worshipped' women, preferred the company of men and cloaked her narrative voice in another (but not exactly opposite) gender. She is as unconscious a 'gay male novelist' as Ernest Hemingway, and as gifted an anatomist of male sexual anxiety as Norman Mailer. Murder was always on her mind, and she usually confused it with love.

'Murder,' she wrote, 'is a kind of making love, a kind of possessing,' and nearly every Highsmith novel is organised around the reverberant psychologies of a homicide. Although love was her lighthouse and she lived for its illuminations, she couldn't live *with* it. So she killed for it over and over again in her writing. A Freudian in spite of herself, she murdered her fictional victims at Greenwich Village addresses where she made love in life.

At twelve, Pat knew she was 'a boy born in a girl's body'. At sixteen, writing was for what she *wished* would happen: she turned her urge to steal a book into a short story about a girl who steals a book. 'Every artist,' she said, 'is in business for his health.' At twenty-one, her focus was fixed: 'Obsessions are the only things that matter. Perversion interests me most and is my guiding darkness.'

Her turbulent love–hate relationship with her erratic mother sundered her psychology and spawned all the Noir bitches in her writing and most of the heartbroken blondes in her bed. Her sentiments for her mild-mannered stepfather were simpler: she wanted to kill him and said so. She grew up to occupy both sides of every question.

In adolescence, Pat began 'double-booking' herself with *cahiers* (notebooks) for her novels, short stories and essays, and with diaries for her love affairs with the beautiful, intelligent women who were her Muses – and the few good men who were not. These lifelong journals – like conjoined twins arising from the vapours of her youthful fascination with doubling – embezzled each other's materials, rehearsed her obsessions before she published them, and gave her the opportunity to renew her vows to the only lasting love match she ever made: the union that joined her intense rushes of feeling with her compelling need to commit them to paper.

At twenty-nine, she published her sensational debut novel, *Strangers on a Train* (1950). The 'deal' at its dark heart – an anonymous exchange of homicides – set up the quintessential Highsmith situation: two men bound together by the stalker-like fixation of one upon the other; a fixation which always involves a murderous, implicitly homoerotic fantasy.* *The Price of Salt* followed in 1952, and its richly figured language borrowed elements from *Strangers* and subdued them to the subject of requited lesbian love – the only 'crime' Pat left out of her other fictions. Published anonymously for forty years, *The Price of Salt* (now reissued as *Carol*) sold hundreds of thousands of copies and made its author uneasy all her life.

Highsmith's industry was staggering. Five to seven neatly typed pages of finished fiction rolled from the platen of her coffee-coloured 1956 Olympia Deluxe portable typewriter each day, followed by book themes, articles, lists of every description, short-story ideas, and four or five personal letters in her oddly impersonal prose. Her thirty-eight writer's notebooks and eighteen diaries were written in five languages, four of which she didn't actually speak. She drew, she sketched, she painted; she made sculptures, furniture and woodcarvings. The simple savageries of gardening – who lives? who goes to the compost pile? – appealed to her American Calvinism, and she took up her secateurs with a will.

Out of her great divide (and in the acid bath of her detail-saturated prose), Patricia Highsmith developed a remarkable

---

* Alfred Hitchcock's wonderful (if skewed towards normality) film version of *Strangers on a Train* (1951) revived his directing career. Raymond Chandler, on the other hand, said that working on the film script drove him crazy.

image of an alternate Earth: Highsmith Country. Its shadow cabinet of homicidal alter egos, displaced guilts, and unstable identities convenes in permanent session in the Nightmare Alley just behind the American Dream. And the deep psychological partitions its citizens suffer (as they count up their culpabilities or slip into measurable degrees of madness) come from its author's unblinking examination of her own wayward tastes:

> I can't think of anything more apt to set the imagination stirring, drifting, creating, than the idea – the fact – that anyone you walk past on the pavement anywhere may be a sadist, a compulsive thief, or even a murderer.

Pat's Suffolk period was the first creatively settled interval in her long, strange European expatriation. And England was ready for her. She had loyal English publishers and agents. Francis Wyndham's crucial survey of her dark materials (part of an extended review of *The Cry of the Owl* in the *New Statesman* in 1963) had provided the public with an elegant introduction to her work: '[T]he reader's sense of satisfaction,' he wrote, 'may derive from sources as dark as those which motivate Patricia Highsmith's destroyers and their fascinated victims.' London-associated writers as diversely distinguished as Julian Symons, Brigid Brophy, Graham Greene, Arthur Koestler, Sybil Bedford, and Muriel Spark admired her writing.* And *The Two Faces of January* (1964) would win the CWA's Silver Dagger Award in 1965.

But it was love alone – and in a magnitude she hadn't yet experienced – that brought the talented Miss Highsmith to Suffolk. In late 1962, domiciled in America, but travelling widely

---

* Muriel Spark adopted Highsmith's favourite cat, Spider, the dedicatee of *The Glass Cell*, when Highsmith moved to England from Italy. Spider, Dame Muriel said, 'brought a bit of Patricia Highsmith with him'.

and restlessly, Pat fell in love ('like being shot in the face', is what she said – still mixing up love and murder) with a cultured, attractive, solidly married Londoner. Obsessed by this woman 'as never before' and so 'killed by pleasure' that she couldn't continue the novel she'd started about a good man wrongly imprisoned (*The Glass Cell*), Pat 'cleared her complicated decks' in America and made her way to Europe and thence to Suffolk, to be nearer (if not closer) to love's inspiring shocks.

Stalking her London romance – but keeping her distance from it, too – Pat wrote most of *The Glass Cell* (1964) in Positano and Rome, and then revised the manuscript extensively in Aldeburgh. Finally, in 1964, she settled in Earl Soham in Suffolk in what had been two country cottages, now knocked together as one dwelling: Bridge Cottage.

The double structure of Bridge Cottage suited her psychology as much as the ambiguities of a love affair with someone else's wife suited her temperament. Lush productivity and plain prose were the results, punctuated by an invigorating volley of complaints. English weather, 'dreary' English pubs and too-infrequent meetings with her English lover encouraged her natural negativity, but only an English Christmas could raise it to the level of simile: 'The holidays here exhaust one, creeping through closed windows like a poisonous gas,' she wrote, sounding just like a Highsmith character.

In fact, Pat was having a better time in Suffolk than she admitted. Enlivened by her new surroundings, she very quickly began to write *A Suspension of Mercy* (1965), and then found a collaborator with whom to plot out a possible television script. She made fast friends with Ronald Blythe, at work on his Suffolk book *Akenfield*, and they gossiped for hours and toured the Suffolk churches. And James Hamilton-Paterson, future author of *Gerontius* and *Cooking with Fernet Branca*, won her heart by walking out on her when she burst into tears. 'I don't blame him,' said Pat, who would have done the same thing herself, 'give him my love.'

Although each of the three novels Pat completed during her Suffolk period was set in a different place (New York, Suffolk, Venice), Highsmith Country is their one, true home.* The first of them, *The Glass Cell*, was sourced from Pat's detailed correspondence with an American convict who wrote to tell her how much he'd enjoyed *Deep Water*. ('I don't think my books should be in prison libraries,' said Pat – and made the convict give her the particulars of prison life.) As always, she followed her unruly feelings in reversing her new novel's line of logic. Philip Carter is a classic Highsmith 'criminal-hero' – with his orphan background and professional training; his high culture and low behaviour; his sluggish libido and ambiguous affections. In *The Glass Cell*, his punishment has been enacted *before* he commits a crime. He is unjustly accused, wrongly imprisoned, physically tortured, and entirely innocent.

Philip Carter and his prison mate Max (a forger who dies in a prison riot) approach intimacy and practise French, and Max seems 'more real' to Carter than his own wife. Carter reads Swift, Voltaire and Robbe-Grillet (and keeps the complete Verlaine in his cell), murders his wife's lover when he's released (guiltlessly and with a piece of classical statuary), and weeps while listening to Bach. He lies to everyone, forces 'guilt' and 'innocence' to change places and exchange definitions, and knows the police will follow him for ever. Still, murder has made his life better: 'Everything was going to be all right now,' he thinks.

---

* Tom Ripley, the 'criminal-hero' of Pat's best-known work *The Talented Mr Ripley* (1955), is Highsmith Country's most prominent ambassador. A socially sinuous, fragilely gendered serial killer, forger, fraudster, and identity impersonator, he is also Highsmith's darker emissary to herself; her *semblable*. It was Ripley, Pat said disconcertingly, who wrote that novel; she was merely taking dictation. And she added Ripley's name to her Edgar Allan Poe award.

But in *The Glass Cell*, the push-broom of Pat's paragraphs sweeps the detritus of confinement steadily before it, trailing strings of objects or mundane actions or simple thoughts in a dogged accumulation of detail as dispassionate as that found in most prisons – or most pornographies. Her gut-punch prose – she's the court recorder here, not the judge, but her style (as spare as a prison bunk) is convincingly mimetic – suggests that Carter has carried his private incarceration (his 'glass cell') into the world with him. The world is his prison now, nor is he out of it.

Nothing if not practical, Pat liked to furnish her houses of fiction with the large and small irritants of her daily life. In *A Suspension of Mercy*, the only novel she both wrote and set in Suffolk, she used her circumstances to make a work at war with itself – a comedy of terrors – and lent her 'criminal-hero' more of her own qualities than even she imagined.

Sydney Smith Bartleby, a young American novelist displaced to Suffolk by his upwardly mobile English marriage, is beginning to chafe. He's in a situation not unlike his author's – and he's burdened with most of her local irritations, too: a collaborator on a television script; a frustrated desire to see a body carried out in a carpet (a gambit Pat considered for other works and parodied in this one by leaving the body *out* of the carpet); a partner in absentia (Sydney's would-be painter wife is taking a holiday from their marriage and its meannesses); some difficult writing to get on with; and an imagination unable to refrain from replacing the dullish realities of his life with the homicidal narratives he wants for his work.

Sydney's names, yoked together by violence, are clipped directly from the baptismal rolls of Highsmith Country. 'Sydney Smith' was the wit, writer and clergyman on whom Jane Austen is said to have based the attractive protagonist of her Gothic satire *Northanger Abbey* – while 'Sir Sydney Smith' was Edinburgh's renowned forensic expert on methods of murder. And 'Bartleby' is Herman Melville's inscrutably persistent Wall Street scrivener. The ways in which Pat uses *A Suspension of Mercy* to juggle these contradictions and toy with the conventions of crime and suspense are both experimental *and* satirical – though the smiles are properly constrained and the laughter suitably stifled.

As Sydney relaxes his ability to distinguish between the fantasies he's staging in his head and what he'd really like to do about his absent spouse, he begins to rehearse the actions, the feelings, and the false identity of a guilty wife-killer; falling under suspicion for his wife's murder after she disappears. In the course of his games, the principles of Highsmith Country, greatly exhilarated by his masquerades, come out to play: deeds before motives, effects before causes, punishments before crimes – and Sydney unintentionally frightens a suspicious neighbour to death, then languidly commits a murder which is both there and not there.

For this ostensible murder – and for his accidental one, too – Sydney feels no guilt. He looks forward to recording what he's just lived through in his writer's notebook. It's a brown notebook, we are told quietly; the same colour as the writer's notebooks Patricia Highsmith used all her life.

Strictly speaking, there is no homicide in Pat's third Suffolk novel, *Those Who Walk Away* (1967). Once again, a murder is there, and not there – and Pat began to imagine the novel's rapid reversals and deep disruptive shocks late in 1966 on a trip to Venice: a city whose end-stopped streets and serpentine canals might have been designed for the psychological volutes of a Highsmith novel.

Pat's first intention for *Those Who Walk Away* sounds like something out of *Sunset Boulevard*: 'A suspense novel from the point of view of the corpse'. But the suicide of the painter Peggy Garrett, wife and daughter, respectively, of the two male protagonists (one of whom, an artist, blames the other, a gallerist, for her death), pre-dates the novel's first page, pervades the work, and tries to pass itself off as the trigger for the purest expression yet of Highsmith Country's 'infinite progression of the trapped and the hunted'.

The dead woman's husband, Ray Garrett, is pursued by Ed Coleman, the vengeful painter who is her father. Ray starts a game of hide and seek with his potential murderer, chasing his own death by following Ed to Venice after Ed tries to shoot him in Rome. Filled with the inspiration of art and artists, Ray seeks what all Highsmith males look for: total oblivion through the dissolution of his burdensome identity.

Just like wrestlers unable to leave the mat, Ray Garrett and his father-in-law try out different holds and postures on each other, different ways of winning and losing, different means of being brutal and being passive. But there is no death in Venice, and Ray and Ed are both caught in the mantrap Highsmith's imagination first sprang in *Strangers on a Train* – and then prised open again in *The Talented Mr Ripley* (1955).

In *Those Who Walk Away*, Pat Highsmith, always a little more frightening than any of her characters, imagines a 'reality' built around the *whole* of the hunt: the hunter, the hunted, their constant exchange of roles, and the terrible necessity of the pursuit itself. Someone as creatively caught up with hunting as Pat was could never choose the hunter over the hunted – or vice versa. Hence her constant shifting of roles and shuffling of identities: a compellingly forceful premise in her fictions – and a cruelly exhausting one in her life.

With her usual discipline, Pat continued to write in Suffolk as her London relationship slowly, then rapidly, declined. She began 'a religious television play' based on a Jesus-like character – and put it to perverse use as a frame for *Ripley Under Ground* (1970). She finished her second snail story, 'The Quest for Blank Claveringii', wrote a 'ghost' tale, 'The Yuma Baby', and in a single month completed a short artistic autobiography disguised as a handbook for would-be writers: *Plotting and Writing Suspense Fiction* (1965). From Earl Soham she travelled to Hammamet in Tunisia for weeks of immersive research for *The Tremor of Forgery* (1969), another book about another American writer losing his sense of moral balance in expatriatism. Back at Bridge Cottage, she finished a film script for her novel *Deep Water* (1957). She never stopped working.

She went on drawing and sketching too, and jotted down little inventions and quirky ephemera in her notebooks: 'The Gallery of Bad Art', a 'sweating thermometer', some free-form 'lamp-shades'. Her 'strychnined lipstick' expressed her feelings for women just as much as her idea for a cookbook, 'Desperate Measures', represented her response to food. The best that can be said of her scheme for the global deployment of children (as tiny territorial ambassadors) is that it adds a new terror to child development.

The final breakdown of her English love affair – she described it as 'the worst time of my entire life' – swept her across the Channel to France and Switzerland, where she moved from region to region, relationship to relationship, and drink to drink. She went on writing as though her life depended on it (it did); monitoring her thoughts the way a searchlight sweeps a prison yard for escaping convicts. And she continued to curate her expatriate's museum of American maladies.

The pearl of a girl from mid-century Manhattan turned into an embittered old oyster in her last home, her Fortress of Solitude (a modernist citadel with jutting twin wings) in a sunny canton in Switzerland: the country, as Scott Fitzgerald wrote, where many things end and few begin.

Even the manner of her dying sustained that volatile attachment to duality which haloed her life and allowed all her contradictory emotions to meet and mate and ignite into art. For Patricia Highsmith – she could have written this ending for herself and perhaps she did – expired of two competing diseases. Her doctors said they could not treat the one without exacerbating the other.

Welcome to Highsmith Country.

Joan Schenkar, 2014

I

Coleman was saying, 'She had no brothers or sisters. Makes things a little easier, I suppose.'

Ray walked with his bare head hanging, hands deep in the pockets of his overcoat. He shivered. The night air of Rome was sharp with coming winter. It didn't make things easier, Ray thought, that Peggy had had no brothers or sisters. It certainly didn't make things easier for Coleman. It was dark in the street where they walked. Ray lifted his head to see a street sign, and found none. 'You know where we're going?' he asked Coleman.

'There'll be taxis down here,' Coleman said, nodding ahead.

The pavement slanted downward. The sound of their footfalls grew higher pitched as their shoes slid a little. *Scrape-scrape-scrapety-scrape*. Ray took hardly more than one step to Coleman's two. Coleman was short and had a quick, choppy gait that was at the same time rolling. Now and again a whiff of Coleman's cigar, which Coleman held between his front teeth, blew past Ray's nostrils, bitter and black. The restaurant Coleman had wanted to go to had not been worth crossing Rome for, Ray thought. He had met Coleman by appointment at eight o'clock in the Caffé Greco. Coleman had said he was to meet a man – what was the name? – in the restaurant, but the man had not arrived. Coleman had not mentioned him once they got there, and Ray wondered now if the man existed. Coleman was odd. Perhaps Coleman had dined or lunched at the restaurant a few times with Peggy, and liked the place for his memories. Coleman had spoken mainly of Peggy in the restaurant, not as resentfully as he had in Mallorca, even chuckling a little tonight. But the grimness, the question, was still in Coleman's eyes. And Ray had got nowhere, trying to talk to him. The evening, for Ray, was simply another evening washing over him. The evening had the atmosphere of others in Mallorca in the ten days since Peggy had died – colourless, muffled somehow from the rest of the world, evenings of food eaten or half eaten simply because it arrived on the table.

'You're going on to New York,' said Coleman.

'Paris first.'

'Any business here?'

'Well, yes. But nothing I can't do in two days.' Ray was going to see some painters in Rome, see if they were interested in being represented by his gallery in New York. The gallery did not exist as yet. He had made no telephone calls today, though he had been in Rome since noon. He sighed, and knew that he had no heart for meeting painters, for convincing them that the Garrett Gallery was going to be a success.

Viale Pola, Ray read on a street sign. A larger avenue lay ahead. Ray thought it should be the Nomentana.

Ray was vaguely aware of Coleman tugging in his pocket for something. Then Coleman faced him suddenly and a shot exploded between them, rocking Ray back against a hedge, making his ears ring, so that for a few seconds he could not hear Coleman's running feet on the pavement. Coleman was out of sight, Ray did not know if a bullet had knocked him backward, or if he had fallen back with surprise.

'Che cosa?' yelled a man's voice from a window.

2

Ray gasped for air, realized he had been holding his breath, then struggled forward, off the hedge on to his feet. 'Niente,' he called back automatically. When he breathed deeply, nothing hurt. He decided he was not hit. He began to walk in the direction Coleman had taken, the direction in which they had been walking.

'That's the man!'

'What happened?'

The voices faded as Ray entered the Nomentana.

He was lucky. A taxi approached immediately from the left. Ray hailed it.

'Albergo Mediterraneo,' he said, and sank back in the seat. He felt a sting, a burning sensation in his left upper arm. He lifted the arm. It certainly hadn't gone through the bone. He touched the sleeve of his coat, and a finger caught in the hole in it. Further exploration, and he found the exit hole on the other side of the sleeve. And now there was a warm wetness in the hollow of his arm where the blood ran.

At the Mediterraneo – a modern hotel whose style did not appeal to Ray, but his favourite hotels had been full today – he claimed his key and rode up with the bellhop, left hand in his coat pocket so no blood would drip on the carpet. The closing of his own room door brought a sense of safety, though Ray found himself glancing in corners after he turned the light on, as if he expected to see Coleman in one of them.

He went into the bathroom, removed his overcoat and tossed it into the bedroom on the bed, then removed his jacket, revealing a splotched streak of blood down his blue-and-white striped shirt-sleeve. Off came the shirt.

The wound was a tiny scallop, hardly half an inch long, a classic graze. He wet a clean face towel and washed it. Ray got a Band-Aid from a suitcase pocket, remembering that this broad Band-Aid had been the only one left in the tin box when he had been clearing out the medicine cabinet in Mallorca. Then, using his teeth, he tied a handkerchief around his arm. He soaked the shirt in a basin of cold water.

Five minutes later, in pyjamas, Ray ordered a double Dewar's from the bar. He tipped the small boy well. Then he turned his light out and went to the window with his drink. He was on a rather high floor. Rome looked wide and low, except for the distant, sturdy dome of St Peter's and column of Santa Trinità at the top of the Spanish Steps. Coleman might think he was dead, Ray thought, from the way he had fallen back into the hedge. Coleman had not looked back. Ray smiled a little, though his brows frowned. Where had Coleman acquired the gun? And when?

Coleman was leaving on a noon plane tomorrow for Venice. Inez and Antonio were going with him, Coleman had said tonight. Coleman said he wanted a change of scene, something beautiful, and that Venice was the best place he could think of. Ray wondered if Coleman would ring tomorrow morning to see if he'd got back to his hotel or not? If the hotel said, 'Yes, Mr Garrett is in,' would Coleman hang up? And if Coleman believed he had killed him, what would Coleman say to Inez? 'I left Ray near the Nomentana. We were taking different taxis. I don't know who could've done it.' Or had Coleman not said he was having dinner with him, but said he was dining with someone else? Would Coleman have got rid of the gun immediately, tonight, dropped it into the Tiber from a bridge?

Ray took a longer pull on the drink. Coleman wouldn't ring his hotel. Coleman simply wouldn't bother. And if he was challenged, Coleman would lie and lie well.

And Coleman would, of course, find out that he was still alive, simply because there would be nothing in the papers about his being dead, or seriously wounded. And if Ray were then in Paris or New York, it would seem to Coleman that he had fled, run

4

from him in a cowardly way before everything could be explained, labelled, analysed. Ray knew that he would go to Venice. He knew that there would be more conversations.

The drink helped. Ray felt suddenly relaxed and tired. He stared at his big open suitcase on the rack. He had packed intelligently in Mallorca, not forgetting cuff-links, drawing-pad, his fountain-drawing-pen, address books. The rest of his things, two trunks, several cartons, he had shipped to Paris. Why Paris and not New York, he didn't know, since in Paris he'd only have to get them sent on to New York. It was not an efficient arrangement, but under the rattling circumstances in which he had packed in Mallorca, it amazed him that he had done as well as he had. Coleman had come down from Rome the day before the funeral and had stayed three days afterwards; and during those days Ray had packed up his things and Peggy's, settled bills with tradesmen, written letters, seen about cancelling the lease with his landlord Dekkard, who had been in Madrid, so that the thing had had to be done by telephone. And all the while Coleman had prowled about the house, stunned, rather silent; yet Ray had seen his thin mouth becoming smaller and straighter as he began to build and harden his wrath against Ray. Once, Ray remembered, he had come into the living-room to ask Coleman something (Coleman had slept on the living-room sofa, declining the guest room he might have had) and found Coleman holding a terracotta lampbase shaped like a large gourd in both hands; and Ray had thought for a moment that Coleman was going to hurl it at him, but Coleman had set it down. Ray had asked Coleman if he wanted to drive to Palma, forty kilometres away, because he had to go in to see about shipping his things. Coleman had said no. The next day, Coleman had taken a plane from Palma and flown back to Rome to Inez, his current woman. Ray had not met her. She had telephoned Coleman twice when Coleman was in Mallorca. Coleman had been summoned to the post office to take the calls, as there was no telephone in the house. Coleman always had women, though Ray could not understand what charm he had for them.

Ray slid carefully into bed, not wanting to encourage more bleeding from his arm. It was annoying that Coleman would be in the company of Inez and the Italian Antonio. Ray had never seen Antonio, but could imagine the type – weak, good-looking and young, neatly dressed, moneyless, a hanger-on now though probably a former boy-friend of Inez. And Inez would be in her forties, perhaps a widow, moneyed, maybe a painter herself, a bad one. But perhaps in Venice, if he saw Coleman alone again just once, he could say it all plainly in words – say the plain fact that he didn't know why Peggy had killed herself, that he honestly couldn't explain it. If he could make Coleman believe that, instead of believing that he, Ray, was keeping some vital fact or secret from him, then – Then what? Ray's mind refused to tackle the problem any longer. He fell asleep.

The next morning he arranged for a night flight to Venice, sent a telegram to reserve a room in the Pensione Seguso on the Zattere quay, and made four telephone calls to painters and art galleries in Rome, which netted him two appointments. From these, he secured one painter for the future Garrett Gallery, a certain Guglielmo Guardini, who painted fantastic landscapes in great detail with fine brushes. The arrangement was a verbal one, nothing was signed, but Ray felt cheered by it. He and Bruce might not, after all, have to start the Gallery of Bad Art in New York. This had been Ray's idea as a last resort, if they couldn't get any good painters, get the worst, and people would come to laugh and stay to buy, in order to have something different from other people who collected only 'the best'. 'All we'll have to do is sit and wait,' Bruce had said. 'Take only the worst, and don't explain what you're doing. We don't have to call it the Gallery of Bad Art. Call it Gallery Zero, for instance. The public'll soon get the

6

idea.' They had laughed, talking about it in Mallorca when Bruce had come to stay last summer. And maybe the idea was not at all impossible; but Ray was glad, that evening in Rome, to be on a soberer track with the painter Guardini.

When he fetched his suitcase at his hotel after his solitary dinner, no telephone call had come for him.

2

The others had arrived first, at least ten hours before him, Ray thought. The plane unloaded its passengers into chilly darkness at 3.30 a.m., and Ray learned that there were no buses at this hour, only boats.

The boat was a good-sized launch, and it rapidly filled with silent, solemn English and blond Scandinavians who had been waiting when Ray's plane landed. The launch backed from the pier, turned smartly, dropped its stern like a charging horse, and shot away at full speed. Cheerful piano music, such as one might have expected in a cocktail lounge, came softly from the loud-speaker, but did not seem to lift anyone's spirits. Speechless, white-faced, everyone faced front as if the boat were rushing them to their execution. The launch deposited them at the Alitalia air terminal pier near the San Marco stop from which Ray hoped to take a vaporetto – his destination was the Accademia stop – but before he realized what was happening, his suitcase was on a trolley and being pushed into the Alitalia building. Ray ran after it, was checked by a jam of people at the doorway, and when he got inside, his suitcase was not in sight. He had to wait at a counter, while two busy porters tried to obey the shouts of fifty travellers and hand them their proper luggage. When Ray got his, and walked out of the building with it, a vaporetto was just pulling away from the San Marco stop.

That meant a long wait, probably, but he did not particularly care.

'Where are you going, sir? I'll carry it for you,' said a husky porter in faded blue, reaching for his suitcase.

'Accademia.'

'Ah, you just missed a vaporetto.' A smile. 'Another forty-five minutes. Pensione Seguso?'

'Si,' said Ray.

'I will accompany you. Mille lire.'

'Grazie. It is not a long walk from Accademia.'

'A ten-minute walk.'

It was certainly not, but Ray waved him away with a smile. He walked to the San Marco pier, on to the creaking, swaying dock, and lit a cigarette. There was nothing moving at the moment on the water. The big church of Santa Maria della Salute on the opposite bank of the canal was only palely lit, as perfunctorily as the street-lights seemed lit, Ray felt, because November wasn't the tourist season. The water lapped gently but powerfully against the stanchions of the pier. Ray thought of Coleman, Inez and Antonio asleep somewhere in Venice. Coleman and Inez might be in the same bed, perhaps in the Gritti or the Danieli, since Inez would be paying the bills. (Coleman had let him know she was wealthy.) Antonio, though probably financed on this trip by Inez, too, would be in a cheaper place.

Two Italian men, well dressed, carrying brief-cases, joined him on the pier. They were talking about expanding a garage some-where. Their presence and their conversation were somehow comforting to Ray; but still he shivered, and glanced around hopefully for the second time for a coffee-bar, and saw none. Harry's Bar looked like a grey glass-and-stone tomb. And not a

9

window was lighted in the red façade of the Hotel Monaco e Grand Canal opposite it. Ray walked in small circles around his suitcase.

At last the vaporetto emerged from a dark curve of canal far to the left, a little blaze of welcome, yellowish light. It slowed to touch at a stop before San Marco. Ray, like the two Italians, stared at it as if fascinated. The boat drew large and close, until Ray could see the five or six passengers on it, and could see the calm, handsome face of the man in the white yachting cap who would fling the mooring rope. On the boat, Ray bought a ticket for himself and a fifty-lire ticket for his suitcase. The boat passed della Salute, and entered the narrower mouth of the Grand Canal. The Gritti Palace's lights were elegant and discreet: two softly lighted electric lanterns held aloft by oversized female statues at the water's edge. Boats arriving at the Gritti would dock between them. Motor-boats under canvas covers bobbed between poles. Their names were *Ca' Corner* and *Aldebaran*. The colour everywhere was black, the rare lights only small yellow splotches against it, sometimes revealing a faint red or green of stone.

At the Accademia stop, the third, Ray walked briskly with his suitcase into the wide, paved way across the island towards the Zattere quay. He cut through by way of an arched passage into what looked like a blind alley, but he remembered that it turned left after a few yards, and remembered also the blue tile plaque on the side of the house straight ahead that said John Ruskin had lived and worked there. The Pensione Seguso was just to the left after the left turn. Ray disliked awakening the porter. He pushed the bell.

After two minutes or so, an old man in a red jacket that he had not taken time to fasten opened the door and greeted him courteously and rode up with him in a small lift to the third floor.

His room was simple and clean and had a view through its tall windows of Giudecca across the water and, directly below, of the small canal that went along one side of the pensione. Ray put on his pyjamas and washed at the basin – there hadn't been a room with bath free, the porter said – and fell into bed. He had thought he was very tired, but after a few minutes he was sure he would not be able to get to sleep. He was familiar with the sensation from the Mallorca days, a tremulous exhaustion that put a faint shakiness in his penline or his handwriting. The only thing to do was walk it off. He got up and dressed in comfortable clothes, and let himself quietly out of the hotel.

Dawn was rising now. A gondolier swathed in navy blue propelled a cargo of Coca-Cola crates into the canal beside the pensione. A motor-boat dashed in a straight line up the Giudecca Canal, as if scurrying home guiltily after a late party.

Ray ran up the arched steps of the Accademia bridge and headed inland for San Marco. He walked through narrow grey streets whose shop-fronts were tight closed, through small squares – Campo Morosini, Campo Manin, familiar, unchanged, yet Ray did not know them well enough to remember every detail of them. He passed only one person, an old woman with a large flat basket of Brussels sprouts. Then the American Express's tiles appeared under his feet, directing him with an arrow to their office, and he saw the lower part of the Piazza San Marco's columns in front of him.

He walked into the giant rectangle of the Piazza. The space seemed to make a sound like 'Ah-h' on his ears, like an unending exhalation of a spirit. To right and left, the arches of two arcades diminished in regular progression. Out of a strange self-consciousness at standing still, Ray began to walk, shy now of the humble brushing sound of his desert boot soles on the cement. A few awakening pigeons fluttered around their nests in the arcades, and two or three came down to peck for food on the Piazza. They paid no more attention to Ray, who walked very near them, than if he had not existed. Then Ray took to the shelter of the arcade.

Jewellers' shops were curtained and barred by folding grillwork. Near the end of the arcade, he went out into the Piazza again and looked at the cathedral as he walked by it, blinked as he always had at its complexity, its variety of styles all crammed together. An artistic mess, he supposed, yet it had been erected to amaze and impress, and in that it succeeded.

Ray had been to Venice five or six times before, beginning when he had come with his parents at the age of fourteen. His mother had known Europe far better than his father, but his father had been stricter about making him study it, making him listen to his teaching records in Italian and French. The summer he was seventeen, his father had presented him with a crash course in French at the Berlitz School in St Louis. Ray had always liked Italy and Italian cities better than Paris, better than the château district which his father so admired and whose scenery had seemed to Ray as a boy like calendar pictures.

It was six-forty-five. Ray found a bar-caffè that was opening, went in and stood at the counter. A healthy-looking blonde girl with large blue-grey eyes and cheeks like peaches took his order for a cappuccino, and made it herself at the machine. A boy assistant was busy filling glass containers with buns. The girl wore a fresh, pale blue smock uniform. She looked into his eyes as she set the cup before him, not in a flirtatious or even personal way, but in the way Ray felt all Italians of whatever age or sex looked at people – as if they actually saw them. Did she live with her parents, Ray wondered, or was she recently married? But she went away before he could glance at her hand for a ring, and in fact he didn't care. He cupped his cold hands round the hot cup, and was aware of the girl's happy, healthy face on the other side of the counter, though he did not look at her again. With his second coffee, he got a croissant, paid the extra to sit down, and went to a small table. Next door, now, he was able to buy a newspaper. He sat for nearly an hour while the city awakened around him, and the street outside began to fill with people hurrying in both directions. The skinny little boy in black trousers and white jacket took out tray after tray of cappuccini for delivery in the neighbourhood, and returned swinging his empty tray between thumb and forefinger. Though he looked no more than twelve and should have been in school, he had a crush on the blonde girl, who treated him like a kid brother, tweaking the back of his hair.

It was up to him to find Coleman and party, Ray supposed, not for them to run into each other in some restaurant or in the Piazza, Coleman perhaps registering shock, or saying, 'Ray, what a surprise to see you here!' But it was barely eight, too early to try to ring them at the Gritti or anywhere. Ray debated going back to the pensione for some sleep, then decided to walk a bit farther. Shopkeepers were arranging their wares now, hanging pocketbooks and scarves outside the doors of cramped shops, rolling up blinds to reveal windows full of leather goods.

Ray looked through a window at a green-black-and-yellow scarf, its floral pattern nearly covering its white ground. A pang had gone through him at the sight of it, and it seemed that only after the pang did he see the scarf, and still a second later realized he had noticed it because it looked like Peggy. She would have adored it, though in fact he did not remember a scarf of hers that was like this one. He walked on, five or six paces, then turned. He wanted the scarf. The shop was not yet open. To kill time, Ray drank an Espresso and smoked another cigarette in a bar in the same street. When he returned, the shop was opening, and he bought the scarf for two thousand lire. The salesgirl put it into a pretty box and wrapped it with care, thinking he was going to give it to a girl.

Then Ray walked back to the Pensione Seguso. He was calmer now. In his room, he hung the scarf over the back of his straight chair, threw away the paper and box, and got into pyjamas again. He sat on his bed and looked at the scarf. It was as if Peggy were in the room with him. It needed no touch of her perfume, no folds from her tying, to look exactly like Peggy, and Ray wondered if he shouldn't remove it, put it away in his suitcase at least? Then he decided he was absurd, and lay back on his bed and slept.

He awakened at eleven to the sound of church bells, though he knew they had chimed every quarter of an hour since he fell asleep. Try Coleman, he thought, or they'll be out for lunch and not back until five. There was no telephone in his room. Ray put on his trench-coat and went into the hall to the telephone that stood on a sideboard.

'Would you ring the Hotel Gritti Palace, please?' he asked.

There was no one named Coleman at the Gritti.

Ray asked for the Royal Danieli.

Again the answer was no.

Had Coleman lied about going to Venice? It seemed rather likely that he had, would have done, whether Ray were killed or not. Ray smiled at the thought that Coleman might be in Naples or Paris or even still in Rome.

There was the Bauer-Gruenwald. Or the Monaco. Ray lifted the telephone again. 'The Hotel Bauer-Gruenwald, please.' A longer wait, then he put the question to the new voice.

'Signor Col-e-man. One moment, please.'

Ray waited.

''Allo?' said a female voice.

'Madame – Inez?' Ray did not know her last name. 'This is Ray Garrett. I'm sorry to disturb you. I wanted to speak to Ed.'

'Ah, Ray! Where are you? Here?'

'Yes, I'm in Venice. Is Ed there? If he's not, I can –'

'He is here,' she said in a comfortingly firm tone, dropping all her aitches. 'One moment, please, Ray.'

It was a long moment. Ray wondered if Coleman was declining to speak. Then Coleman's voice said:

'Yes?'

'Hello. I thought I'd let you know I'm in Venice.'

'Well, well. Quite a surprise. How long are you here for?'

'Just a day or so – I'd like to see you, if possible.'

'By all means. And you should meet Inez? – Inez Schneider.' Coleman sounded just a trifle rattled, but recovered as he said, 'Dinner tonight? Where is it we're going, Inez? – Da Colombo around eight-thirty,' he said to Ray.

'Maybe I can see you after dinner. Or this afternoon? I'd rather see you alone.' An explosive blast like a Bronx cheer from the telephone numbed Ray's ear for a moment, and he lost what Coleman was saying. 'Could you say that again? Sorry.'

'I said,' Coleman's taut, ordinary American voice said in a bored manner, 'it was high time you met Inez. We'll see you at eight-thirty at Da Colombo, Ray.' Coleman hung up.

Ray was angry. Should he ring back and say he wouldn't come for dinner, that he would see him at any other time? He went into his room to think about it, but within a few seconds he decided to let it go and to turn up at half past eight.

3

Ray was deliberately fifteen minutes late, but not late enough, as Coleman had not arrived. Ray walked twice through the big restaurant, looking for him. He went out and entered the first bar he saw. He ordered a Scotch.

Then he saw Coleman and a woman and a young man walking by the bar, Coleman laughing loudly at something, his body rocking back. Not quite two weeks after his only child had died, Ray thought. A strange man. Ray finished his drink.

He entered the restaurant when he thought they had had time to be seated. They were in the second room he looked into. Ray had to go very close to the table before Coleman deigned to look up and greet him.

'Ah, Ray! Sit down. Inez – may I present Inez Schneider? Ray Garrett.'

'Enchantée, M. Garrett,' she said.

'Enchanté, madame,' Ray replied.

'And Antonio Santini,' said Coleman, indicating the dark, wavy-haired young Italian at the table.

Antonio half stood up and extended a hand. 'Piacere.'

'Piacere,' Ray said, shaking his hand.

'Sit down,' said Coleman.

Ray hung his coat on a hook and sat down. He glanced at Inez, who was looking at him. She was a darkish blonde, about forty-five, slight, and she wore good jewellery. She was not quite pretty; she had a receding and rather pointed chin, but Ray sensed a warmth and femininity, perhaps something maternal in her, that was most attractive. And again, looking at Coleman's bloating face, his unappetizing brown moustache, his balding head freckled from Mallorca, imagining the bulging belly below the table level, Ray wondered how he could attract women as fastidious as Inez seemed to be. Coleman had been with another woman very much the type of Inez, when Ray had met him and Peggy the spring before last at an exhibition in the Via Margutta. *My father's always the one who says good-bye*, Peggy's voice said in his ear, and Ray hitched himself forward nervously in his chair.

'You're a painter?' asked Antonio on his right, in Italian.

'I'm a poor painter. I'm a better collector,' Ray answered. He hadn't the energy or the inclination to inquire into Antonio's work. Coleman had said Antonio was a painter.

'I'm very happy to meet you finally,' Inez said to Ray. 'I wanted to meet you in Rome.'

Ray smiled slightly, and could think of nothing to say. It didn't matter. He sensed that Inez would be sympathetic. She was wearing a good and rather powerful perfume, earrings with a pendant green stone, a green and black jersey dress.

The waiter arrived, and they ordered. Then Inez said to Ray:

'You are going back to the States?'

'Eventually, but I go to Paris first. I must see some painters there.'

'Doesn't care for my work,' Coleman mumbled across his cigar.

'Oh, Edward,' Inez said, pronouncing the name 'Édouard.'

Ray tried to look as if he hadn't heard. He was not fond of Coleman's current pop art phase, but it had simply never crossed his mind to invite Coleman to join his gallery. Coleman now considered himself 'European'. As far as Ray knew, he was not and did not want to be represented by a New York gallery. Coleman had given up his job as a civil engineer when Peggy was four years old and had started painting. For this Ray liked him, and for this Peggy's mother had divorced him, claiming Peggy. (And perhaps there had been another woman in the picture, too.) Then in less than a year, Peggy's mother had been killed in a car she was driving. Coleman, in Paris, had then been informed that he had custody of his daughter, and that his deceased wife, who had been rich, had settled a trust fund on Peggy which Coleman could not touch, but which would pay for her education and bring her an income when she became twenty-one. All this Peggy had told Ray. Peggy had become twenty-one while they were married, and had enjoyed four months of the income. It could not, Peggy had said, be passed on by her to her father or anyone else. On her death it had reverted to an aunt in America.

'You are going to start a gallery in New York,' Inez said.

'Yes. My partner – Bruce Main – hasn't got the space as yet. We're trying for it.' Ray could scarcely talk, but he made an effort. 'It's not a new idea of mine. It's an old one. Peggy and I – We'd –' He glanced inadvertently at Coleman, and found Coleman's small eyes fixed calculatingly on him. 'We were planning to go to New York after our year in Mallorca.'

'A little more than a year,' Coleman put in.

'Peggy wanted to stay on,' Ray said.

Coleman shrugged, as if to express disbelief or that what Peggy had wanted was of no consequence.

'Are you seeing painters in Venice, too?' Inez asked.

Ray was grateful for her civilized voice. 'No,' he said.

Their food arrived. Ray had ordered cannelloni. Meat was repellent, the cannelloni merely uninviting. Coleman ate with appetite.

18

'What did you want to talk about?' Coleman asked Ray, pouring wine from the carafe for himself first, then for Ray.

'Perhaps I can see you some time tomorrow,' Ray replied.

Antonio was listening to every word, hanging on their conversation, and Ray was inclined to dismiss him as of no importance; but as soon as he thought this, it occurred to him that Antonio might be a partner with Coleman, a young man who would help Coleman get rid of him, for a little money. Ray glanced at Antonio's shiny dark eyes, his serious rather crude lips now gleaming with olive oil, and came to no conclusions about him. And Coleman, talking to Inez, had not answered his suggestion that they meet tomorrow.

'Where are you staying?' Coleman asked Ray.

'The Pensione Seguso.'

'Where is that?'

'At Accademia.'

A big table of men at the back of the room was extremely noisy.

Ray leaned forward and said to Coleman, 'Is there any time tomorrow when I could see you?'

'I'm not sure – about tomorrow,' Coleman said, eating and not looking at Ray. 'We've got some friends here. They're joining us tonight, matter of fact.' Coleman glanced towards the door, then looked at his watch. 'What time did they say?' he asked Inez.

'Nine-thirty,' Inez replied. 'They eat early, you know.'

Ray cursed himself for having come tonight. Under the circumstances, there was nothing to do but be polite and leave as soon as possible. But he could think of nothing, absolutely nothing, to say to Inez. Nothing to say to her even about Venice.

The time dragged on. Antonio talked to Inez and Coleman about the horse races in Rome. He was enthusiastic. Ray could not listen.

Coleman stood up, letting his napkin fall. 'Well? Better late than never. Here they are!'

A man and woman approached the table, and with difficulty Ray tried to focus on them.

'Hello, Laura!' Coleman said. 'Francis, how are you? Mr and Mrs Smith-Peters, my – former son-in-law, Ray Garrett.'

Ray stood up and acknowledged the rude introduction politely, and found an extra chair that was needed. They looked like very ordinary Americans in their mid-fifties, and they looked as if they had money.

'Oh, yes, we've eaten, thanks,' Laura Smith-Peters said, sitting down. 'Americans, you know. We still like eating around eight.' She was speaking to Inez. She had reddish hair, and her voice was too high and rather nasal. From her hard 'r' Ray gathered she was Wisconsin or Indiana.

'And we're on demi-pension at the Monaco, so we thought we had to eat there tonight, because we were out to lunch,' Mr Smith-Peters said with facetious precision, his thin, birdlike face smiling at Inez.

Ray became aware that Mrs Smith-Peters was gathering herself to speak to him, no doubt about Peggy, and he braced himself.

'We're really very sorry to hear about the tragedy in your life,' she said. 'We'd known Peggy since she was eighteen. But not well, because she was always away at school. Such a lovely girl.'

Ray nodded.

'We're from Milwaukee. I am. My husband's a Californian, but we've lived most of our lives in Milwaukee. Except for the last year. Where're you from?'

'St Louis,' Ray said.

Coleman ordered another litre of wine, and glasses for the Smith-Peters. But Mrs Smith-Peters did not want any wine, and at last, on Coleman's insistence that she have something, asked for a cup of tea.

'What do you do?' Ray asked Mr Smith-Peters, feeling the question wouldn't bother him.

'Manufacturer of sporting equipment,' Mr Smith-Peters responded briskly. 'Golf balls, tennis rackets, skin-diving stuff. My partner's carrying on in Milwaukee, but the doctor ordered complete rest for me. Heart attack a year ago. So now we break our necks climbing three flights of stone stairs in Florence – we live there now – and chasing around Venice –'

'Darling, since when are we *chasing* around?' his wife put in.

He was a man who liked to move quickly, Ray saw. His hair was nearly white. Ray could not imagine him young, with more weight on him, but it was easy to imagine his wife young, bright-blue-eyed and pert, with a rather common Irish prettiness that needs youth or else. Mr Smith-Peters's face reminded Ray of certain old baseball players' faces he occasionally saw on sports pages in the States and never cared to read about. Lean, hawk-nosed, grinning. Ray did not like to ask if he had been keen on any sport before he started his business. He knew the answer would be either baseball or golf.

Ray felt Mrs Smith-Peters's eyes on him, looking him over perhaps for signs of grief, perhaps for signs of brutality or coldness that might have precipitated Peggy's suicide. Ray did not know what Coleman had told them, but it would not have been anything favourable, not a single thing, except perhaps that he had money, a fact Coleman would have stated with faint contempt. Yet Coleman had a nose for money himself, witness his wife, and the woman he was with now. And the Smith-Peters. The Smith-Peters were typical of the people Coleman collected for social and economic reasons. They probably cared little about art, but Coleman could sell them one of his paintings. Coleman could take a woman, with whom he contemplated an affair, to a party given by people like the Smith-Peters, and impress her. Peggy, for all her rather primitive terror of and respect for her father, had deplored his sponging and his hypocrisy.

'We were so surprised when Ed came up to us this morning in

the plaza,' Mrs Smith-Peters said to Inez. 'We had no idea he was here. We're just here for a couple of weeks while they're installing the central heating in our Florence house.' She looked at Ray. 'We met Ed and Peggy in St Moritz one Christmas.'

'Laura, would you like to sweeten that tea with a cognac?' Coleman interrupted.

'No, thank you, Ed. Cognac keeps me awake,' Mrs Smith-Peters replied. She turned to Inez. 'Are you here for long, Mme. Schneider?'

'You will have to ask Edward that,' Inez said with a wave of a hand. 'He said something about painting here, so – who knows?'

Her frankness, the fact she admitted being in Coleman's charge, seemed to surprise Mrs Smith-Peters, who might have suspected their relationship but hadn't expected the female half to reveal it. 'Paintings – of Venice?'

Ray tried to imagine what Coleman's heavy black outlines and flat expanses of unvaried colour would make of Venice.

'You seem quite depressed,' Mrs Smith-Peters said gently to Ray, and Ray hated Coleman's hearing it.

Coleman listened.

'That can't be helped,' Ray said just as quietly, and in a way that he hoped dismissed the subject, but Coleman said:

'Why shouldn't he look gloomy – a man who saw his wife die, a girl die, two weeks ago.' Coleman waved his cigar for emphasis.

'He did not *see* her die, Edward,' Inez said, leaning forward.

'He saw her die by inches before he found her dead,' Coleman retorted. He was certainly feeling his liquor, but he was also far from drunk.

Mrs Smith-Peters seemed to want to ask a question, but thought better of it. She looked like a distressed little Irish girl.

'It happened while Ray was out of the house for several hours,' Inez said to Mrs Smith-Peters.

'Yes, and where was he?' Coleman smiled towards Antonio,

who still listened with serious attention, then turned towards Mr Smith-Peters, whom he wanted to draw into the conversation. 'He was at the house of a woman neighbour. On a morning or an afternoon when his wife was obviously in trouble, he was somewhere else.'

Ray could not look at anyone at the table. But Coleman's words did not hurt so much now, strangely, as they had in Mallorca when he and Coleman had been alone. 'She was not obviously in distress that day,' Ray said.

'No more than any other day, you mean,' said Coleman.

'Edward, I am *sure* we don't want to hear all this again,' Inez said, tapping with a table-knife hilt on the tablecloth, the knife held straight up. 'I am sure the Smith-Peters don't.'

'There was no one in the house?' Mrs Smith-Peters asked softly, perhaps meaning to show polite interest, but it was awful.

'The maid was there, but she left at one after fixing the lunch,' Coleman told her, glad of an ear. 'Ray came home after three and found Peggy in the tub. Cut her wrists. Drowned also.'

Even Antonio squirmed slightly.

'How awful!' Mrs Smith-Peters murmured.

'Good God!' whispered Mr Smith-Peters, and cleared his throat.

'Ray wasn't back for lunch that day,' Coleman said, meaningfully.

Nor did that hurt so much. Ray had been at the house of Elizabeth Bayard, American, aged twenty-six or so; and he had been looking at her drawings, which were better than her paintings. She was new in the village, and he and Peggy had been to her house only once. She had served him a Dubonnet and soda with ice, and he had talked and smiled a great deal that day, he remembered, enjoying Elizabeth's company because she was attractive, decent and well-meaning; though not even those qualities were needed to make him enjoy those two or three hours with her, because he was tired of the handful of Americans and

English in the village. He had said, 'I'm sure Peggy doesn't care if I'm back for lunch or not. I said I mightn't be.' Lunch was always cold, and they could eat it or not eat it, and at whatever hour they wished. And it was quite true, as Coleman implied, that he found Elizabeth Bayard attractive (Coleman had put it more strongly in Mallorca, but Ray had conceded nothing on this point), and he remembered thinking that afternoon that he could, if he were so inclined, probably start an affair with Elizabeth and conceal it from Peggy, and that Elizabeth would be casual and affectionate and that it would be a most salubrious change from Peggy's mysticism for him. Ray also knew he never would have begun an affair. One couldn't, with a girl like Peggy for a wife, a girl for whom ideals were real, even indestructible, maybe the realest things on earth. And certainly physically he had scarcely had energy for an affair, anyway.

'He does look gloomy enough to do away with himself, and maybe he will,' said Coleman, mumbling again.

'Edward, I insist you stop this,' said Inez.

But another question was rising in Mrs Smith-Peters. She looked at her husband, as if asking his permission, but he was staring at the tablecloth. 'Was she painting at all?' she asked Ray.

'Less and less, I'm afraid. It was too bad. We – Because we had plenty of servants. There was lots of time.'

Coleman was again listening critically.

Ray went on: 'It was a lazy atmosphere, though. I had a certain routine, an easy one, but – people fall apart without one. Peggy dropped her morning painting, and then she'd paint in the late afternoon, if she painted at all.'

'Sounds utterly depressing,' Coleman said.

But Peggy had not acted at all depressed, Ray thought. He could not say this. It sounded self-justifying. And what right had these strangers to hold a tribunal about him and Peggy? Ray tossed his napkin nervously on to the table.

Mrs Smith-Peters looked at her watch and said they must go. She turned to Inez. 'I wondered if you and Ed would like to go to the Ca' Rezzonica? I love the place. I was thinking of tomorrow morning.'

'May we ring you at breakfast?' Inez asked. 'Is nine or nine-thirty too early?'

'Oh, heavens, no, we're up at eight,' said Mrs Smith-Peters. Her husband rose first.

'Perhaps you'd like to come, too,' Mrs Smith-Peters said to Ray as she stood up.

'I'm afraid I can't,' Ray said. 'Thank you.'

The Smith-Peters departed.

'Can you get the check, Inez? Back in a minute,' Coleman said, getting up. He walked towards the back of the restaurant.

Antonio stood up as soon as Coleman's back was turned. 'If you excuse me,' he said in English. 'I think I go back to my hotel. I am very tired. I must write my mother.'

'Oh, of course, Antonio,' said Inez. 'We'll see you tomorrow.'

'Tomorrow.' Antonio bent over her hand and deposited a token kiss. 'Good night,' he said to Ray. 'Good night, madame.'

Inez looked for a waiter.

Ray raised his arm, but failed to catch the waiter's attention.

'Ray, I wish you would leave Venice,' Inez said to him. 'What good does it do for you to see Edward again?'

Ray sighed. 'Ed doesn't understand yet. I somehow need to explain more to him.'

'Did he have dinner with you the last night in Rome?'

'Yes.'

'I thought so. But he said it was someone else. Listen, Ray, Edward will never understand. He was so mad about his daughter –' She closed her eyes, tilted her head back, but wasted only a second in this, because she was trying to speak before Coleman returned. 'I never met Peggy, but I heard about her from lots of people. Head in the clouds, they say. She was like a goddess to Edward, someone not even human. Too good for humans.'

'I know.'

'He thinks you are very callous. I see that is not true. But I see also that he will never understand it was not your fault.'

What she said did not surprise Ray. Coleman had called him callous in Mallorca, and probably would have called any husband of Peggy's that, even if Peggy had had a happy marriage, with lots of children, even if Peggy had been radiating joy, fulfilment, and all the rest of it.

'Is it true that Peggy was frightened of sex?' Inez asked.

'No. No, really, on the contrary – he's coming back.'

'Can you leave Venice tomorrow?'

'No, I—'

'I must see you tomorrow. Eleven o'clock at Florian's?'

Ray had no time to answer, as Coleman was sitting down, but he gave her a nod. It was easier than refusing.

'Our waiter is so busy,' said Inez, with convincing exasperation as if they'd been trying to get him all the while.

'Jesus God!' Coleman said with a sigh, squirming around in his chair. 'Cameriere! Conto, per favore!'

Ray pulled out two thousand-lire notes, more than his share.

'Put that away,' said Coleman.

'No, I insist,' Ray said, repocketing his wallet.

'Put it away, I said,' Coleman said rudely. He was paying, no doubt with money Inez had given him at some time.

Ray said nothing. He stood up. 'I'll say good night, if I may.' He made a bow to Inez. Then he got his coat from the hook. It was the coat, the only overcoat he had with him, in which the two bullet-holes were in the left sleeve, but the coat was almost black, the holes not very noticeable. He raised his left arm and smiled as he departed.

4

The morning was brilliant with sunshine. Below Ray's pensione window, workmen sang as if it were spring or summer, a cleaning girl sang as she mopped the hall outside his door, and a bird in a cage sang in a window of the Embassy of Monaco across the small canal.

When Ray left the pensione at ten-thirty to meet Inez, he had two letters in his pocket, one to his parents and one to their gardener Benson, who had written him a note of sympathy to Mallorca. To his parents Ray had written his thanks for their asking him to come home for a while, but said that he had business still to do in Europe, and that he thought it best to get down to work with Bruce Main on the New York gallery. It was an answer to the second letter his parents had written him, after he had cabled and written them about Peggy. He went to a tobacco shop under the arcade of the Piazza, bought stamps, and dropped the letters into a box outside. He was ten minutes early. He walked slowly about the square, until he at last saw Inez walking briskly in high heels, a small trim figure, coming from the San Moisè corner.

'Good morning!' he said, before she saw him.

'Oh!' She stopped. 'Hello. Am I late?'

'No. In fact you're early,' Ray said, smiling.

A pigeon banked low above her head, its wings creaking. Inez had a small yellow hat of feathers, with a few peacock feathers at one side. In the sunlight, Ray saw the wrinkles under her eyes, and the deeper ones on either side of her mouth. They did not in the least diminish her attractiveness, Ray thought. He wondered if such a woman might ever be interested in him as her lover, and he felt a wave of inferiority which he could not lift by telling himself it was irrational. A woman like Inez might like him very much because he was younger, and because she would be flattered.

There were not many tables outdoors at Florian's, and those few who sat there wore coats and mufflers.

Ray held Inez's chair for her.

She wanted simply a caffè.

'Well,' she said when they had ordered. She had planted her forearms flat on the table, elbows spread, her fingers in pumpkin-coloured suède gloves locked. 'I repeat, I would like you to leave Venice. Today, if you can.'

The cold, clear air made her words crisp, too. They were both smiling. It was impossible not to smile on such a morning and in such a place. 'Well, perhaps I can leave tomorrow. I'm quite willing.'

'You want to talk to Edward, but I tell you it's no use. You could produce a *diary* of Peggy's with the whole truth, whatever that is, and Edward would still believe what he wishes to believe.' She had removed one glove now, and she gestured passionately to emphasize her words.

'I do know what you're saying. I understand, but—' Ray adjusted his trench-coat under him and leaned forward. 'I may have to go over the whole thing again with Ed, but I could do it in five minutes, if I organized it properly.'

'And what would you tell him?'

'I would tell him about Peggy. And about me. The atmosphere. What we did and talked about. I think that's what Ed is interested in.'

Inez shook her head hopelessly. 'Is it true Peggy was trying dope? Taking this LSD?'

'No. Good Lord, not Peggy. She wasn't even curious about it. I know, because we've been to parties where they had it. Lots of people had it there.'

'You see? Edward thinks she was taking dope.'

'Well, that's one of the things I might put him straight about.'

Their coffee arrived, the tab was put under the ashtray.

'And then he would think of something else. Such as that you had other women. I don't know.'

'He inquired about that in Mallorca. He met several of our friends. No luck for Ed, I'm afraid.'

A silence for a few seconds. Ray felt the futility of this meeting with Inez.

'I feel that you mean the best for me,' Ray said, 'but you can see how many things Ed has wrong. I can't just leave things like this.'

'But I think it is better if you do and if you don't try to write to him about them, either.' She looked down at the pigeons bobbing around on the pavement. 'I am older than you. And I know a little about Edward. I am giving you my best advice.'

'I do appreciate it,' Ray said, but his tone sounded as if he had no intention of taking it, which was true.

'Edward wants to blame you entirely. I have even thought he might try to kill you,' Inez said in a lower voice.

Ray sat back and laughed a little. His heart had begun to beat faster. 'Why? Is he carrying a gun?'

'Oh, no, but – he might get someone else to do it.'

'Matter of fact, I was going to ask you about Antonio. Do you think he would hire Antonio?'

'Oh, no! Be assured. Not Antonio. Antonio hates quarrels.

They make him sick. He is not a bad boy, but he is not from the best of Italian families. You know. Last night he was almost sick. He listen, he listen, and then he can't stand any more. He rang me this morning to apologize for leaving so soon.'

Was that true, that Antonio had been almost sick? Inez certainly thought so. 'Do you think I can see Ed this afternoon? Can you help me make an appointment with him? Then I can leave tomorrow.'

'I know he will postpone. He will make you wait two or three days, just to annoy you. He knows that you want to see him.'

'It shouldn't be impossible. I saw him alone in Rome,' Ray said in a voice that suddenly rose, so that he glanced to his right to see if anyone had noticed. 'The trouble was, that night, he only wanted to talk about the past.' Ray was telling the truth, but he felt that he manufactured, because he was going to leave out the gunshot. 'He was in a good mood, really, talking about Peggy's schooldays, the holidays they had when she came home from school in Switzerland. He talked about not having enough money to keep up with her, and about saving for places like Venice and Paris, because she had her own money and lots of it.'

'Oh, I can imagine,' Inez said.

'When I tried to talk about what had just happened – he didn't want to hear it. But now you see he does. You can tell that.'

'He only wants to whip his anger up. Like last night. You can see *that*. How old are you, Ray?'

'Twenty-seven,' Ray said.

'I was twenty-one when you were born. You see, I am bound to know a lot more. For one thing, I have had two husbands.' She repressed a sudden mirth. 'My last husband left me more than a year ago for another woman. *They* are now not together. I knew just that would happen. I know, for instance, that you would not frighten a girl like Peggy with bed – with sex.'

'I told you that last night.'

'No, you answered my question was Peggy frightened by it. It's different.'

Ray took a moment to collect his words. 'No, I wouldn't call it frightened. She was very fond of it. In a way. But not the usual way. I mean – I think she expected something fabulous out of it, something mystical. There *is*, of course, something mystical in it, but she wanted something more. And more and more.' This burst of eloquence finished him for a few seconds. Plainer words that he might have said became mixed in his mind until he no longer knew what they were. Trying to put it into words brought out the ludicrous side: Peggy thinking it would be 'better' if they changed their position in bed a little bit, whereas all had been perfect as it was, and trying to make any improvement ruined everything. Ray bit his lip in nervousness, and to keep from smiling.

'That I can also imagine,' Inez said. 'She liked it very much.'

'Yes,' Ray said gratefully. 'But somehow not in the right way. I never said that to Ed. It's so difficult. Also I never tried to talk to Peggy about it. Or I think when I did once, she didn't know what I meant, or I didn't go far enough. You see, I blame myself there, for not talking to her, because I was so much older and certainly knew more about the world.'

'Peggy seems to have known nothing about the world,' Inez said, tapping her ash into the tray from which the wind at once removed it.

Inez's words and the flat way she said them were the most comforting thing Ray had known since Peggy's death. Then the vision of the red-filled bathtub came to his mind, as it did ten times a day. He saw, superimposed upon Inez's yellow and tan clothing, the ugly white and red picture of the bathroom in Mallorca, Peggy's long dark hair floating just under the surface at the back of the tub. She had not drowned, because there was not much water in her lungs, the police had said. And the tub had of course not been filled entirely with blood, because it was too full for that, but the

31

colour had looked to Ray as if gallons of blood had run from her by some process of her will to give up life utterly, with a bang.

'You loved her,' Inez said.

'Yes, I certainly did. I'm sorry you never met her.' Ray hesitated, then pulled the folded scarf from his coat pocket. 'This – it's not hers. I bought it here yesterday. But it's so like her. Like her personality. That's why I bought it.'

Inez smiled and touched the scarf with her finger-tips. 'Decorative and romantic.'

He said with sudden embarrassment, 'In a way, it's like a picture of her,' and put the scarf back into his pocket. 'But I'm sure you've seen photographs of her.'

'Did you keep other things of hers?'

'No. Her clothes I gave away in the village – to poor people. I gave Ed her jewellery. Most of her things were in Ed's apartment in Rome.'

There was a silence. A string orchestra began to play something from *South Pacific*.

'What do you feel guilty about?' Inez asked.

'I don't know. I suppose when someone commits suicide – the person or persons nearest them always feel guilty, don't they?'

'Yes, they do generally.'

'If I am guilty,' Ray said, 'and of course that's possible, it's for something I haven't thought of as yet.'

'Then you shouldn't look guilty – as yet.'

'Do I?'

'Yes. It's your manner. If you are not guilty, then you should not look guilty,' Inez said, as though it were quite simple.

Ray smiled a little. 'Thank you. I'll try.'

'If you leave tomorrow, would you give me a ring at the hotel first? If I'm not in, leave a message. "Everything's all right." Just that. Would you?'

'Yes.'

32

'Or whenever you leave, ring me first.' Inez drank the last of her coffee.

'What do you like about Ed?' Ray asked, feeling naïve, but unable to keep the question back.

Inez smiled and looked suddenly younger. 'A certain courage that he has. He doesn't give a damn about the world, what the world thinks. He has conviction.'

'And you like that? Just that?'

'He has a certain strength, and women like strength. I don't suppose you understand that. Or not yet.'

Ray could understand it, if the man looked like Errol Flynn, flouting convention, even flouting the law, but not someone as ugly as Coleman; so this comment left him as baffled as Inez thought he was. 'He doesn't look a bit like Peggy, do you think? Or Peggy didn't look at all like him. Not even the colouring.'

'No, not from the pictures I've seen. She is like her mother.'

Ray had seen a photograph of her mother. Her mother had died at thirty, and the picture of her in Coleman's apartment in Rome – Peggy had had none in Mallorca – had shown a striking brunette with a faintly smiling mouth like Peggy's, intense eyes, like Peggy but more arrogant than Peggy's dreaming face.

'I must go now,' Inez said, getting up. 'I told Edward I was going out to buy shoes. I shall just tell him I couldn't find any.'

Ray, not finding a waiter, left the money on the table. 'I'll walk with you.'

'Not all the way. I don't want Edward to see you.'

They walked towards the end of the square.

'Not that I will be with Edward for ever,' Inez said, lifting her head higher. She had a light and graceful step. 'But he is very nice when one is lonely, and I was lonely – six months ago. Edward is a man without complications for a woman. He doesn't say, "Stay for ever", and when he says, "I love you", which is almost never, I don't believe it anyway. But he is a nice companion—'

33

She broke off, and Ray felt she had been going to say, 'in bed'. It was beyond him.

'– and a nice escort,' she finished, the wind carrying away the words so Ray barely heard them.

Yes, he was an escort, Ray supposed. Women liked escorts.

'You mustn't come any farther,' Inez said, stopping.

They were now in the street of the Bauer-Gruenwald. Ray would have walked into the hotel with her, but he realized she would bear the brunt if Coleman saw them. 'How long are you staying?'

'I really don't know. Five days?' She shrugged. 'You must promise me you will leave tomorrow. Edward is angry that you are in Venice and staying here will accomplish nothing, believe me.'

'Then I'd like to see him today.'

Inez shook her head. 'This afternoon we go to the Ca' Rezzonica, and tonight all of us go to the Lido for dinner. I am quite sure Edward would not see you anyway today. Don't let him humiliate you like this.' The sunlight made her eyes a fiery yellow-green.

'All right. I'll think about it.' Because he was keeping her, Ray raised a hand and turned away abruptly.

He would lunch at the pensione, he thought, but before lunch, whether Inez was present or not in Coleman's hotel room, he would try to arrange a meeting with him. And after lunch, he would write to Bruce, tell him about Guardini in Rome, and give Bruce a date when he would be in Paris at the Hôtel Pont Royal.

The girl at the desk in the Seguso handed Ray a message with his key. It said:

Mr Coleman telephoned at 11.00. Would you dine at Lido tonight. Telephone Hotel Bauer-Gruenwald.

Coleman proposing another bullying evening. Ray approached the desk for the Bauer-Gruenwald number, as there was a booth downstairs, but two elderly English ladies were ahead of him, inquiring about the best way to go to the Ca' d'Oro. The girl told them, then one said:

'We thought of going by gondola. Can you tell us where to find a gondola? Or can you have one fetch us here?'

'Oh, yes, madame, we can arrange for a gondola to come here. At what time?'

Ray stared at a tall ticking clock in the hall, at its brass pendulum behind the etched glass. He should take his coat today and find a place that did reweaving, he thought. At last, he put in his request to the girl, and she dialled the Bauer-Gruenwald number.

Ray took it in one of the two booths. Coleman answered.

'Ah, Ray. We're having dinner tonight at the Excelsior on the Lido. Would you like to join us?'

'I'd be glad to come over, if I can see you alone for a while after dinner,' he said, as politely as ever.

'Sure we can,' Coleman said affably. 'Okay then, eight-thirty or nine at the Excelsior?'

'I'll join you after dinner, thanks very much. Good-bye.' And he hung up.

5

Ray thought that eleven would be early enough to arrive at the Excelsior. At ten, he had a toasted cheese sandwich with a glass of wine, standing at a counter, then walked to the pier on the Riva degli Schiavoni from which the boats to the Lido departed. There was a quarter of an hour wait. Grey-blue clouds passed slowly over the stars, and Ray thought it might rain. A middle-aged couple also waiting for the boat were having a depressing quarrel about rent money which the husband had lent or given to the wife's brother. The wife was saying that her brother was worthless. The husband shrugged miserably, looked into space, and answered his wife in the terse language of ancient matrimonial warfare:

'He paid it back before.'

'Half of it. Don't you remember?' she asked.

'It's done now.'

'It's gone now. We'll never see it again.'

The husband lifted a string-tied cardboard box and shuffled to the gate as the boat pulled in, as if he would love to creep away from his wife, on to the boat, anywhere, but the wife was right behind him.

He and Peggy had never quarrelled, Ray thought. Perhaps that had been part of what was wrong. Ray considered himself – because he had been told it often enough by other people – easy-going, which was on the helpful side in a marriage, he supposed. On the other hand, Peggy had never been demanding, had never held out for anything he thought unreasonable, so there had simply been no occasion for quarrelling. He hadn't particularly wanted to spend a whole year in Mallorca, but Peggy had (*some place very primitive and simple, simpler even than southern Italy*), so Ray had decided to look on it as a long honeymoon, and had decided he could spend the time well by painting and reading, especially reading art history books, so he had agreed. And the first four months, she had been amused and happy. Ray could even say the first eight months. The novelty of the rather bare-foot life had worn off by then, but by then she had been painting, fewer hours a day but more constructively, he had thought. His thoughts trailed off, and he was as lost as ever for a reason for her dying. Coleman now had her paintings, had corralled every one, and also all her drawings, and had shipped them to Rome, not asking Ray if he might like one. Ray reproached himself for having let it happen. For this, Ray felt extremely bitter against Coleman, so bitter he tried to forget it whenever he recalled it.

He looked now at the Lido lights, a long low streak ahead. He thought of Mann's *Death in Venice*, of the hot, festering sun beating on that strip of land. Passion and disease. Well, this was not at all the weather, there was no disease, and the passion was only in Coleman.

Ray followed the now silent couple on to what seemed a colder dock at Piazza Santa Maria Elisabetta, set his teeth against the wind, and went to ask the man in the ticket-booth in which direction the Excelsior lay. It was a ten-minute walk across the island on the wide Viale Santa Maria Elisabetta, then a right turn at the Lungomare Marconi. The dark, glass-fronted houses to right and left, built for summer residence, looked desolate. A few bar-caffès were open. The Excelsior was a large, lighted place, and one could tell at a glance that it would be well heated. Ray turned the collar of his trench-coat down, smoothed his hair, and went into the dining-room.

'Thank you, I'm looking for some people,' he said to the head waiter who had come up to him. There were not many people in the dining-room, and Ray saw Coleman's table almost at once. He grimaced slightly when he saw that the Smith-Peters were here, too. Ray was glad to see that they had been served coffee.

Inez lifted a hand to him and smiled.

'Hello, Ray!' said Coleman.

'Good evening,' Ray said to everyone. Antonio was also present, and tonight his smile looked more genuine.

'How nice of you to come all the way out here,' said Mrs Smith-Peters to Ray.

Ray sat down. 'It's a pleasant trip.'

'That's why we came,' Coleman said, a little pink in the face. 'I can't say the food would bring anybody. I've had better in lots of trattorias.'

'Sh-h! After all, Mrs Perry is inviting us,' Inez said to Coleman, frowning.

A slender, sixtyish woman in a blue evening dress, neck and wrists glittering with jewellery, an Edith Sitwell type, was approaching, and Ray then noticed that there was an extra setting, a full cup of coffee, where she had been. Ray got to his feet.

'Mrs Perry,' Inez said to her, 'this is Mr Garrett, Mr Coleman's son-in-law.'

'Former son-in-law,' Coleman corrected. He had not stood.

Mrs Perry shot him a worried look, but the expression on her face was permanently worried, Ray saw.

'How do you do, Mrs Perry?' Ray said.

'How do you do?' Mrs Perry sat down. She smiled and lifted her head, like someone under strain, and said, 'Well! Shall we all have a brandy? What kind does everyone prefer? Or does anyone care for something else?' Tendons stood out under her chin, slack under delicately wrinkled skin. She wore mauve shadow on her thin eyelids.

'I would like a brandy, thank you,' said Antonio.

'Courvoisier, please,' said Ray, seeing that orders from her guests would please her.

When the brandy arrived, Mrs Perry engaged Ray in conversation about his art gallery. She had been told by Inez, she said, that he was starting one in New York. She asked Ray its name.

'That's not decided yet. Just the Garrett Gallery, unless we think of something better. I'm hoping to get space on Third Avenue.'

Mrs Perry said she loved paintings, and had two Gauguins and one Soutine at home. Her home was in Washington. She seemed very sad, and Ray felt automatically sorry for her, perhaps because he did not know what had made her sad, and if he had known, could have done nothing about it. He also realized he would never know, because he would not ever know Mrs Perry long enough to find out. Ray watched Coleman for signs of departure. Inez had finished her brandy. The Smith-Peters were gathering themselves.

'We were told there was a boat back at midnight, and I think Francis and I ought to catch it,' Mrs Smith-Peters said. 'It's been so lovely, Ethel.'

'Must you go? We can always hire a motoscafo,' said Mrs Perry.

But they were determined, and Inez too was saying to Antonio in Italian that they should go back with the Smith-Peters, because Edward wanted to talk with Signor Garrett. Antonio obligingly stood up.

'Edward, we can leave the *Marianna* for you, and you can bring Ray back with Corrado,' Inez said to Coleman.

Coleman started to protest at this arrangement, then said, 'Oh, well, if the twelve is the last vaporetto—'

'I'm sure it's not,' Ray said, but he wasn't really sure.

'It might be.' Inez turned to Ray and smiled. 'We engaged a motor-boat for four days. Maybe you will take some rides with us if you are here.'

Ray nodded and smiled at her. He supposed Corrado was the pilot.

Inez, Antonio, and the Smith-Peters left. Mrs Perry lit another cigarette – she smoked only half before putting her cigarettes out – then said that since they wanted to talk, she would say good night. Coleman stood up now, as Ray did, and they both thanked her, and Coleman said carelessly, as if he did not mean it, that he would give her a ring tomorrow. Coleman walked with her across the dining-room, a clumsy and reluctant escort of the woman, who was taller than he. He turned back. Coleman was going to talk to him. Or at least they were alone now.

'Another brandy? Coffee?' Coleman sat down.

'No, thanks.'

'Well, I will.' Coleman signalled to the waiter, and ordered another brandy.

Ray picked up the water pitcher and poured some into a clean glass. Neither said anything until the waiter had brought the brandy and departed.

'I wanted to talk to you,' Ray began, 'because I feel you don't quite understand still that –' He hesitated only a second, but Coleman interrupted quickly.

'Don't understand what? I understand you weren't the right man for my daughter.'

Ray's cheeks grew warm. 'That may be. Perhaps he exists somewhere.'

'Don't get fancy with me, Ray. I'm talking plain American.'

'So am I, I think.'

'All this "perhaps", "I *think*". You didn't know how to handle her. You didn't know, until it was too late, that she was at the very

40

end.' Coleman looked directly into Ray's eyes, his round, bald head tilted.

'I knew she was painting less. She didn't act depressed. We still saw people quite often and Peggy enjoyed seeing them. We'd given a dinner-party two nights before.'

'And what kind of people?' Coleman asked rhetorically.

'You met a few. They aren't scum. The point is, she wasn't depressed. She was dreamy, yes, and she talked a lot about orchards full of fruit, birds with coloured feathers.' Ray moistened his lips. He felt he was talking badly, that it sounded as if he were trying to describe a film he had seen by starting the story in the middle. 'The point I want to make is that she never mentioned suicide and never talked as if she were depressed. How was a person to know? She actually looked happy. And I told you in Xanuanx that I went to see a psychiatrist in Palma. He could have seen her a few times – in fact for as long as Peggy wanted. She didn't care to see him.'

'You must've suspected something was very much the matter or you wouldn't've looked up a psychiatrist.'

'Not *very* much the matter. But I would have had the psychiatrist come to the house, if I'd known how badly off she was. She ate normally—'

'I've heard that.'

'I thought Peggy needed to talk with someone else besides me, someone who'd try to explain to her – what reality was.'

'*Reality?*' Coleman's tone was angry and suspicious. 'Don't you think she got a big dose of it with marriage?'

To Ray, it was a complex question. 'If you mean the physical aspects—'

'I do.'

'It was like reality and not reality with Peggy. She wasn't frightened. She—' He simply could not go on with it to Coleman.

'She was just surprised. Shocked, maybe.'

'Not at all. The trouble was not that. It might have been going away from you. Having me as the centre of her life, presumably, instead of you, after all those years when she had only you.' He rushed on, though Coleman wanted to interrupt. 'She was an extraordinarily sheltered girl, you must know that. Private schools all her life, very much supervised by you when she was on her holidays. You must know you didn't give her the freedom that most girls her age have when they're growing up.'

'Do you think I wanted her to grow up knowing all the – the dirty side of life the way most girls do?'

'Of course not. I do understand that. And I appreciate the fact that Peggy was not like that. But maybe she wanted more magic than I had to give her – or than there is in marriage.'

'Magic?'

Ray felt baffled and vague. 'Peggy was very romantic – in a dangerous way. She thought marriage was another world – something like paradise or poetry – instead of a continuation of this world. But where we lived, it couldn't've been more like a paradise. The climate, the fruit on the trees right outside the door. We had servants, we had time, we had sunshine. It wasn't as if she were saddled with children right away and up to the elbows in dishwater.'

'Oh, money couldn't make Peggy happy. She's always had money,' Coleman said tersely.

And Ray knew he had said the wrong thing, used the wrong comparison, because Coleman resented his having money, though he would never have let his daughter marry anyone who hadn't it. 'Of course it wasn't merely money. I'm trying to describe the atmosphere. I tried many times to talk to Peggy. I wanted us to move to Paris for a while, take an apartment there. That would've been a step towards reality. The climate's worse, there's noise and people and – and there's a calendar and a clock to watch in Paris.'

'What's all this nonsense about reality?' Coleman demanded, puffing on the cigar between his teeth. His eyes were a little bloodshot now.

Ray realized it was hopeless, as Inez had told him. And during his silence, Ray saw Coleman's anger harden again, as he had seen it do in Mallorca. Coleman sat back in his chair with an air of finality, of dignity in his bereavement. Peggy had been the reason for his existence, his only true source of pride, Peggy whom he had begotten and raised single-handed – or at least since she had been four or five – a paragon of beauty, grace and good manners. Ray could see all this going through Coleman's mind, and no explanation, apology, atonement from him would ever change it. Ray realized now that he could never do it on paper, either. Coleman's eyes as well as his ears were closed.

'I am utterly sick of discussing it,' Coleman said, 'so let's take off.' He looked swimmingly, absently about as if for a waiter. 'And let bygones be bygones,' he mumbled.

That was not a phrase of reconciliation, as Coleman said it, and Ray did not take it as such. He got his trench-coat and followed Coleman out. Neither had tried to do anything about paying for the last brandy. Ray fumbled in the left pocket of his trench-coat, checking to see if he had his lighter. He pulled out his Seguso key, which he thought he had left at the desk, and with it came the folded scarf. He pushed the scarf back with the key, but Coleman had seen the scarf.

'What's that?' Coleman asked.

They were walking into the lobby.

'My hotel key.'

'The scarf. The handkerchief.'

Ray's hand was in his pocket, and he pulled it out again, with the scarf. 'A scarf.'

'That's Peggy's. I'll take that, if you don't mind.'

Coleman's voice was audible to the man behind the Excelsior's

43

desk and to the young bellhop by the door. Coleman's hand was out. Ray hesitated an instant – he had a right to the scarf – then rather than have an argument, he gave the scarf to Coleman. 'Take it.'

Coleman let the scarf drop from a corner, as they went through the hotel's doors, looked at it, and said, 'Just like Peggy. Thank you.' On the pavement, he said, 'After all, you gave away her clothes in Mallorca.' He pushed the scarf into his overcoat pocket.

'I didn't think you wanted any,' Ray replied. 'After all, you took all her work – her paintings and drawings.' He was sorry that his bitterness was audible. But the scarf was phoney, in a way, and this gave him a rather nasty satisfaction.

Their steps crunched again on the gritty road with the rhythm of the night in Rome, three nights ago. Ray was watchful for a sudden move from Coleman, a draw of the gun, perhaps – Coleman thought his life worthless – so he walked some two feet to one side of Coleman. Coleman wanted him to know he considered his life worthless, Ray realized. It was part of Coleman's punishing him. They passed only two people, two men walking separately, in the walk across the island.

'I don't have to go back with you,' Ray said. 'I'm sure there's a vaporetto.'

Coleman seemed to shrug slowly. Then he said, 'No trouble. Same direction. Here it is. The "*Marianna* number two".' He walked towards a group of three motor-boats, moored against the dock which turned at right angles from Ray and Coleman.

On the stern of one of the boats, Ray saw MARIANNA II. None of the boats had a canvas cover.

Coleman looked around. Only three or four young Italian boys were in view, huddled in their coats, not far from the ticket-booth of the vaporetto, twenty yards away. The ticket-booth was closed, Ray had noticed. He looked out at the lagoon for an approaching vaporetto, but saw none. It was 1.20 a.m.

'Damn Corrado. He's probably gone home,' Coleman mumbled. 'Well, let's go. We don't need him, anyway.' Coleman stooped on the wharf, went down a short ladder and got himself awkwardly on board, into the pit at the stern.

Coleman was going to drive it. Ray recoiled at once, sought for an excuse, a good excuse to get out of going, and, realizing both the difficulty and the absurdity of having to invent an excuse to protect his life, he smiled with amusement and felt blank. 'You're going to drive it?' he asked Coleman.

'Sure. I drove it all day. Corrado just comes along for the ride. He lives on the Lido, but I don't know where.' Coleman was fishing keys out of his pocket. 'Come on.'

I can stand up to him, Ray thought. Coleman wouldn't catch him a second time by surprise. If Coleman tried, he might have the pleasure of hitting Coleman, at least, of knocking him out. Anyway, retreating now would be blatant cowardice, and Coleman would gloat. Ray stepped aboard. A low brass rail ran around the stern, and the boat had a covered cabin where the controls were.

Coleman started the motor and backed out cautiously. Then the boat turned, and they picked up speed. The noise of the motor was unpleasant. Ray turned his trench-coat collar up and buttoned the top button.

'I'll head for the Giudecca Canal! Put you off somewhere on Zattere!' Coleman yelled at him.

'Schiavoni's okay!' Ray yelled back at him. He was sitting in the stern on the low seat. It was certainly fast transport, but it was cold. Ray started into the cabin for shelter, just as Coleman turned from the controls and moved towards him.

'Got the wheel set!' Coleman said, jerking a thumb behind him towards the motor.

Ray nodded, keeping his hand on the cabin door-top for balance. The boat was bouncing about. In view of the buoys around,

45

not to mention possibly other boats, Ray did not think it very safe to set the controls. He looked ahead anxiously, but saw nothing between them and the bobbing lights of the mainland of Venice. Coleman bent and turned sideways to Ray to relight his cigar. Ray started into the cabin again, and Coleman came towards him, so that Ray had to step back, but Ray still kept his hand on the cabin top. Then Coleman, with the cigar between his teeth, lunged against Ray with his whole weight bent low, catching Ray in the stomach. Ray fell half over the gunwale, but his right hand caught the slender brass rail. Coleman hit him in the face with his fist, and shoved a foot in his chest. Ray's right arm was bent awkwardly, and his grip was broken as his weight swung over the side.

Ray had a sickening backward fall for a second, then he was in, wet, sinking. When he had struggled up to the surface, the boat was many yards away, its buzzing motor faint in his water-clogged ears. His shoes and his trench-coat were pulling him down. The water was icy on his body, and already he could feel the approach of numbness. He cursed himself. *It's what you deserve, you ass!* But his body, like an animal's body, fought to keep afloat, to gasp for air. He tried to remove a shoe, but couldn't without his head going under. He concentrated on keeping afloat, on finding a boat to hail. The water was outrageously rough, as if the sea itself had taken up Coleman's cause. He saw no boats anywhere. Venice looked farther away than it had from the boat, but the Lido was still farther, Ray knew. One of his ears popped and cleared of water, and then he heard a bell faintly. A buoy's bell. For several seconds, he could not tell its direction – or see its lights, if it had any – but he decided it was on his left, away from Venice, and he bent his efforts in that direction. His progress could not have been called swimming. It was a series of jerks of legs and body and arms, and these he made with caution, not wanting to exhaust himself. He was a fair swimmer, only fair, and clothed and in icy water he was a rotten swimmer. He realized, very profoundly, that he was probably not going to make it.

'Help!' he yelled. Then, 'Aiuto!' wasting valuable breath. The bell sounded closer, but his strength was going faster than the bell was coming. Ray rested, anxious about cramp. He felt it in his left calf, but he could still move the leg. Then he saw the buoy, a light grey blob, closer than he had dared hope. It had no light. The wind was blowing the sound away from him, and Ray hoped blowing the water towards the buoy. Now Ray stayed afloat, and tried only to steer himself, progressing by inches.

The buoy rose like a smooth teardrop that had half fallen into the water. He saw no handhold, and the top – a mess of bars enclosing the bell – was too high out of the water to be leapt for. Ray touched the buoy with his finger-tips, at last felt its fat, slippery body with the palm of one hand. It took energy to cling to it, arms outspread, but it was immensely encouraging to his morale to have reached it. It warns ships away from it, Ray thought, and found a macabre amusement in that fact. He groped hopefully with his feet for some kind of hold, and didn't find any. The water was at his neck. The metal bars were twelve inches above his finger-tips when he reached for them. With one hand – the other pressed gently against the inward-sloping buoy – he loosened his tie, removed it, and tried to fling one end of it across a bar. The bars were nearly vertical, but bowed out slightly. He tried from a direction in which the wind would help him. On the fourth or fifth try, one end of the tie went through, and Ray jiggled it patiently. When the two ends were even, he leapt for it, and it held. Cautiously, he put his weight on it, letting himself be borne as much as possible by the water, then grabbed for the metal bar and missed, released the tie so as not to break it, and went under. He struggled up, waited for a few seconds, to recover his breath, then tried again. Using knees against the buoy and careful tugs on the tie, he lunged again for the bar and this time caught it. He half knelt against the buoy and locked both arms around the bar.

Now, he supposed, it would be a test of muscular strength, a test of how long he could stand the cold before fainting or freezing or falling asleep or whatever people did, but at least he was out of the water, and he was also in a better position to see a ship.

He saw one, perhaps a quarter of a mile away, a boat that looked like a cargo barge with a motor at its stern.

'Aiuto!' Ray shouted. 'Soccorso! – Soccorso!'

The boat did not change its course.

He yelled again. But it was evident whoever was aboard did not hear him.

It was a disappointment to Ray, because he felt that this was the only boat destined to pass him. He also had a strange feeling that he did not very much care, not as much as he would have cared five minutes ago, when he had been in the water. But he supposed that now he was just as much in danger of dying. The idea of removing his trench-coat and somehow tying himself with it to the metal bars was too complicated to consider. But the barge's oblivious progress away from him seemed a blatant rejection, a shameless (because there was no need for the barge to have shame) denial of his right to live. For several seconds, he felt drowsy, bowed his head against the wind, but set his arms hard to hold himself. The ache of cold in his ears grew worse, the bell's clangour fainter to him.

Ray lifted his head and looked around again, saw what he thought was a bobbing light far away over his left shoulder, then it disappeared. He kept his eyes on the spot, however, and the light reappeared.

He gathered himself and shouted: '*Hello-o!*'

He got no answer, but at least he heard no motor, which was a fact in favour of his being heard. Or was this a buoy with a light instead of a bell? Now, far behind the light, something that looked like a vaporetto was moving in the Lido's direction, but for hailing purposes, it might as well have been a million miles away.

'Hello-o! Soccorso!' he yelled toward the light. He was sure it was moving now. Ray's lightless buoy swung and banged its bell, warning boats away. He could not tell in which direction the light was moving, obliquely towards or from him. 'Soccorso!' His throat felt raw from cold and salt.

'Ah-ool!' a voice answered from the light's direction. It was a gondolier's cry. 'Somebody there?'

Ray did not know the word for buoy. 'The bell! Sulla campana! Veni, per favore!'

'La campana!' came the firm, corroborative reply.

Ray realized that he was saved. His arms felt instantly twice as tired. The man was rowing. It could take easily another ten minutes. He did not want to watch the slow approach, and kept his head sunk on his chest.

'Ah-ool!' It was like an automatic cry, a natural sound like a cat's miaow, an owl's hoot, a horse's whinny.

Ray heard a plash as the gondolier made a bad stroke or a wave exposed his oar. 'Qua,' Ray said, much more feebly, hoarse now.

'Vengo, vengo,' replied the deep voice, sounding very close.

Ray looked and saw him behind his bow light, standing and rowing at the stern of his bobbing boat.

'Ai! – What happened? Did you fall off a boat?'

It was in such dialect, Ray barely understood. 'I was pushed.' It was what Ray had planned to say, that he was pushed off by joking friends. But he had no strength for talking, dangled a limp foot over the side of the gondola, let himself drop, and was dragged aboard by the Italian's strong arms. Ray rolled helplessly on to the gondola's floor. The hard ribs of the boat felt delicious, like solid earth.

The Italian bent over him, invoked the names of a few saints, and said, 'You were pushed? How long were you there?'

'Oh—' Ray's teeth rattled, and the syllable was falsetto. 'Maybe ten minutes. It is cold.'

'Ah, si! Un momento!' The Italian stepped deftly past Ray, opened the locker in the prow of his boat, swiftly produced a folded blanket, then a bottle. The Italian's shoe brushed Ray's nose as he turned, stooped. 'Here. Drink from the bottle. Cognac!'

Ray held the bottle, a wine bottle, to his open mouth, keeping his teeth clear of the glass. One big swallow, and his stomach heaved, but the drink stayed down. It was bad and watered brandy.

'You go inside,' said the Italian, then seeing that Ray could not move, he took the bottle from him, corked it and laid it on the boat's floor, then caught Ray under the arms and dragged him into the covered part of the gondola, on to the bench seat made to hold two people. Ray sprawled, quite without strength, felt vaguely apologetic, and realized that his right hand, which lay flat on the carpeted seat, felt nothing at all and might have been dead flesh.

'Santa Maria, what friends! On a night like this!' The Italian held the bottle again for Ray. He had draped the thick blanket over him. 'Where do you want to go? To San Marco? You have an hotel?'

'San Marco,' Ray said, unable to think.

'You have an hotel?'

Ray did not answer.

The Italian, a wiry figure clad in black, his head small and squarish, was framed for a moment in the low grey door of the gondola. Then he went away, scrambled towards the stern of the boat. A rattle of the oar, and then Ray became aware of the forward movement of the boat. Ray wiped his face and hair with a corner of the blanket. He felt colder as his strength returned. He should have told the man Accademia, he thought. On the other hand, San Marco was closer, and there he could find a bar, an hotel lobby, in which to get warm. A vaporetto crossed their bow, looking like a furnace of warmth with all its lights, full of calm, comfortable people facing forward.

'Have you an hotel? I'll take you to your hotel,' said the gondolier.

He must give him a tremendous tip, Ray thought, and his numb hand moved towards his inside jacket pocket, could not open his trench-coat buttons, pressed the side of his coat, and Ray thought but was not sure that the wallet was still there. 'It's in the vicinity of San Marco,' Ray said. 'I think I can walk, thank you.'

Swish – swish went the gondola, attacking the distance with soft lunges. The wind whipped past the open front of the cabin, but Ray no longer felt the brunt of it. It was probably the most unromantic gondola ride anyone ever had, Ray thought. He wrung out the ends of his trench-coat, then trouser cuffs. San Marco was drawing nearer. They were headed for the Piazzetta, between the Ducal Palace and the tall column of the campanile. 'I am sorry to have wet your gondola,' Ray said.

'Ah, *Rosita* is not a ... boat. Not now. Anyway in the winter she carries oil and vegetables. It is more profitable than tourists when there aren't any.'

Ray could not understand every word. 'You're finishing—' he began hoarsely, 'finishing work this late?'

A laugh. 'No, I start. I go to the railroad station. I sleep a little in the boat, then we start around five-thirty, six.'

Ray stamped his feet, assessing his strength. Perhaps he could make it to the Hotel Luna from San Marco.

'A fine joke, your friends. Americans, too?'

'Yes,' Ray said. The land was very near. 'Anywhere here. I am very grateful. You saved my life.'

'Ah, another boat would have come along,' said the Italian. 'You should have a hot bath, lots of cognac, otherwise you ...'

The rest was lost on Ray, but he supposed that he would catch his death.

The gondola's gold-combed prow, after heading dangerously for the stern of a large excursion boat, swerved and slid neatly into a slit between striped poles. The gondola braked, the prow kissed the pier gently, bobbing. The Italian grabbed something on the pier, braced his legs and turned the boat sideways, made it go forward, and steps appeared on their left. Ray stood up on shaking legs, then on all fours debarked, placing hands on the stone steps before he climbed. A fine sight for the doges!

The Italian laughed, worried. 'Is everything all right? Maybe I should walk with you.'

Ray did not want that. He stood up on hard, flat stone, feet apart for balance. 'Thank you infinitely.' He struggled desperately with trench-coat buttons, pulled out the wallet. Vaguely, he realized he had some twenty notes folded in squares, and he pulled out about half of them. 'With my thanks. For another bottle of cognac.'

'Ah, signor, è troppo!' A wave of the hand, a laugh, but he accepted the money, and his face widened with his smile. He had a stubble of grey beard.

'It is not enough. A thousand thanks. Addio.'

'Addio, signor.' He shook Ray's hand hard. 'I wish you health.'

Ray turned and walked away, aware that two men paused briefly to stare at him. Ray did not look at them. He walked slowly, shook his clothes so they would not cling, and shivered violently. Everything looked shut. San Marco's showed only two or three lights of places that were closed and cleaning up. Ray turned right, making for the Luna. But the Luna lobby was too big and open, Ray remembered; he would be noticed, asked his business. Ray veered suddenly into a small bar-caffè. There was a counter. He stood and asked for a cappuccino and a cognac. The cognac the boy poured was Stock. Ray did not like it, but was in no state to protest. While he waited for his coffee, a sudden hostility against Coleman rushed through him, as if the perilous events of the past hour or so had somehow held his emotions back. The sensation lasted only a few seconds, and ebbed as his strength had ebbed. The hollow-eyed boy behind the counter looked at him from time to time. Ray pulled the collar of his trench-coat straighter. It was a new trench-coat, waterproof, and it was beginning to look presentable. Only his shoes and trouser cuffs were a mess. Ray decided to go to a small hotel near by that might not insist on his passport, because his passport was at the Seguso. He had another cappuccino, another cognac, and bought cigarettes and matches. The iron door of the bar came down with a rattle and a bang. There was a smaller door in it through which he could get out, and a ring of keys dangled from its lock. Ray paid and left.

He saw the kind of hotel he wanted a minute later in a narrow lane, a blue-lit sign over its short, filigree marquee saying Albergo Internazionale or something like that. The décor of the lobby was imitation old-Venetian. At the bar to the left of the lobby, two Italians sat talking.

'You wish, sir?' The white-jacketed barman had come to the unattended desk.

'A room for one tonight?' Ray asked.

'With bath, sir?'

'Yes. Is the water hot?'

'Oh, yes, sir.'

A few moments later he was in a small room by himself, empty-handed, without luggage. What had the boy said? *You can register tomorrow morning. The manager has locked up the desk.* He had given Ray the white card that hotel guests had to fill out for the police. Ray turned on the hot water in the tub, and smiled at the sight of steam rising. He undressed and eased himself into the water, which he had been careful to make not too hot. He began to feel sleepy, or faint, so he got out and dried himself as briskly as he could with a smallish towel. There was an enormous towel hanging folded on a rod, but Ray had not the energy to deal with it. Then he hung up his clothes with some care, slowly because he was exhausted, and got naked between the sheets. His throat was already sore, and he did not know what he was in for.

In the morning, he sat up, blinked, and realized where he was. He had slept with the light on. He turned it off. His throat was fiery now, his head light and empty as if he might faint. He was frightened, and not merely because he might have pneumonia. It was a nameless, vague fear that he had, combined with a sense of shame. His trousers were still wet. He looked at his wrist-watch – still running because it was waterproof – and saw that it was 9.20. A small plan came to him, so small he felt moronic for finding pleasure in it: he would order breakfast, have his suit pressed, and try to sleep again while they were pressing it. He put on his trench-coat, which was only slightly damp in its lining, and picked up the telephone and ordered. He felt a lump inside his coat, up on the right, and recalled that his book of Traveller's Cheques was in the buttoned pocket there. He pulled them out. What luck that he'd put them there, left them there, rather, after buying them in Palma. Two thousand dollars' worth of hundred-dollar bills. There was a smaller book of Traveller's Cheques in his pensione, left over from Xanuanx days, only a few hundred in it, Ray thought. He flattened the book of cheques out. He had signed them in India ink with his fountain-drawing-pen, so the signatures were intact, but the pages were stuck together. He laid the book on the four-barred radiator.

His breakfast tray arrived, and Ray sent the girl away with his damp suit and also his shirt. She looked a little surprised, but said nothing.

After his breakfast, he filled out the card with a made-up name and passport number, because he felt for some reason ashamed to write his own.

He was awakened at eleven, when his suit was brought back. He hung the suit in the closet and went back to bed, thinking to wake up around one, leave the hotel, and have a good lunch somewhere. He awakened at a quarter to one, and got dressed. He had no tie and he could use a shave, but those things could be easily remedied. Ray stood at his window, which looked out on to tile roofs and a few tree-tops and vines in people's gardens, a view that might have been Florence or several other Italian towns, and again he felt the nameless, paralysing fear, a sense of helplessness and defeat. *You might have been dead. How is it you're alive?* Ray squirmed under his jacket. He had almost heard the voice. And once more, Coleman probably thought he was dead. Once more, Coleman didn't give a damn, wasn't very interested in whether he was alive or not. *Because you simply don't matter.* Ray forced himself to think what he had to do next. Pay the bill here. He didn't want to go back to the Seguso. That was it. Play dead for a few days. See what Coleman would do. The thought brought a curious relief. It was a kind of plan.

Downstairs at the desk, he asked for his bill. Number eighty-four. The name, Thompson. Ray handed in his card. He paid the four thousand, six hundred and sixty lire. No passport was asked for. Ray went out the hotel doors and was immediately aware of the fact he did not want to run into Coleman. Or Inez, or Antonio. He regretted not having looked out through the glass doors before going out, and now he walked stiffly and glanced at people so frequently that a few eyes were attracted to him, so he made himself stop that. The shops were beginning to close for the long midday break. Ray went into a shop and bought a pale blue shirt and a blue-and-red striped tie. There was a cubicle for trying on clothes, and he put on the new shirt and tie in there.

Warily, Ray walked into the street the Hotel Bauer-Gruenwald was on, and turned left, away from the hotel. No Coleman, no Inez, only streams of strangers who paid him no attention. Ray went to a trattoria called Citta di Vittorio, too modest a place for Inez and Coleman to go to, he thought, but still he looked around as he opened the door. He had bought a newspaper. Ray had a slow lunch, ate all he could, but failed to finish what he had ordered. His cheeks felt hot, and his face had been pink in the mirror at the haberdasher's. Unfortunately, he was about to be ill. It was curious to think that he might now have something that would prove to be fatal, Coleman's follow-up blow. He debated going to a doctor for a shot of penicillin. *I fell into a canal last night and . . .*

Ray went to a doctor about four o'clock, in a dusty old building in the Calle Fiubera behind the Clock Tower. The doctor took his temperature, said he had a fever, would not give him penicillin, but gave him an envelope of large white pills and told him to go home and to bed.

The day was grey and cold, but it did not rain. Ray walked to the tailor's shop where he had left his overcoat to be repaired, and picked the coat up. It seemed a strange transaction like one life invading another, or a bridge between two existences, the overcoat. But Coleman's bullet-holes were gone, erased, the overcoat was like new, and he put it on. It was a good silk-lined coat from Paris. He went into a bar for a caffè and a cigarette. He had to think what to do, because the night would come soon. With a glass of water, he took two of the huge pills, tilting his head back to get them down. He remembered being ill once in Paris, when he was a child, being given a large pill to swallow, and asking the doctor in French, 'Why is this so big?' 'So the nurses won't drop them,' the doctor had said, as if it were self-evident, and Ray still recalled his shock and sense of injustice that a nurse's fingers should be thought of before his own throat. The doctor here had told him six per day. With the delicious, inspiring caffè, Ray felt full of ideas and anything seemed possible. He might strike up an acquaintance with a girl, tell her an interesting story, be invited to her flat, be allowed to stay, especially if he gave her some money. Or he could pick up some Americans, tell them he was hiding from a girl, an Italian girl who was inquiring at every hotel in Venice for him. But he realized the difficulty of finding Americans who (*a*) had a flat or a house in Venice and (*b*) would be Bohemian enough to take in a stranger. Ray thought again, and tried to be more logical. For the third time, the peach-faced girl in the bar-caffè north of the Piazza came to his mind. A nice girl, that was evident. He would have to tell her a decent story. The nearest to the truth was best, or so he had always heard. He could ask her a perfectly honourable question: did she know of any place, any family, any person who would take him in for a few days, if he paid them rent? Private houses would not ask for his passport, because they did not report their income from lodgers.

Ray left the bar, and went in search of a barbershop. In the barbershop – where a ten-year-old boy lay sprawled on a bench with a transistor, enraptured by some quite good old-style American jazz – Ray asked the barber to leave the beard along his jawbone and his upper lip. He was not trying to change his appearance, and the beard wouldn't do so to any extent; he simply wanted a change. He had grown such a beard in Mallorca for a few months. Peggy had liked it at first, then she had not liked it, and he had shaved it off. The barber's mirror was long and clear, covering half the wall. Ray looked directly at himself over the double row of bottles of hair tonic and lotions, his eyes burning now in a fine frenzy of fever, he supposed, but they seemed very steady.

He had heavy dark brown eyebrows, a wide straight mouth, the lips more full than thin. His nose was strong and straight, a heavier version of his mother's, but in his mother it had been a final asset that made her 'a beauty'. His red-brown hair was not in his parents, but had been the hair colour of his mother's brother Rayburn, for whom he was named. When Ray received letters addressed to Raymond Garrett, he knew whoever had written did not know him well. From his father, an oilwell worker in his youth, a self-made man, now a millionaire with an oil company of his own, Ray had inherited wide cheekbones. It was an American face, slightly on the handsome side, hopelessly marred by vagueness, discretion, the second thought, if not downright indecision, Ray thought. He disliked his appearance, and always saw himself leaning slightly forward as if to hear someone who was speaking softly, or as if incipiently bowing, kowtowing, about to retreat backwards. And he felt that because of his parents' money, he had had life too easy. It was still un-American to take money from one's parents. Among his friends, lots of them painters without much money, Ray was inclined to pick up any tab, but this also was forbidden: it was showing off. He was afflicted by a constant feeling that he was not in the mainstream of life, because he did not have to hold a job. With friends, he divided bills rather too pointedly, perhaps, and each paid his share, except when he had had a couple of drinks and was able to do what he felt like, which was to say, 'This is on me.'

Sitting in the barber's chair, Ray recalled a childhood incident which stood out absurdly, and returned to him at least twice a year. When he was nine or ten, he had stayed in the house of one of his school friends, an apartment house. He had realized that his school friend's parents didn't own the apartment, only rented it, and that other people had lived there before them and would live there after them. He had spoken to his father about it that evening, saying, 'Our house always was ours, wasn't it?' 'Of course, I built it,' said his father. (Ray had thought then, his father *might* have built it with his own hands before Ray was born, because his father could do anything.) Ray had felt different then, rather special, but in a way that he did not want to be. He had wanted to live in a house or an apartment in which other people had lived before. He had felt that it was vaguely unfriendly and arrogant of him and his family to live in a house they had built themselves and owned. The apartment of his school friend had been by no means a shabby one, but rather luxurious. But years later, even into the present, the sight of a row of brownstones in New York, of ordinary house-fronts here in Venice, brought back the incident to him, and the same disquieting emotion: other people lived in layer upon layer of humanity and history; his own family had a thin but rich new surface. Therefore there was, somehow, nothing for him to stand on.

At twenty, while going to Princeton, Ray had become engaged to a St Louis girl whom he had known since he was eighteen. He had thought he was in love with her, but he hardly knew how the engagement had happened. Of course, he had done the proposing, verbally, but in a way the girl had, and both their families had exerted pressure simply by 'approving'. A year later, just before graduating, Ray had realized he didn't love her at all, and he had had to break it off. The experience had been traumatic. He had barely passed his examinations. He had felt a heel, thinking he had wrecked the girl's world, and one of the happiest moments of his life had been just after graduating, when he heard that the girl had got married. He really hadn't hurt her at all, he realized. His parents, Ray thought, hadn't had an inkling of what he had gone through that last year in university, though they took great interest in his grades, and whom he knew, and whether he was 'happy and doing well'.

He listened – with more pleasure than he usually listened to jazz, which in Mallorca had nearly driven him mad – to the free and easy expertise coming from the boy's transistor, music that the plump barber cutting his hair now, and the other two barbers and the men in the chairs, seemed not to hear at all, and Ray felt that anything in the world that he wished might be possible. It was, theoretically, possible and true. Yet he realized also that he lacked the dash to make any of it come true, and that the thought had come to him because of the jazz and because of his fever. He was timid, quite unlike his father whose word was law and who did what he wanted to do, or what needed to be done, in one slashing stroke. Ray hated his self-effacement, which even sometimes caused him to stammer with strangers. He detested his money, but there were always places to get rid of it, and Ray was using them – helping to support a couple of painters in New York, anonymous gifts (small compared to millionaires' gifts, but he hadn't come into his father's money as yet) to broken-down churches in England, to relief committees for Italian and Austrian villages buried under landslides, to a couple of organizations for the improvement of racial relations. Ray could have had even more money. He had instructed his trust fund bankers to send him a sum he considered adequate; but because he did not use all his income, money was piling up in the trust fund, making more daily, despite the whacks of income tax and his occasional request for five thousand dollars for a car, ten thousand for the boat he and Peggy had bought in Mallorca.

When he left the barbershop, he walked in the direction of the bar-caffè near the Campo Manin. It was after five o'clock and growing dark. The girl might not be working now, Ray thought, if she started so early in the morning.

He found the bar-caffè, and she was not behind the counter. Ray felt very disappointed. He stood at the counter and ordered from the small boy a cappuccino he did not want. He debated asking the boy about a room somewhere. Italians were very helpful about such things, and the boy looked bright, but Ray could not bring himself to risk it. The boy might tell other people. Then the blonde girl in her pale blue uniform came in through a door at the back of the shop. A slow shock went through him at the sight of her, and he looked down at his cup; but his eyes had met the girl's, and she said with a smile, 'Buona sera,' as she must have said to two hundred people that day.

She served two men who had come in. Glasses of red wine at the counter.

He should speak before it became any more crowded, Ray thought, and began to form his sentences in Italian. When the girl was dunking cups into the sink of hot water directly before him, Ray said, 'Excuse me. Do you know of a house in the vicinity where I might rent a room? It is not necessary that it be in the vicinity.'

'A room?' she asked, her grey eyes wide. Then her eyes closed half-way as she thought, wet dishcloth in left hand on the chromium sink edge. 'The signora next door to me. Signora Calliuoli. In the Largo San Sebastiano.' She pointed.

The direction meant nothing to Ray. 'Can you tell me the number?'

The girl smiled and looked bewildered. 'It's a long number and there is no name on the bell. If you want, I will show you when I leave. If you want to wait' – a glance over her shoulder – 'I finish at six.'

It was seventeen minutes to six. Ray finished his coffee, paid, and left a tip in the saucer on the bar. He nodded to the girl, trying to look efficient and proper, said 'Until six,' and went out of the bar.

The Signora Calliuoli might not have a room free, he thought, in which case the girl might not know of another place. But Ray felt carefree and happy, actually happy, and realized at once that it was due to fever and quite specious. He turned up at the bar-caffè on the dot of six.

The girl was putting on a black cloth coat. She gave him a smile and a wave. A heavy-set young man in a white mess jacket came from the door at the rear, perhaps to take the girl's place for the evening, and she spoke to him, too, eliciting a smile from him and a glance at Ray.

'It's not far. Four minutes,' said the girl.

Ray nodded. He wanted to tell her his name, for politeness'

sake, then realized he had to make up a new one. 'My name is Philip. Filipo. Gordon,' he added.

She nodded, uninterested. 'Mine is Elisabetta.'

'Piacere.'

'You want it for how many nights?' The girl walked quickly.

'Three, four. Say a week, if the signora prefers.'

They turned a corner, the wind blew straight at them, and Ray shuddered. Suddenly the girl stopped, and rang a bell in a narrow doorway directly on the street. Ray looked to right and left, then up at a five-storey house, narrower than it was high. He saw no canal near by.

'Who is it?' called a voice from an upstairs window.

'Elisabetta.' There followed a longish sentence which Ray could not understand at all.

A buzz opened the door. They went in, and met the woman who was descending the stairs. She beckoned Ray to come up and see the room. To Ray's relief, the girl came with them, exchanging conversation or gossip with the woman.

Ray was shown a square, medium-sized room with a red-and-yellow flowered counterpane on a lumpy-looking three-quarter-sized bed. A tall wardrobe was the closet, and there were pictures on the wall. But it was clean.

'You understand? Eight hundred lire per day with breakfast,' Elisabetta said.

'Very good,' Ray said. 'Benone, I shall take it,' he said to Signora Calliuoli.

Signora Calliuoli smiled, and deep, friendly creases formed on either side of her mouth. She wore black. 'The bath is downstairs. One floor. The toilet' – she pointed – 'one up.'

'Grazie.'

'Va bene?' said Elisabetta, smiling also.

Ray wanted to embrace her. 'Thank you so much,' he said in English. 'Grazie tanto.'

'Your valise?' asked Signora Calliuoli.

'I'll fetch that tomorrow,' said Ray casually, and pulled out his wallet. He produced a five-thousand-lire note. 'I shall pay you for five nights, anyway, if that is satisfactory. I am sorry not to have change now.'

The woman took the note. 'Thank you, sir. I shall bring you mille lire.' She went off.

Ray stood aside for the girl to precede him out of the room. They went downstairs. Ray had an impulse to ask her to have dinner with him, to ask if he could call for her at eight o'clock, but he thought he had better not.

Signora Calliuoli met them downstairs with his change. 'Grazie, Signor Gordon. You are going out now?'

'Just for a few moments,' Ray said.

'There is someone always here. You won't need a key.'

Ray nodded, hardly listening. A curtain of unreality had come down between him and the world. Ray felt energetic, happy, courteous and optimistic. The girl looked at him oddly on the street, and Ray said:

'I thought I would accompany you home.'

'I live right here.' She had stopped suddenly, her hand on the knob of another door like the one they had just left, but this door had a circular knocker of braided metal.

'Thank you once more for finding the room for me,' Ray said.

'Prego,' said the girl, and now she looked a little puzzled, perhaps suspicious of him. She was groping in her purse for a key.

Ray took a step back and smiled. 'Good evening, Signorina Elisabetta.'

This brought a small smile. 'Good evening,' she said, and turned to put her key in the lock.

Ray went back to his new house and his room. He meant to lie down for only a few moments, but fell asleep and did not awaken until half past eight. The tiny pinkish reading lamp was on. He had dreamed about an earthquake, about schoolchildren swimming adeptly through canals made by the earthquake, and climbing on to the land like otters. He had held a frustrating conversation with a couple of girls who sat on a high wall while he stood below, knee-deep in mud, trying to make them hear him. They had snubbed him. Fallen and damaged buildings were everywhere in the dream. Ray took two more of his pills. His fever was worse. He should have some hot soup somewhere and go straight back to bed, he thought.

He put on the blue shirt he had removed for his sleep, and made himself as presentable as possible with his limited wardrobe. A good brace of drinks, he thought, before his soup. He went to a bar and had a couple of Scotches, then walked towards the Rialto and the Graspo di Ua. He might as well have a good bowl of soup, if that was all he was eating, and the Graspo di Ua was an excellent restaurant. The walk tired him, but he reflected that he could take a vaporetto back, and that the Giglio stop should be the closest to the Largo San Sebastiano.

Ray opened the door of the Graspo di Ua and went in, grateful for the warmth that enveloped him at his first step. Ahead of him, a little to the right, Coleman faced him, laughing and talking to Inez, whose back was to Ray. Ray stared at him. Coleman's mouth was open, his spoon lifted, though his voice was lost in clatter and brouhaha.

'How many, sir?' asked the head waiter.

'No. No, thank you,' Ray replied in Italian, and went out again. He turned automatically in the direction he had come from, then reversed and walked towards the Ponte di Rialto, the nearest place from which to catch a vaporetto. Inez, too, had been laughing, he thought. What did Inez think? What did Coleman think about whether he was alive or not? Had Coleman telephoned the Seguso? Hadn't he, without Inez knowing? Now Ray thought perhaps he hadn't. Somehow it was a shattering, dumbfounding thought. Ray concentrated on reaching the Rialto and the waterbus stop.

The Seguso would pack up his suitcase by tomorrow, probably, and keep it somewhere downstairs. Would they notify the police or the American Consulate? Ray doubted if they would be in a hurry to do that. Surely whimsical guests had before departed suddenly for somewhere, and had written days later for their luggage to be sent on.

Coleman laughing.

Of course, Coleman wouldn't have said anything to Inez, except that he had let Ray off on the Zattere quay. If Inez remarked that Ray hadn't rung them, Coleman would say, 'Oh, he's probably gone on to Paris. Why should he tell us?' Inez might remember she had asked him to ring her before he left. But then what would she do?

Ray felt suddenly weak and very ill. His nose was running. He went back to the house in the Largo San Sebastiano, was let in by a plain adolescent girl he had not seen before, climbed the stairs to his room and went to bed after taking two pills.

He dreamed of fire, and of pink, dancing bodies, slender, naked, sexless, in a place that was neither heaven nor hell. He woke up hot, his chest and back sleek with sweat, and was happy because he believed the fever was breaking. God bless the pills, he thought sleepily, and put his head down again on the damp pillow. He awakened at a knock on the door.

The plain-faced girl brought in his breakfast tray. Ray pulled the covers over his naked shoulders.

'The signora asks are you sick?' the girl said.

'Better now, thank you.' His voice was hoarse.

The girl looked at him. 'You have a cold?'

'Yes, but it's better,' Ray said.

The girl withdrew.

He took two more of the pills. He had eight more to go.

For the first hour he was awake, he did not try to think or plan. He treated himself gently, like one still balanced between sickness and health, even life and death, grateful to feel more well than ill. He would buy a sweater today, and another pair of shoes, possibly a suitcase, a nice one, if he had enough money. He thought he had seventy or eighty thousand lire in his wallet. He would have to think about how to get more, using his Traveller's Cheques without a passport, but he would worry about that later. At some point today, he might go to the bar-caffè where Elisabetta worked, and invite her to dinner.

Ray bought a razor, shaving soap, toothbrush and toothpaste, and a pair of shoes. He took these things home and made use of the razor, shaving around the growing beard. It was now nearly one. He went out and walked in the direction of the Campo Manin. On the way, he encountered Elisabetta, evidently going home for her lunch.

'Buon' giorno,' Ray said to her.

'Buon' giorno.' She stopped. 'You are feeling better.'

'Yes. Why?'

They walked in the direction the girl had been walking.

'Because yesterday I thought you were sick.'

'Just a cold. I'm better, yes.'

'I saw Signora Calliuoli last night in the bar on our corner. She said you looked sick and went to bed early.'

'Yes, I did. I was very cold two nights ago. Caught a cold.' He did not know the word for chill.

'Venice can be very cold.'

'Very.'

'Excuse me, I must buy bread.' She disappeared into a bakery shop.

Ray waited in the street for her. The shop was full of women and housemaids, buying bread for lunch. He mustn't look like an ass, tagging after her, Ray thought, and stood up straighter as she came out. 'I was wondering,' he said, 'if you might have dinner with me tonight. I would like to invite you, to say thank you.' His limited Italian came to an abrupt stop at the end of this sentence. He had spoken solemnly and stiffly, like a formal old man, he felt. And as soon as he thought this, the girl's attraction, which had been formidable a second before, disappeared as if a fire had gone out. Yet he depended terribly on what her answer would be.

'I can't tonight; my aunt is coming for dinner,' the girl said rather carelessly as she began to walk on. 'Thank you.'

'I am sorry. Tomorrow night?'

She looked sideways at him – she was not much shorter than he – and her smile was lovely, quick, amused. 'Oh. I can see you tonight. My aunt comes every Saturday.'

'Very good! At what time? Eight? Seven-thirty?'

They had arrived at her house door.

'Seven-thirty. I must not be too late. The bottom bell.' She indicated without pushing it. 'Arrivederci.'

At seven-thirty precisely, Ray pressed the bottom bell. He had a new shirt, new tie and new shoes. And he had made a reservation (in the name of Gordon) at the Graspo di Ua, since he thought it unlikely that Coleman and Inez would dine there two nights in a row.

Elisabetta opened the door. She wore a pale blue dress, lighter than her work smock. The colour became her. 'Buona sera. Come upstairs. I will be ready in a moment.'

Ray went upstairs and met her parents and her aunt, who were drinking glasses of red wine in the dining-room, where an oval table was set for four. Soup bowls stood ready on plates. The aunt and the father resembled each other. The mother was large and blonde like Elisabetta, and smiled easily, but Ray could see that she was looking him over carefully.

Ray was not asked to sit down, and after she had introduced them Elisabetta reappeared almost at once in her coat.

'I am staying next door with Signora Calliuoli,' Ray said – he was sure unnecessarily – to Elisabetta's mother.

'Ah, si. Are you here for a long time?'

'For a few days.'

'You should be home by eleven, Elisabetta,' said her father.

'Don't I know I have to get up with the pigeons!' said Elisabetta.

'Where are you going to have dinner?' asked her mother.

Ray cleared his throat, which was still husky. 'I thought at the Graspo di Ua.'

'Ah, very good,' remarked her aunt, unsmiling.

'Yes, I think it is quite good,' said Ray.

'Let's go,' Elisabetta said. 'Good night, Aunt Rosalia.' She embraced her aunt's shoulder and gave her a kiss on the cheek.

6

Elisabetta – her last name was Stefano – was pleased by the restaurant. That Ray could see as they went in.

And there was no Coleman in sight.

Ray ordered a Scotch, the girl a Cinzano. She was perhaps twenty-four or -five, Ray thought. He felt still far from well, was vaguely shaky and full of aches, but he tried to conceal this by a slow and formal manner, and made conversation with such questions as, 'Have you always lived in Venice?'

Elisabetta had been born in Venice, and so had her mother, but her father was from a town south of Florence which Ray had not heard of. Her father was manager of a leather goods shop near the Ponte di Rialto. 'Are you a police agent?' Elisabetta asked, looking at him with a smiling earnestness across the table.

'*Dio mio*, no! What made you think that?'

'Or a spy?' she said, giggling nervously.

Much of her glamour dropped away then. 'Not a spy either.' But she had a lovely complexion, a really spectacular complexion. 'If I were a spy,' he began carefully, 'my government would give me all I needed – a passport, a name, an hotel.'

She hung her pocketbook on a hook provided by the waiter.

The hook rested on a disc flat on the table and curved over the edge. 'Did you tell me your real name?'

'Yes. Philip Gordon. You wonder why I'm not in an hotel. I shall tell you why. I am trying to avoid some friends for a few days. American friends.'

She frowned, sceptical. 'Really? Why?'

'Because they want me to go back to Rome with them. They are going on from Rome to London. If I went to an hotel, they would find me, because they did not believe me when I said I was leaving for America. You understand?' It sounded unconvincing and he felt it was made vaguer, rather than more straightforward, by his rather simple Italian. He could see that she didn't believe him, that she was uneasy because of this. He looked at his wrist-watch. 'You must help me watch the time, if you have to be back by eleven. It is five past eight now.'

Her lips spread in a smile then. 'Oh, they are not so severe.'

She had large white teeth, a full, generous mouth. She would be lovely in bed, Ray thought, and wondered if she could possibly be a virgin? If she was twenty-five, or maybe only twenty-two? He sought to bolster his story, but the waiter arrived.

'My friends are all young men,' Ray said when the waiter had taken their order. 'Old college friends. A little rough. When I said I was not going back to Rome with them, they threw me into the water. Two nights ago. That is why I had a cold yesterday.'

'The water *where*?' asked Elisabetta with alarm.

'Oh, one of the canals. I got out right away, but it was cold, you know. I had a long walk home. To my hotel. I told my friends I was leaving, and I packed, but—'

'Did they apologize?'

'Oh, yes, in a way.' Ray smiled. 'But I know they did not believe I was leaving. I checked in my valise at the railway station. I thought it would be nice to be free for a few days.'

The girl's first course arrived, and she picked up her fork

70

with an anticipatory smile. 'I do not believe you. Not any of it.'

'Why do you not believe me?'

'What work do you do in the United States?'

'I have an art gallery,' Ray replied.

Elisabetta giggled again. 'I think you tell one lie after another.' She looked to right and left of her, then said softly, 'I think you have done something wrong and you are hiding.'

Ray also looked around him, but only for Coleman. 'I think you want to insult me,' he said with a smile, and began on his soup.

'I am so tired of Venice,' she said with a sigh.

'Why?'

'It is always the same. Cold in the winter, crowded with tourists in the summer. But always the same people. Not the tourists, the people I am with.' She rambled on in this vein for two or three minutes, not looking at Ray, her face childlike with petulant dissatisfaction, with boredom, with – Ray saw to his dismay – a lack of intelligence.

Ray listened politely. There was only one thing to suggest to such girls, he thought, and that was to get married, to exchange one kind of boredom for another, perhaps, but with a different scene and a different person. At last he said, 'Can't you take a trip somewhere? Or go to another city to work? Like Florence?'

'Ah, Florence. I was there once,' said Elisabetta without enthusiasm.

There was nothing left but marriage, so Ray said, 'Do you want to marry?'

'Oh, some day. I am in no hurry. But I am already twenty-two. That is not old though, is it? Do I look twenty-two?'

'No. I suppose you look twenty,' Ray said.

This pleased her. She drank her wine, and he poured more. 'That boy in the bar, Alfonso,' she said, 'he wants to marry me. But he is not very interesting.'

71

Ray supposed it was the husky young man he had seen coming on duty as Elisabetta left last evening. He felt that she was talking to him as she might to another man, or to another girl, even, which gave a sudden feeling of flatness to the evening. On the other hand, in the last few minutes, the girl's sexual attraction had disappeared for him. Her body might be very nice, but what she said bored him and killed his desire.

Now she talked about her parents, their small quarrels about everything. Her mother was interested in investing more and more money. Stocks. Her father wanted to buy a farm near Chioggia to retire to, and he wanted to start buying it now. She had no brothers or sisters. She did not know which side she was on, her father's or her mother's, and she said their quarrels were tearing her apart. She gave half her salary to her parents, and she let them quarrel over what they did with it. Now her Aunt Rosalia was a lot more sensible, but the trouble was she had no influence – no *influenza* – on either of her parents.

They reached the dessert. The girl wanted something with ice cream. Ray poured the last of the wine for himself, as the girl's glass was nearly full.

'Shall I tell you the truth about myself?' Ray asked in a moment of silence.

'Yes.' Elisabetta looked at him with serious eyes, sobered by the recounting of her own life.

'My father-in-law is in Venice and he wants to kill me. My wife died a month ago. It was my father-in-law who pushed me into the water. The water between the Lido and the land.'

'In the lagoon.' Elisabetta's eyes seemed to retreat as she stared at him. Her full lips were solemn. 'Your wife died?'

'She was a suicide,' Ray said, 'and her father thinks I am to blame. I – I don't think I am. But he wants to kill me, so I must hide to protect myself.'

'Why don't you leave Venice then?'

Ray did not answer for a moment, and he could see his silence tip the scales of the girl's mind. She didn't believe him.

'You are telling me another story. Why do you tell me lies?' Now the lips smiled. 'You do not need to tell me lies. Or even the truth,' she added with a gesture, lifting her left hand from the table. 'Do you think you have to explain everything? At least make up better stories when you do!' She laughed.

Ray looked at her, at her round, strong shoulders, yet without really seeing her. He could not decide if she was something he had to deal with, or something he should let alone.

'Why don't you get your valise from the railway station?' she asked. 'You know what I think? I think you did something wrong.' She leaned forward and whispered. 'Maybe you stole something. Maybe jewellery. Meanwhile – maybe you have a big bill at an hotel where you cannot pay. So you leave the hotel and you hide. There.'

'There,' Ray repeated, for want of anything else to say.

'I think you stole something, and you are worried,' Elisabetta said, and began to eat her dessert.

'Do I look like a thief?'

She lifted her eyes to his. Her eyes looked golden now. 'I do in truth think you look guilty about something.' She looked a little afraid of him after she had said it.

Culpa. Mea culpa. Ray resented it and felt embarrassed also, as if she had told him that he had some unattractive trait such as B.O., halitosis, or a hunchback, something he couldn't get rid of. 'In this case, you're wrong,' he said, but he saw he had made no impression on her.

She watched him with gleaming, mischievous eyes. 'Of course you do not have to tell what it is you did, if you do not want to. I do not think you look like a real criminal. Not professional.'

Just an amateur, Ray supposed. A mistake-maker. The jazz music of the barbershop went through his head. *Sweet Lorraine* distorted almost beyond recognition, a trumpet cavorting above the piano. In Mallorca, the constant jazz had prevented him from reading, painting, even thinking. Peggy had wanted L.P.s on all the time, stacks of them, all morning, all afternoon, and the damned jangling jazz was one of the things, a major thing, that had driven him out of the house the noon of the afternoon she died. But yesterday in the barbershop he had enjoyed the same kind of music, or had at least been tolerant of it. He could not come to any conclusion about this, but he had been glad yesterday that he felt tolerant and even enjoyed the music. Had he been anaesthetized by fever? He was not going to tell the girl the most important thing about his relationship with his father-in-law, Ray thought, and that was that his father-in-law probably thought he was dead. Elisabetta wouldn't believe it, anyway, and it was a dark and precious secret to Ray, not one to waste, even unbelieved. Then his mental rejection of her brought a feeling of guilt, a surge in the opposite direction, towards her.

'Do you like dancing?' he asked.

She cocked her head, smiling. 'You are very strange. Always changing the subject.'

They went to a night-club some distance away, through a dozen streets, around corners, a dark maze away from the Graspo di Ua. The girl knew the way exactly, and filled Ray with wonder at her sense of direction. Without a thread, she led him through a labyrinth and brought him before an open red door from which steps led down.

Ray ordered champagne, because it seemed the thing to do. The lights were dim, the place small, and only half filled. Two or three of the girls who were dancing obviously worked there. The orchestra had four men.

'I was here only once before,' Elisabetta confided to Ray as they were dancing. 'With an officer in the Italian Navy.'

The girl was pleasant to hold, but he did not like her perfume.

And he felt extraordinarily tired. Tomorrow he would look up Coleman, he thought, and give him a surprise. He did not yet know how or where, but an idea would come to him. And if Coleman had left the city, he would track him down.

The orchestra stopped for a few seconds, then began a samba. Ray did not want to dance any longer.

'You are tired,' Elisabetta said. 'Let's sit down. I think you still have fever.'

It was difficult to talk over the music. Elisabetta did not want any more champagne. Ray poured for himself. He looked at the doorway, where the steps descended, and imagined Inez coming down them, followed by Coleman. Inez must know by now, Ray thought. She must have tried to ring him at the Seguso, probably not telling Coleman that she had tried, and the Seguso might well have said that Signor Garrett had not come in for two nights. The girl at the Seguso would say it in a tone of some alarm, Ray was sure. Inez would question Coleman, and Coleman would say he had put him off at Accademia or at the Zattere quay, but Inez might not believe him. Yes, probably a great deal was going on between Inez and Coleman now, and what would Inez's reaction be? What would she do? What would anybody do? That was a question, a problem, and perhaps different people would behave in different ways.

'What are you worried about?' asked Elisabetta. She was smiling, a little merry on the champagne.

'I don't know. Nothing.' He felt faint, blank, dead or perhaps dying. Distant, high-pitched bells rang in his ears. The girl was saying something that he could not hear, looking off to one side now, and her unconcern at his condition made him feel quite alone. He breathed deeply, one deep breath after another of the tobacco-laden air. The girl did not notice. The faintness passed.

A few moments later, they were out on the street, walking. The girl said it was not far back to where they lived, and there was no boat that could be of any help. The lanes were moist under their shoes. The girl held his arm and chattered on about her last summer's vacation. She had gone to visit relatives in the Ticino. They had cows and a big house. They had taken her to Zurich. She thought Zurich was much cleaner than Venice. Ray could feel the warmth of the girl's arm next to his. He did not feel faint now, but he felt alone and lost, without purpose, without identity. Wouldn't it be strange, he thought, if he really *were* dead, if he were dreaming all of this, or if by some strange process – which was the assumption on which nearly all ghost stories were based – he was a ghost visible to a few people, like this girl, a ghost who tomorrow would not be in the room at Signora Calliuoli's, would have left not even an unmade bed behind him, only a strange memory in the minds of the few who had seen him, the few whom other people might not believe when they spoke of him?

But the dark canals were very real, and so was the rat that crossed their path twenty feet ahead, running from a hole in a house wall to a hole in the stone parapet that bordered the canal, where a barge stirred sleepily against its rope mooring, making a piggish sound like *schlurp*. The girl had seen the rat, but had interrupted what she was saying by only a brief 'Ooh!' and gone on. A light, fixed on the corner of a house so it would illuminate four streets, seemed to burn with patience, waiting for persons not yet arrived, persons who would carry out some action below it.

'How long are you really going to be here?' asked Elisabetta.

Ray saw that they had entered their street. 'Three or four days.'

'Thank you for this evening,' Elisabetta said in her doorway. She looked quickly at her watch, but Ray doubted if she could see the time on it. 'I think it's before eleven. We are very good.'

He had reached a state of not hearing what she said, and yet he did not want to leave her.

'Something worries you, Filipo. Or are you just very tired?' She whispered now, as if in her own street she did not want to disturb the neighbours because she knew them.

'Not very tired. Good night, Elisabetta.' He squeezed her left hand in his for an instant, had no desire to kiss her or to try to, yet he felt that he loved her. 'You've got your key?'

'Oh, but certainly.' She opened the door softly, and waved him good-bye before she closed it.

An old woman in black, whom Ray had never seen before, opened the door for him. Ray murmured an apology for his lateness, and she assured him cheerfully that she never slept, so it was no trouble to her. Ray climbed the stairs quietly. Never slept? Never undressed then? The mother of Signora Calliuoli? Ray leaned over the stair-well at his floor. The light below was extinguished now, and he heard not a sound.

7

At a quarter past ten the next morning, Ray entered the Calle San Moisè, the street of the Hotel Bauer-Gruenwald. He felt it was the ripe time of the morning, when most likely Coleman and Inez would be setting forth for their morning's activities – shopping, a bit of tourism, or simply a walk. Ray walked with his head a little down, as tautly as if he expected a gunshot, a bullet in his body, at any second. He waited at the door of a shop across the street from the hotel's entrance and some thirty feet to one side of it. It was Sunday, and only a few shops were open. And for twenty minutes, nothing happened, except that ten or fifteen people, including bellhops, went in and out of the hotel. Ray did not know exactly what he wanted or intended to do, but he wanted to see Coleman, or Inez, and see the way they acted. When they did not appear, he pictured them arguing upstairs in one of the rooms about whether he was alive or dead, though he knew this was irrational. They might be still breakfasting, or chatting casually as Coleman stood in the bathroom shaving.

Ray walked on and found a bar with a telephone. He looked up the Bauer-Gruenwald number and dialled it. 'Signor Col-e-man, per favore,' Ray said.

"Allo?" said Inez's voice. "Allo?"

Ray did not answer.

'Is this Ray? – Ray? Is it you – Edward, come here!'

Ray hung up.

Yes, Inez was upset. Coleman would be more upset, Ray thought. Coleman – if he knew Ray had not gone back to the Seguso, and Ray had not much doubt Coleman did know that – would assume he had drowned. Coleman would think, therefore, the silent telephone call was an accident, that the hotel switchboard had made a mistake, or cut someone off. But Coleman would suffer a little doubt, too. And whatever Coleman had told Inez, the telephone call would stir up the mystery again in her mind. Had it been Ray telephoning? If not, then where was Ray? Could Coleman tell her? Ray walked slowly past the Bauer-Gruenwald, and jumped slightly as he saw Inez in a black fur coat coming out the glass doors. Ray stepped into a narrow street to his left.

Inez walked briskly past him, only twenty feet away.

Ray followed her at a distance. She turned right into the Calle Vallaresso, which led to Harry's Bar on the corner and to the vaporetto dock at its end. Ray saw that she was going to take a boat. There were several people on the dock, waiting. Ray walked to the right side of the dock and turned his back on the crowd, facing the water. Inez did not take the first boat. She was going in the other direction then. Ray wanted very much to see her face, but was afraid to look lest his eyes attract hers. He had not been able to see her face clearly when she came out of the hotel.

Another boat arrived, and Inez boarded it, as did most of the people on the dock. Ray got on among the last, and stood at the rear of the boat. They stopped at Santa Maria della Salute on the other side of the canal. Inez did not get off. Ray could see her through the stern window of the boat, seated on one of the bench seats, her back to him. She wore the yellow-feathered hat. The boat rushed on.

79

'*Giglio!*' called the conductor.

A creak of dock as the boat touched.

Inez did not move.

'*Accademia the next stop!*' shouted the conductor.

They chugged smoothly towards the arched wooden bridge at Accademia. Inez stood up, moved forward and to the left where the boat's door was. Ray walked along the port deck, keeping behind the ten or twelve debarking passengers. Inez, on the pavement in front of the Accademia di Belle Arti, looked all around her as if she did not know her way, and stopped a passer-by. The man pointed to the broad street that went across the island.

Ray followed her slowly. No need to rush now, to watch her turnings, because he knew where she was going. In the wide courtlike area behind the Seguso, Ray walked left, a direction that would bring him to the canal that went along the side of the pensione, but which was also a dead end, because no pavement bordered the canal just here. Inez also disappeared in the *sotto-porto* which led to the Ruskin house. Ray retraced his steps quickly, crossed the open area diagonally, found another street which led to the little canal, but here, he knew, were pavements and also a bridge. He crossed the bridge over the canal, and turned right on the pavement. Now the Seguso lay on his right, across the canal from him. An arched stone bridge spanned the canal on the Zattere quay. Ray remained at the foot of the bridge, the end away from the Seguso.

Inez was not in view. Was she still talking inside the pensione, or had she left already? He could not see her on the quay. Ray rested his arms on the bridge parapet, and looked over his shoulder at the Seguso's entrance. He looked up at the Seguso's windows, at the fourth window from the bottom which had been his, giving on the little canal, and just then, Inez's light hat, dark coat appeared in its greyness, and Ray looked away, out towards the length of Giudecca.

Inez had asked to see his room. They had not yet packed up his things, Ray supposed. He was sorry he had a bill there, but at least they had his suitcase. What was Inez telling them? Not, surely, that he might be dead. What was she asking them? That could be any number of things, what he had said to them, if he had said anything, if he had telephoned – questions that were quickly answered, leaving the mystery still there. Ray had disappeared. Ray felt an instant's shame at his behaviour, at his silent telephone call less than an hour earlier, and the shame almost immediately became anger, anger against Coleman.

Well I'm not going to his hotel. I don't give a damn, Ray could hear Coleman saying. *Why do you think something's happened to him? He's probably run off, chucked everything and run off. You know damned well he's got Peggy on his conscience.*

Would Inez believe that? No. Would she question Coleman until he told her the truth? Ray could not imagine Coleman telling the truth about that night to anyone. Was Coleman expecting daily that the body would be reported? Washed up somewhere? Probably.

Inez was coming out of the pensione.

Ray grew tense, hoping she would not turn in his direction because she was walking forward from the hotel, past the Ruskin turn, more slowly and thoughtfully than she had walked from Accademia. She turned right on the Zattere quay, so that her back was to him. Ray followed her, but at such a safe distance now, the following was purposeless for observing her. He observed the black spot that was her fur coat. She passed the Zattere boat stop and turned right.

He followed her back to Accademia, where she crossed the bridge. She walked at a moderate pace, though the air was nippy and most people on the street hurried. She stopped now and then to look into a shop-window – a closed stationery shop, a fancy goods shop – completely demolishing Ray's fantasy that she was thinking about him, and making Ray feel slightly hurt and also absurd for feeling so. After all, what was he to Inez? Just someone she'd known for a few days, son-in-law of her current lover, and the legal relationship had been erased, in fact, by the death of her lover's daughter.

Inez looked as if she were passing time because she had an appointment somewhere later. It was a quarter past eleven. Ray watched her enter a bar-restaurant, in front of which tables and chairs stood out on the pavement, chairs tipped in and leaning on the tables as if they were cold also. Ray realized that his teeth were chattering, and reproached himself for not having yet bought the obvious, a sweater. He walked past the restaurant, and saw Inez standing at the cash register. Unfortunately, no shop was open near by in which to take shelter. Ray hovered round a corner, stamping his feet, ducking his chin into the upturned collar of his coat. He stared down a narrow street whose curving perspective was cut off by vertical reddish sides of houses. Used houses. Laundry stretched across the street appeared frozen stiff – men's shirts, dishtowels, shorts, white bras. He was going to become ill again after yesterday's improvement, he thought, but he did not want to turn loose of Inez. He saw a tobacconist's shop, and went in. He bought cigarettes and lit one, and examined postcards on racks, at the same time keeping an eye on the street in case Inez walked past. Ray was afraid to step out lest he run straight into Inez.

But at last he did go out as a stream of five or six young men went by the door, heading left. As Ray passed the bar-restaurant he saw that Inez was having a coffee and writing something at one of the little tables inside. The sight of her in the dim interior, framed in the rhomboid of the bar's front window, suggested a Cézanne painting. He took up his vigil in front of a little shop whose windows were full of ribbons, dress fasteners, boxes of wool, and woollen underclothing for babies. Five minutes passed. When

Inez came out and turned in his direction, Ray, taken by surprise, entered a grocery-and-wine shop where there were several customers, so no one paid him any attention. After Inez went by, Ray walked out into the street again.

Another pause, as Inez gazed into a sweet shop's window. She looked over her shoulder, once to the right, once to the left. She was probably looking for him, perhaps without much hope, but still, anyone would look, Ray thought, under the circumstances. Inez walked on, came to San Marco and walked its length. She appeared to be going back to her hotel. But at Calle Vallaresso, she turned left. Harry's Bar, Ray thought, which was disappointing, as he could not enter the small place without being seen, and it was impossible to see into it from the outside. But Inez turned right, and went into the Hotel Monaco directly across the street from Harry's. Hadn't the Smith-Peters been staying at the Monaco?

Perhaps she had a date with Coleman here; he had better watch out for him, Ray thought, and looked behind him in the narrow street. The only place to run would be into Harry's Bar or on to the boat dock. His watch said twelve thirty-five. Ray walked past the hotel entrance, quite close to it, and did not see Inez in the lobby; but the lobby had a section to the right, and she might have been in its far corner. He passed five uneasy minutes, feeling he had lost Inez and that Coleman might appear and see him at any moment. Ray decided to go into the hotel. He walked coolly towards the sign straight ahead that said BAR, past the lounge on his left, and he had almost reached the bar, when he saw Inez in the left corner of the lounge near the door, and she was apparently looking straight at him. She was cut off from his view in the next instant by the door-jamb of the lounge. He stopped, waiting. He was in a short, wide corridor which was now empty, and he watched the door of the lounge for Inez's figure.

The Smith-Peters appeared from the left, approaching the

lounge, and Ray turned his back and walked on towards the bar. There were only two people there, the barman and a customer. Ray looked back down the corridor, just as Coleman came in the front door fifty feet away. Ray turned slowly, sideways to Coleman, and when he looked again, Coleman had vanished, no doubt into the lounge. They might all come into the bar, Ray thought, and he decided to leave at once. He walked out at a pace neither fast nor slow, tensed as he passed the glass-panelled doors of the lounge where they sat, the four, only a few feet away.

Ray went out of the hotel. Sooner or later, he thought, if he continued doing this, one of them would look up, happen to look at him, and the game would be over. But just now, they had all been in animated conversation, Inez gesticulating, Mr Smith-Peters leaning forward and laughing. If Inez was going to tell them about having been to the Seguso, she was saving it for later.

In a shop in the Calle Vallaresso, Ray bought a dark blue sweater, and put it on under his jacket. He was able to see, while buying the sweater, that Coleman and his party had not passed by. They were perhaps lunching at the Monaco with the Smith-Peters.

Ray walked back slowly towards the Monaco, and now he was on guard for Antonio, who might be joining them.

The group of four had left the lounge corner, but they were not in the dining-room. Harry's Bar, perhaps. Or they could have boarded a vaporetto while he was buying the sweater. Or they could be in the bar of the hotel. It was not wise to stick his nose into the bar, but Ray felt compelled to do so. He advanced once more to the bar, where four or five people were now, none of them Coleman or of his group. Ray ordered a Scotch at the bar.

Fifteen minutes later, Inez and Coleman and the Smith-Peters came into the hotel and went into the lounge. They had probably been at Harry's Bar. Ray let another five minutes pass. Then, not permitting himself to debate, because there was too much against the idea, he went to the lounge and looked in. They were not there. Ray walked on to the dining-room, which was only half full, and was met by the head waiter. Ray saw Coleman's table on the far right, and requested a table for one on the opposite side of the room. Ray followed the head waiter to the table. He did not look towards Coleman's table for several minutes, not until he had chosen his meal and ordered a half-bottle of wine.

Whatever they were talking about, they were quite merry. Not falling about with laughter, but there was a smile on all their faces. Had Inez brought up her Seguso visit in Harry's, and had they finished discussing Garrett's disappearance? Or was Inez not going to mention it in front of other people? Was she going to speak to Coleman about it later when they were alone?

But it was the fact that Inez *knew* which fascinated Ray as he watched her laughing and talking, waving a hand gracefully. She might think him dead, murdered by Coleman, but it was not influencing her manner at luncheon. Ray found this fact absorbing. And at any minute she might look in his direction – he was perhaps fifty feet away – and look again and recognize him, provided she was not shortsighted.

Again a curious anger stirred in Ray as he slowly ate his food. Coleman looked so pleased with himself, as if he had done the right thing, something commendable, something at any rate for which he would never have to apologize to anyone. In a way, it was as if the whole group, Antonio also if he knew, accepted his disappearance, maybe his murder, as no more than fitting.

Ray suddenly could eat no more. A cheese tray arrived anyway, a basket of fruit to choose from, and Ray declined them. He finished his wine, paid the bill, and made an unobtrusive exit. No cry followed him. It was as if he were invisible, a ghost.

A few flakes of snow were falling, but they disappeared near the pavement, or as soon as they touched the ground. The shops were mostly closed now, but Ray found a tobacconist open. He wanted something to read. The shop had some Penguin books. Ray chose one on drawings of the fifteenth and sixteenth centuries. It had a section of illustrations. His walk homeward took him past the bar-caffè where Elisabetta worked. Ray glanced in, not expecting to see her, but she was there, smiling her wide, healthy, blonde smile at a dumpy woman who stood at the counter, maybe one of Elisabetta's neighbours or friends. Ray remembered now that Elisabetta had said she was going to work from nine until two today. Elisabetta and the woman were real, Ray thought; they were connected. But he felt that, if he had walked into the bar, he might not have been seen by Elisabetta or by anyone else.

He began to trot against the cold and in order to get home sooner. There was no doubt, he still had some fever.

Signora Calliuoli opened the door for him, smiling. 'It's a cold day. A little snow.'

'Yes,' Ray said. The house smelled rather pleasantly of tomato sauce. 'I was wondering if I could have a hot bath?'

'Ah, si! In fifteen minutes the water will be hot.'

Ray went up to his room. He had thought, an hour ago, of writing to his friend Mac in Xanuanx. Now he realized he could not write to anyone as long as he was pretending to have vanished. Ray felt depressed and lonely. His anger against Coleman had mysteriously disappeared. He thought of Peggy as he lowered himself into the tub of hot water. In the corner of the bathroom, an electric stove radiated an orange heat. The linoleum had an ugly pattern of red and green on a cream ground, and was worn in spots, showing dark red weaving. Not beautiful, but in a Bonnard it might have been. Ray owned a Bonnard in St Louis, and as he recalled it, he immediately attached a present value to it – about fifty-five thousand dollars – since he was now a dealer. He could foresee a time when the sudden view, the contemplation of paintings, would lose their wonder. Well, he *could* lose it, he supposed, but he did not intend to let that happen. *Do you ever feel that the world is not enough?* Peggy had asked him that at least twice. Ray had wanted to find out from her how the world was not enough, and Peggy had finally said she meant that the stars and the atoms, the systems of religion which stretch the imagination and still remain unfinished, and all painting and music – all *this* was not enough, and the human mind (or maybe the soul for Peggy) desired more. It might have been her death cry, Ray thought, if she had had one. *The world is not enough, therefore I leave it to find something bigger.* It was certainly the way she had felt about sex, because time after time—

Ray's memory boggled and dodged. He had always, always had the feeling that no matter how good it was, how much Peggy had enjoyed it, she was thinking that she must have missed something, missed somehow the essence, and for Peggy the only help was, 'Let's do it again.' Or 'Let's get away early and come home and go to bed.' It had been delightful at first, a sexy girl, a dream-wife and all that. Then sameness, even fatigue had begun to set in, camouflaged for a very long time, eight months perhaps, by physical pleasure, the feeling that the sex organs had separate existences of their own, weren't even connected with Peggy or him. Ray remembered thinking this many times when, not having wanted to make love, he had found his body quite willing. Then he remembered times, maybe three times, when they had gone to bed before going out to dinner, made love twice (or for Peggy six times), and Ray had become short-tempered, ready with a cutting remark to Peggy or to anyone, some of which he never made, some of which he had, afterwards feeling ashamed of himself. He had begun to be busy around five or six in the afternoons, going out to do errands, or busy with his painting. He had also been frank enough to put it in words to Peggy: 'If we go to bed in the afternoon, I'm a little tired for the night.' Mild enough. Peggy's face had fallen, briefly, when he had said that, Ray remembered.

And though she hadn't again proposed any afternoons in bed, Ray had seen that she had wanted to a few times. But no one, no friend, if they'd known the situation, no doctor, no Coleman could have possibly said that he neglected Peggy in the bed department, or overstrained her as far as he could tell. (Ray wished now he'd had a friend to talk to. Would that have helped? Mac, for instance. He had thought of talking to Mac, but he had felt he hadn't known Mac long enough, or didn't know him well enough. Prudishness.) And this was something he hadn't yet said clearly to Coleman, who still thought he had made demands on Peggy, or shocked her. This was what he had wanted to say the night of the Lido. Ray knew he suffered the damnable torture of being misunderstood and maligned, combined with the inability to speak to defend himself or even to find an ear: a circumstance ludicrous rather than pitiable to anyone who was not in it. From a big jolt like this, one could go on to little jolts, he foresaw, bitter reactions to little slights, and thus a paranoid would be created.

And, as another example of their never having quarrelled and of Peggy's wanting something 'better', she had never arrived at the right moment to have a child. Ray had very much wanted a child, conceived and gestated in Xanuanx, born, maybe, in Rome or Paris. It was always 'Not yet – but soon' with Peggy. Since she would have been bearing the brunt of it, Ray hadn't insisted or argued. Should he have insisted? It seemed brutal and vulgar to insist, and he knew he never could have. But a child on the way might have prevented her suicide. Funny Coleman had never mentioned that. Perhaps it was too earthy for Coleman. Ray remembered, wincing, his father's P.S. to one letter after they had been married for a year: 'Any chance of a grandchild any ways soon? Tell me the news.' There wasn't any news.

Ray turned on a trickle of hot water from the big scratched nickel tap, and dragged the hand towel, which he was using as wash-cloth, absently over his chest.

It was too bad that Peggy's painting hadn't been 'enough' for her, that she hadn't been sufficiently fascinated by that struggle towards mastery or perfection or whatever it was, which was endless and quite big and absorbing enough for artists like Michelangelo, da Vinci, Braque and Klee. But it was impossible for Ray to imagine Peggy working really hard, the way her father did. Coleman definitely worked. Whether Ray liked his painting or not, he had to admit Coleman threw himself into it. Whereas Peggy had for only short stretches, three weeks here and there. Ray had heard about and seen these stretches in Rome in the months before they were married, but there had been no such stretches in Mallorca. The year and more in Mallorca suddenly seemed to Ray a prolonged honeymoon – from Peggy's point of view. One couldn't build a life in that atmosphere. Ray got out of the tub, impatient with himself for thinking nothing but platitudes.

He was still ill, he realized, and he thought he had better get rid of whatever he had before he tried to do anything else.

8

Coleman at that moment, ten minutes to three in the afternoon, was entering his and Inez's two-room suite in the Bauer-Gruenwald, having left Inez and the Smith-Peters at the San Marco boat stop, whence they were taking a boat for some sightseeing. Coleman had said he wanted to work on some ideas, which was true, but he also wanted to get away from Inez for the afternoon. She was being chilly, was on the brink of questioning him again about Ray, Coleman knew. He did not intend to let her think he was worried, because he wasn't. Least of all did he worry or care what Inez thought.

The quiet and solitude of the two primly tidied rooms were a pleasure to Coleman, and after he had taken off his jacket and tie and changed into floppy, moccasin-like house slippers, he rubbed his hands together and slowly walked, like a comfortable bear now, from his and Inez's bedroom through the bathroom which separated the rooms and into what he thought of as his room. Here he was accustomed to drawing, and writing an occasional letter (he had not answered every single one concerning Peggy's death, but had convinced himself he didn't have to, as he was above, or maybe even below, this kind of bourgeois convention), but so far had not slept, though Inez made him rumple the bed every night for the benefit of the maid. Coleman got a Venus pencil from his writing-table drawer, and picked up a sixteen-by-twelve-inch pad. He began to sketch an imaginary cathedral seen from above, its arms coming down to make an enclosure in the foreground of the picture. In the foreground, he drew seven figures, showing only the tops of their heads and some of their noses, a few gesticulating hands, a few knees and feet.

This was his new tack: the human figure seen from directly overhead. He felt this view, showing little, still showed much. His sketch, as he had anticipated, gave a mischievousness and duplicity to his assembled conspirators. That was to be the title, 'The Conspiracy'. One of the shoes on the standing men was a black business shoe, another a jester's pointed shoe, another a tennis shoe. One of the men was bald, another wore a bowler. The shoulders of one bore the epaulets of a naval officer, American. Coleman worked for nearly an hour on his sketch, tore it out of the pad and propped it up against his paintbox on the writing table, and retreated into the bathroom to get a view of it.

He thought of an improvement in the composition, and went back to his drawing pad and a new page. Before he had finished this, Inez returned, and entered by the other room. Coleman greeted her without turning round. By now one slipper was off, and he had pulled his shirt out of his trousers.

'Well, how was the afternoon?' Coleman asked, still drawing, as Inez came in.

'I couldn't face the museum. Too cold. So we had another coffee, and I left them.' She turned away to hang up her coat.

Coleman heard her close a door, he thought the bathroom door, but glancing round, he saw that it was her room door. Faintly, he heard her saying something on the telephone. He went on with his work. She was probably trying the Seguso again for Ray, he thought, and who knew? Ray might answer.

A couple of minutes later, Inez came in, knocking perfunctorily on the bathroom door which stood open. 'Listen, Edward –
if you have a moment. I'm sorry to disturb you, but it is something
important.'

Coleman turned round on the bed and sat up straighter.
'What, dear?'

'I went to the Seguso this morning – to see if they had any
news of Ray. They have not and he has left no message.'

'Well, you knew that,' Coleman interrupted.

'I know, but they were a little worried also, because all his
things are there still. They had not packed up his things, but I
think by now they have. And his passport was in his room.' Inez
stood in her silk-stockinged feet, a small, straight, earnest figure
framed in the open bathroom door.

'Well? – I've told you, I think he ran off, just chucked everything.' Coleman shrugged. 'How am I to know?'

'I just rang the American Consulate,' Inez continued. 'They
know nothing about him, where he is, but the Pensione Seguso
this morning telephoned them about the passport in his room.
Not only passport but toothbrush, Traveller's Cheques, every –
little – thing.' She pumped with her arms for emphasis.

'It's not my business,' Coleman said, 'and I don't see that it's
yours.'

Inez sighed. 'You said you put him down at the Zattere quay.'

'Yes, right *at* the hotel. The hotel door wasn't fifty feet away.'
Coleman gesticulated also. 'He obviously decided not to go
home that night – if that was the night he didn't turn up. Seems
to be.'

'Yes. He wasn't drunk, was he?'

'No, he wasn't drunk. But I told you he was in a hell of a state
of mind. He feels guilty. He feels awful.' Coleman stared in front
of him for a moment, and longed to get back to his drawing. 'I'm
sure he was carrying some money. He always does. He could've

gone to the railroad station and got the next train out. Stayed at some other hotel and just beat it the next day.'

'Beat it?'

'Vanished.' Another shrug. 'But as I say, it does support what I think, doesn't it? What I believe, what I know is true. Ray could've prevented Peggy's death, and he didn't take the trouble.'

Inez looked up at the ceiling, wrung her hands briefly. 'You are obsessed by that. How can you know?'

Coleman smiled gently and impatiently. 'I've talked to him. I know guilt when I see it.'

'The Consulate told me they are going to notify the parents in America. In—'

'St Louis, Missouri,' Coleman said.

'Yes.'

'Very good. So they should.' Coleman turned back to his drawing, then felt compelled to stand up, to give Inez his attention, because she expected it. She was upset. She had left the Smith-Peters to come back and talk to him. He went over and put his short, heavy hands lightly on her shoulders, kissed her cheek. She looked older, because she was worried, but she lifted her face to his expectantly, awaiting words of strength, even orders, and Coleman said, 'Honey, I don't see that it's our business. Ray knows where *we* are. If he wants to go off by himself – vanish, even – isn't that his business? Matter of fact, did you know the police have no right to interfere with a person who wants to disappear? I read that in an article somewhere the other day. Only if a man is deserting a family or has debts can they track him down and bring him back.' Coleman patted her shoulders and laughed, happily. 'An individual's got some rights still in this bureaucratic society,' he said, turning away back to the bed and his drawing.

'I think I saw Ray today,' Inez said.

'Oh? Where?' Coleman asked over his shoulder. He blinked to conceal a sudden annoyance.

'It was – oh, I don't know, somewhere between Accademia and San Marco. One of the streets. I could be wrong. It looked like his head and shoulders. From the back.' She looked at Coleman.

Coleman shrugged. 'Could be. Why not?' He knew she was thinking, asking herself again, or was about to ask him again, 'Did you have a quarrel on the Lido that night? Did you fight on the boat?' Inez knew – because Coleman had been wise enough to tell her outright before she found out from Corrado – that he had driven the boat back alone with Ray that night. And she had asked him two nights ago, after he had told her he had dropped Ray at the Zattere quay, if he had not had a fight with Ray on the boat, and Coleman had said no. A fight on the boat meant one thing, that he might have pushed Ray overboard, unconscious or dead. Coleman's annoyance grew as he looked at Inez, and he wished he hadn't thrown away the gun. He had bought the gun in Rome, had had it twelve hours only, and had thrown it away wrapped in a newspaper in a rubbish basket that night, after he thought he wouldn't need it any longer, after he thought Ray was dead. Coleman tried to calm himself and asked, 'I gather you didn't go up and see if he was Ray?'

'He went down a street, the man. I lost him. Yes, I would have gone up to see if he was Ray.'

'My dear, your guess is as good as mine.' Coleman sat down on the bed, but on the other side of the bed so that he was more or less facing Inez. The body hadn't been washed up, Coleman reminded himself. Bodies always were washed up. Of course only three days had passed. But with all the islands around Venice, the Lido, San Erasmo, San Francesco del Deserto (the cemetery island, bristling with cypresses), his body should have washed up by now if he were drowned. Coleman watched the papers daily, morning and evening. He wished now that he had made sure he was dead before pushing him off the boat. He had been in too much of a hurry. Very well, if it had to be done still again, it would

94

be done again, Coleman thought with grim resignation, and looked at Inez. 'What do you expect me to do? Why are you telling me all this?'

'Well—' Inez said, folding her arms. She put one stockinged foot atop the instep of the other, an awkward, untypical stance. 'They will surely question you – the police, no? Maybe all of us, but you are the one who saw him last.'

'The police? I don't know, dear. Maybe the porter at the Seguso saw him last.'

'I asked that. He didn't come in at all Thursday night.'

'Let them question me,' Coleman said. Then he had a brief feeling that Ray was really dead. But he knew it was unfounded. He didn't *know*, and that was what was so maddening. Ray could tell the police that he, Coleman, had made two attempts on his life. Coleman gave a splutter of laughter suddenly, and looked at Inez. Ray hadn't the guts to do that. Ray wouldn't.

'What is funny?'

'The seriousness with which we're taking all this,' Coleman said. 'Come here and see my new drawing. My new idea.'

Inez came towards him, arms still folded until she drew near him, and then she put her hand on his shoulder and looked at his drawing. 'These are people?' she asked, smiling.

'Yes. Seen from overhead. There's my first drawing.' He pointed, but the drawing had slipped flat from its prop against the paintbox. Coleman went round the foot of the bed and stood it up again. 'I like them, don't you? These people seen from the top?'

'It's very funny. With the noses.'

Coleman nodded, pleased. 'I want to try it in colour. Maybe from now on I'll just paint people seen from above. An angel's-eye view.'

'Edward, let's go away. Let's leave here.'

'Leave Venice? I thought you wanted to stay another week.'

'You don't need Venice for painting. You're not painting

Venice.' She gestured towards his two drawings. 'Let's go to my house. Central heating, you know. Just installed. Not like the Smith-Peters, who will probably never get theirs.' She smiled at him.

She meant her house near Ste Maxime. The South of France. Coleman realized that he did not want to leave Venice until he knew about Ray, that he would not. 'We've hardly been here a week.'

'The weather's so awful.'

'So is it in France.'

'But at least it's my place, our place.'

Coleman chuckled. 'I've never seen it.'

'You can have a studio of your own there. It's not like an hotel.' Inez circled his neck with her arms. 'Please let's go. Tomorrow.'

'Aren't we going to that thing at the Fenice the day *after* tomorrow?'

'That's of no importance. Let's see now if we can get a plane tomorrow to Nice.'

Coleman took her arms down gently from his neck. 'What do you mean I'm not painting Venice? Look at that drawing.' He pointed to the first. 'That's a Venetian church.'

'I am not happy here. I feel uncomfortable.'

Coleman did not want to ask her why. He knew. He went to his jacket and took the next to last cigar from his tortoiseshell case. He must remember to buy more this evening, he thought. The telephone rang in Inez's room, and Coleman was glad, because he could not think of anything to say to her.

Inez went to the telephone more quickly than she usually did. ''Allo? Oh, 'allo. Antonio!'

Coleman groaned mentally, started to shut the bathroom door, then thought perhaps Inez would think it rude if he did. Antonio was downstairs, Coleman learned from what Inez was saying.

'Oh, please don't. Antonio. Not yet. Antonio, I would like to see you. Let me come down. I'll just be a minute. We'll have a coffee. I will see you in two minutes.'

Coleman watched her put on her shoes. He was getting a glass of water at the bathroom tap.

'Antonio's downstairs,' she said. 'I am going to see him for a few minutes.'

'Oh? What's he up to?'

'Nothing. I just thought I would see him since he's here.' She put on her fur coat, but not her hat, and glanced at herself in the mirror. 'I won't bother with lipstick,' she said to herself.

'When'll you be back?'

'Maybe in fifteen minutes,' she said with a graceful backward turn of hand. 'Bye-bye, Edward.'

Her air of urgency was unusual, and Coleman guessed what Antonio had said. Antonio was going back to Naples, or Amalfi, and Inez wanted to persuade him to stay on. Coleman did not like Antonio. He did not dislike him violently, he had seen worse parasites, but he disliked him. Coleman thought Antonio suspected that he had something to do with Ray's disappearance – maybe even had killed him, and Antonio wanted to keep clear of any mess. Coleman had no doubt that Inez had arranged to see Antonio alone at least once since Thursday night, and that they had had a good chat. Coleman sighed, then took a reassuring puff of his cigar.

He walked to the window and looked out. It was a beautiful view, over the tops of some houses, towards the Grand Canal, with lights of ships and shore in the gathering darkness. And the rise of abundant steam heat into Coleman's face from the radiator just below the window gave him a sense of security and luxury. All over Venice, he knew, people were huddled round stoves, or with chapped hands were doing their chores about the house or outdoors, and no doubt several artists were chafing their hands at wood stoves – stubborn bastards, that red-tile variety which

97

abounded in Italy – before going back to their canvases. But he had glorious heat and a beautiful woman to share it with. Coleman realized and admitted to himself, and to anyone who might ask him or imply a question on the subject, that he had not the least scruple about taking money from women like Inez. Antonio did, in a funny way. Antonio thought sponging was a fair game, one to do and get away with if one could, but he had a faintly skulking attitude about it. Not so Coleman.

And about the other thing, Coleman thought, bouncing his warm feet and puffing his cigar, Ray Garrett, he had no scruples about that. Ray Garrett was his fair game. If he got caught for it, too bad, a piece of bad luck, but Coleman considered the game worth it, because he didn't give a goddam if he did get caught for murder. At least Garrett would be dead. And Garrett deserved to die. If not for Garrett, and his pusillanimous brain, and his upperclass American destiny, Peggy would be alive now.

Coleman started towards his jacket which hung over a chair, towards Peggy's picture, then restrained himself. He had looked at it once today. Lately he had been in the habit of staring at it at least twice a day for several minutes; yet he knew every shade of light and dark in the photograph that made up the flat, fleshless image called 'Peggy', could have drawn the photograph precisely from memory, and in fact on Friday had, as a kind of celebration of what he thought was Ray's death. Well, he still thought Ray was dead. If he used his common sense, the logical thing was to assume that he was dead. The body would wash up a few days from now, that was all, maybe even tomorrow.

Then it dawned on him that Inez would guess that he wanted to stay on in Venice in order to find out from a first-hand position if Ray were dead or not. This made Coleman feel slightly uncomfortable, as if he had let Inez in on a little too much. Inez had always defended Ray. She kept talking about 'being fair in the situation', but what it amounted to was a defence of Ray. Inez would not like him, might say good-bye to him, if she knew he had killed Ray. On the other hand, and Coleman had thought of this before, of course, if Ray's body were to wash up anywhere, who was to say if he had been pushed in or had jumped off some fondamento of his own accord? A young man committing suicide a few weeks after his wife's, practically his bride's, suicide, was not unknown in the world.

But Coleman reminded himself that he didn't care what Inez thought or what she did. Or what she said to the police, but he didn't think she would say anything. What had happened on the boat simply could not be proven, because there had been no witnesses.

There flashed before Coleman's mind the fight he had had with his father when he was sixteen. Coleman had won it. They had exchanged two blows each, and his father's had been harder, but Coleman had won the fight. The fight was over whether Coleman would go to an architectural school or to a college that specialized in engineering. Coleman's father had been a mediocre architect – doing bungalows for middle-class people in Vincennes, Indiana – and he had wanted his son to be an architect, too, a better one, of course, but still an architect. Coleman had always been more interested in machinery and in inventing. The thing had erupted when he was sixteen, because he had had to put himself down for one school or the other. Coleman had taken a stand, and won, and that had been a turning-point in his mother's attitude towards him, Coleman remembered with some pleasure. His mother had respected him and treated him like a man from then on. Coleman was not proud of having hit his old pop, but he was proud of having stood up for himself. Just after that fight, he had stood up for his right to see a certain girl named Estelle, whom his father considered 'cheap'. His father had forbidden him the car every time he had a date with Estelle, and finally had forbidden him the car entirely. One night, Coleman simply took the car and drove it out of the garage, not fast but steadily, towards his father who stood with arms outstretched in the driveway to stop him. His father had got out of the way, banged his fist in anger on the top of the car as Coleman drove by; but after that, there had been no argument about the car.

Coleman had never thought he was violent, but perhaps he was, compared to most men. He wondered what had happened to the five or six fellows he used to go around with at engineering school? Maybe they were a little more violent than most men, too. Coleman had lost touch with all of them in the last fifteen years since he had become a painter. But when they were all about twenty, they had menaced an old watchman at school. Denis had hit him in the ribs once, Coleman remembered, and that was what had liberated them. The old watchman had guarded a certain back door of the dorm, and he sat inside or outside the door, depending on the weather. But Coleman's group, if they wanted to get out and go on the town around midnight, did. They simply demanded that the door be unlocked. The old man opened it always. And he had never reported them to the dean for fear of another blow.

Then there was one occasion of near-violence, Coleman remembered, and smiled, then chuckled. A certain Quentin Doyle in Chicago, who had played around with Coleman's wife Louise, trying to start an affair. Coleman simply acquired a pistol, and one evening casually showed it to Doyle. Doyle had let Louise strictly alone after that. And it had been so easy, Coleman thought with amusement. He hadn't fired the pistol, he had had a legal permit for it, and the mere showing of it had had such splendid effect.

Coleman opened a flat drawer in the wardrobe and took from below a stack of handkerchiefs (brand new, given him by Inez) the scarf of Peggy's. He glanced at the door and listened, then opened the scarf and held it so the light made its colours their brightest. He imagined it round Peggy's smooth, slender neck, and around her head when the wind blew in Mallorca. He saw her grace when she walked, heard even her voice, when he looked at the Florentine Art Nouveau design. The black in the scarf added drama, but suggested death to Coleman. Nevertheless, it was Peggy. He pressed it gently to his face, kissed it. But no scent was on it. Coleman had washed it once, Thursday night late after returning from the Lido, to remove Ray's touch from it. He had hung it at the back of the wardrobe in his room, from a hook. It was not ironed, but at least it was clean. He folded the scarf quickly, his back to the door, and replaced it where it had been.

He might, of course, marry and have another child – a son or another daughter, it didn't matter. Coleman admitted that he was as paternal as any mother was ever maternal. But a daughter, for instance, would never be another Peggy. And there simply wasn't time any longer to watch her grow up. No, never, never would there be anything for him like Peggy.

From the floor of the wardrobe, Coleman got a bottle of Scotch. He did not permit himself a Scotch before 6 p.m., but now it was 6.05. He poured some in a bathroom tumbler and sipped it straight, enjoying its burn in his mouth. He stood again at the window. *And by God*, he swore to himself, *if that bastard is still alive and hanging around Venice, I'll get him.* Ray Garrett was asking for it, that was the funny part. His eyes were begging for it. Coleman rocked back on his slippered heels and laughed, and felt pleased and comforted by the richness of his own laughter.

Then he heard behind him the closing of a door, and stopped.

Inez had come in, and had put on the light. 'What were you laughing at?'

'I was thinking – of another painting. With my aerial view. You weren't very long with Antonio.'

'He had a date at seven.'

'Oh, with a girl? That's nice.'

'No, two young men he met in Venice.'

More talking, Coleman supposed. Antonio would tell his friends about his American painter friend Edward Coleman and the woman Antonio would claim he shared with him, and the interesting disappearance of Ray Garrett. But they wouldn't do anything about it, Coleman thought. It would be as remote from them as an item in the newspaper about people they didn't know.

Inez had removed her blouse and skirt, put on her dressing-gown, and was washing her face at the bathroom basin.

Coleman could not understand her maternal tolerance for crumbs like Antonio – men she'd sleep with only two or three times, yet was so slow to get rid of. There'd been one hanging about when he'd first met Inez in Ascona a year ago. 'I hope you didn't give him any more money,' Coleman said.

'Edward, I gave him just a few thousand lire,' Inez said patiently, but in her tone Coleman heard her irritation with him, the start of resistance. 'After all, he has no money and I did invite him on this trip.'

'It's quite natural that if a person doesn't work, he has no money. Just wondering how long it's going to go on, that's all.'

'Antonio said he was leaving in a few days. Meanwhile he is at a very cheap hotel.'

Coleman thought of saying that if Antonio met another rich woman, he'd move out of the cheap hotel and into her palazzo or whatever, and that would be the last Inez ever saw of him, but he decided not to say this.

Inez was putting lotion on her face. Coleman liked the smell of it. It reminded him of a bouquet of old-fashioned flowers. He went up behind her and put his arms around her, pulled her against his body. 'You're looking very ravishing today,' he said, and put his lips to her ear. 'How about a nice little split of champagne?' That was Coleman's phrase for going to bed. Sometimes Inez ordered a split of champagne, sometimes not.

A moment later, Coleman was stubbing out the cigar he had left in the ashtray in his room. It was a lovely time to go to bed, six-thirty in the evening, before dinner, and Inez's little smile as she said, 'Yes, let's,' made Coleman feel very happy, cheerful, contented. Coleman removed his clothes in his own room. 'Come into my room,' Coleman said.

Inez did.

9

During the next two days, Coleman more than once – in fact, three times – felt that Ray's eyes were on him. Once it was while crossing San Marco's, though in that open space maybe anybody would have felt observed, if he suspected the presence, the observant presence, of someone like Ray Garrett. No place for an agoraphobe, San Marco's Square. Another time was at lunch in the Graspo di Ua. Coleman had looked over both shoulders – if Ray had been there, he was behind him, because he was not among the people in front of Coleman – and Inez had noticed his looking. From then on, Coleman had been careful not to appear to be looking for Ray. If he were alive and in Venice, Coleman wondered what he was waiting for, or hiding for?

On another occasion, Coleman had felt while walking past a tobacconist's, that Ray was inside, that Ray had seen him as he walked by. Coleman had turned and walked back and looked directly into the shop through the door. Ray had not been inside. Then there was what Inez had said about the head and shoulders of some man in the street resembling Ray. Coleman did not know what to make of his feelings, but he knew he was not inclined to imagine things that weren't there. And Ray could, of course, be spying on the Bauer-Gruenwald. If Coleman had been alone, he would have moved, but he did not want to propose moving to Inez.

Meanwhile, Coleman waited for a new development because of the American Consulate's notifying Ray's parents. It was a wealthy family. They would do something.

On Thursday morning, 18 November, there was a telephone call in Inez's room. It was from Mrs Perry of the Lido. Coleman, in his dressing-gown and sitting on Inez's bed, had answered it.

'I wonder if you've seen this morning's paper, Mr Coleman?'

'No, I haven't.'

'Your son-in-law – his picture's in the *Gazzettino*. They say he's missing. Missing since last Thursday night. That's the night we had dinner.'

'Yes, I did know,' Coleman said, with a successful attempt at casualness. 'That is, I knew just in the last couple of days. Not missing. I think he's gone off on a trip somewhere.' Coleman put his hand over the telephone and said, 'Mrs Perry.'

Inez was listening attentively, standing six feet away, her comb in her hand.

'I'd forgotten his name,' said Mrs Perry, 'but I did recognize his face. I suppose you've spoken to the police?'

'No. I didn't think it was necessary.'

A knock on the door. Inez let the breakfast tray in.

'I think maybe you should,' Mrs Perry said, 'because the police want to know the last people who saw him. You went back with him that evening, didn't you?'

'Yes, I dropped him on Zattere by his pensione.'

'I'm sure the police would want to know that. I could say I saw him that evening, until just after midnight, but you saw him after I did. I haven't rung Laura and Francis yet, but I thought I would. Is he apt to go off on a trip, just like that?'

'Oh, I think so. He's a free agent. Used to travelling.'

'But he left his passport, the paper said. I couldn't translate all of it, but I got the manager to help me. I just happened to see the newspaper on someone else's breakfast tray in the hall. He seems to come from a nice family in the States. They've been notified. So you see, it doesn't sound like just a trip.'

Coleman wanted to hang up. 'I'll get a paper and see what I can do, Mrs Perry.'

'And do keep in touch, would you? I'm very interested. I thought he was such a nice young man.'

Coleman promised that he would.

'What's in the paper?' Inez asked.

'Let's have some coffee, dear.' Coleman gestured to the tray on the writing-table.

'Have they found out something?'

'No.'

'Then what is in the paper? What paper? We'll get it.'

'The *Gazzettino*, she said.' Coleman shrugged. 'It's to be expected, if the Consulate was notified.'

'Nothing about where he is? In the paper?'

'No, just a report he's missing. I wish I'd thought to order orange juice. Wouldn't you like some?'

Inez brought Coleman his coffee, then picked up the telephone and ordered two orange juices and asked if she could have a *Gazzettino*.

The Smith-Peters would ring up next, Coleman thought. They had gone to the theatre with the Smith-Peters last evening, and Francis had asked him how Ray was. Coleman had said, before Inez could answer anything, that they hadn't seen him lately. 'He's still in Venice?' Laura had asked. 'I don't know,' Coleman had replied. The Smith-Peters were leaving for Florence as soon as their central heating and plumbing were ready, but that was running into Italian delays, and they kept themselves informed by telephoning their housekeeper. It looked as if they would be here another week. Coleman wished they weren't here.

'Perhaps you should speak to the police, Edward,' Inez said.

'Wait till I see the paper. I'll speak with them if I have to.'

The paper and the orange juice arrived.

Ray Garrett's picture, probably his passport picture, was one column wide on the front page, and the item below it some two inches long. It stated that Rayburn Cook Garrett, 27, American, had not returned to his room at the Pensione Seguso, 779 Zattere, since last Thursday evening, November 11th. His passport and personal effects were still in his room. Would anyone who had seen him that evening or since come forward and speak to the police at their local police station? It went on to say that Garrett was the son of Thomas L. Garrett of so-and-so address, St Louis, Missouri, president of the Garrett-Salm Oil Company. The police or the American Consulate had perhaps spoken to Ray's parents by telephone. Coleman, however, was as yet unworried.

'If he is in Venice, I should think they can find him – with this picture,' Inez said. 'Where could he be staying without a passport?'

'Oh – if he's here, maybe some private house where they take in roomers,' Coleman said. 'Not every place asks for a passport.'

Inez poured their orange juice from two small cans. 'Promise me you'll speak to the police today, Edward.'

'What can I tell them? – I put him on the Zattere quay and that's the last I saw of him.'

'Was he walking towards his pensione? Could you see?'

'Seemed to be. I didn't stay to look.'

He could see that Inez would not rest until she got him to a police station. It crossed his mind to refuse, even if it meant making Inez angry with him, if it meant leaving her and going back to his Rome apartment, but if he did not speak to the police, she or eventually the Smith-Peters or Mrs Perry would, Coleman thought; he would be mentioned in that case, so the best thing to do was to speak to the police on his own. It was damned annoying. Coleman would have given a lot to get out of it. If Ray hadn't had money, if he'd been an ordinary American beatnik, his disappearance wouldn't have raised this stink, Coleman thought. Ray's parents had probably cabled the Consulate in Venice, asking them to do everything they could.

So Coleman promised to go to the police that morning.

He and Inez left their room by 10 a.m., and Coleman was congratulating himself on the fact he hadn't had to deal with the Smith-Peters, when the telephone rang. They heard it from the hall, and Inez went back into the room. Coleman wanted to walk on to the elevators, but he was curious as to what Inez would say, so he went back into the room with her.

'Yes . . . Oh, she did? Yes, she rang us up also . . . We are going this morning to speak to the police . . . The last time was when Edward dropped him at the Zattere near his pensione Thursday night . . . I don't know him that well . . . Yes, oh yes, of course we will, Laura. Good-bye.' Inez turned to Coleman and said, as if she were rather happy about it, 'Mrs Perry rang up the Smith-Peters. They hadn't seen the paper. Let's go, darling.'

At the first police station they tried, near San Marco, Coleman was pleased to learn that the chief officer there had not heard of Ray Garrett. He made a telephone call, then Coleman was told that another officer was coming over. Coleman and Inez had a ten-minute wait. Inez's feet were getting cold, so they went out for a coffee and came back.

The new official was a bright-looking man of around forty, greying at his temples, in dapper uniform. His name was Dell' Isola.

Coleman explained his relationship to Rayburn Garrett, father-in-law, then said that he and the Signora Schneider and three other people had seen Garrett last Thursday evening until after midnight on the Lido, and that Coleman had then taken him home in their rented motor-boat, the *Marianna II*.

'You put him off exactly where?'

Coleman told him, near the Pensione Seguso on the Zattere quay.

'At what time was this?'

The conversation was in Italian, in which Coleman was adequate though not perfect. 'As nearly as I can remember one-thirty in the morning.'

'Was he a little drunk?' asked the officer politely.

'Oh, no. Not in the least.'

'Where is his wife?' asked Dell' Isola, pencil ready, taking it all down.

'My daughter – died about three weeks ago,' said Coleman, 'in a town in Mallorca called Xanuanx.' He spelled it for the Italian, and explained that she and Garrett had been living there.

'I am sorry, sir. She was young, then?' Dell' Isola's sympathy sounded genuine.

Coleman was touched, unpleasantly, by his kind tone. 'She was just twenty-one. She was a suicide. I think – I know Signor Garrett was unhappy about this, so I can't tell what he might have done that night. It is possible he decided to leave the city.'

Three or four policemen were now standing around listening, standing like tailors' dummies, their eyes fixed on Coleman and Dell' Isola alternately.

'Did he say anything that evening about going away?' Dell' Isola looked towards Inez, too. She was standing a few feet away, though someone had offered her a chair. 'He was depressed, you say.'

'Naturally – he had not been happy since my daughter's death. But he did not say anything about going away,' Coleman answered.

There were a few more questions. Did Signor Garrett suffer from blackouts, amnesia? Was he trying to hide from anyone? Had he any large debts? To these questions Coleman answered in the negative 'as far as he knew'.

'How long will you be in Venice, Signor Coleman?'

'Two or three days more.'

He asked for Coleman's hotel, his permanent address – Rome, and Coleman gave street and number and telephone – then thanked Coleman for his information and said he would pass it on to the American Consulate. 'You were present the evening on the Lido, Signora?' he asked Inez.

'Yes.'

Dell' Isola took Inez's address in Venice also. He seemed pleased to be in charge of inquiries here, though he said the building was not his headquarters. 'Were there other people present? – May I have their names, please?'

Coleman told him, Mr and Mrs Francis Smith-Peters, now at the Hotel Monaco, and Mrs Perry at the Hotel Excelsior, Lido.

It was over.

Coleman and Inez walked out into the chill day again. He wanted to visit the church of Santa Maria Zobenigo, which he told Inez cheerfully had no ornament on its façade with any religious significance. Inez knew this and was familiar with the church. She wanted to buy a pair of black gloves.

They went to the church first.

It was after three when they returned to their hotel for a rest. Coleman wanted to make a drawing, and Inez suggested they have tea sent up, as she felt chilled to the bone. At four, the telephone rang and Inez answered it.

'Oh, 'allo, Laura,' Inez said. She listened for a moment. 'That sounds very nice.' She was lying back on her pillows in her dressing-gown. 'Let me speak to Edward. They would like us to have dinner tonight at the Monaco, and a drink first at Harry's Bar.'

Coleman grimaced, but agreed. It was hard to manufacture prior engagements in Venice, since he knew so few people here, only three, and unfortunately every one of them was out of town.

Inez said yes. Harry's Bar at seven. 'Yes, we did. No, they know nothing. À bientôt.'

Inez and Coleman were a little late at Harry's. The room was three-quarters full. Coleman looked around first for Ray, quickly, then saw Laura Smith-Peters's red-blonde head at a back table. She was sitting opposite her husband. Coleman followed Inez towards them. Waiters in white jackets swooped gracefully about with trays of martinis in small straight tumblers and plates of tiny hot sandwiches and croquettes.

'Well, hello!' Laura said. 'It's so nice of you to come out to meet us on a night like this!'

It was raining lightly.

Coleman sat down beside Inez.

'What have you been doing all day?' Laura asked.

'We went to a church,' said Inez. 'Santa Maria Zobenigo.'

They ordered, an americano for Inez, Scotch for Coleman. The Smith-Peters had their martinis.

'Delicious drink, but awfully strong,' said Laura.

As if a martini could be weak unless it was full of ice, Coleman thought.

'How can a plain martini be weak?' Francis said brightly, and Coleman hated that his thought had been echoed by this bore.

They had not yet been questioned by the police, Coleman decided.

Coleman girded himself for a deadly evening, and determined to order another Scotch as soon as he could catch the waiter's eye. A waiter did come, with a saucer of olives which he set down, and a plate of hot croquettes which he offered. The Smith-Peters accepted, and the waiter served them a croquette each in a paper napkin folded in a triangle.

'I should be dieting, but we only live once,' said Laura, before taking a bite.

Coleman put in his Scotch order. He glanced at the door ahead of him as a man and woman came in.

'So you went to the police today, Ed,' Francis said, leaning towards Coleman. His grey hair was neatly combed over his bony head. His hair looked damp, as if he had just applied tonic.

'I told them what I knew,' Coleman said, 'which isn't much.'

'Do they have any clues at all?' Laura asked.

'No. The police station hadn't even heard of Ray Garrett. They had to send for someone who didn't know much either, but he took a few notes from me.' That was all he ought to say, Coleman thought.

'Did he say anything about taking off some place?' Laura asked.

'No.'

'Was he depressed?' her husband asked.

'Not very. You saw him that night.' Coleman took an olive.

Francis Smith-Peters cleared his throat and said, 'I was going to go to the police just as a matter of duty. You know, as a fellow-American. But I thought since you'd seen him last—'

'Yes,' Coleman said. Francis's tenor voice was as unpleasant as a rotary saw to Coleman. And Francis's eyes were on guard, Coleman saw, beneath their bland friendliness. If Francis had gone to the police, he might have felt obliged to tell them – only after leading questions, of course – that Coleman hadn't liked Ray Garrett, and that there had been some unfriendly words from Coleman to Garrett. Coleman sensed all this, and sensed it in Laura, too.

'I felt the same way,' Laura put in. 'You knew him so much better and you'd seen him last.'

It was probably Laura, Coleman thought, who had kept her husband from going to the police – although Francis's Italian was so non-existent Coleman could understand his reticence. 'Let's stay out of it, Francis. You know Ed doesn't like him, and we don't know *what* happened that night.' Coleman could imagine the conversation in their hotel room.

'I don't know that neighbourhood,' Francis said, 'around the Zattere quay. What kind of neighbourhood is it?'

'Oh, quieter than here, certainly,' Coleman answered.

'What do *you* think happened, Inez?' Laura asked. 'You're so intuitive.'

'About *this*? – No,' Inez answered. 'He's—' She lifted her hands in a helpless shrug. 'I just don't know.'

'What were you going to say?' asked Francis. 'He's what?'

'If he's so depressed, maybe he went off somewhere – left everything – I suppose that's possible.'

Coleman felt the Smith-Peters doubted this, and that they felt Inez did not believe it herself.

'The alleys,' Coleman said, 'the alleys in Venice, if someone wants to hit you over the head and take your money – there's always a canal handy. Just roll the body in.' The American table on his right was noisy. One of the men had a laugh like a dog's bark.

'What a horrible *idea*!' Laura said, rolling her blue eyes, looking at her husband.

'See anyone around when you let him off?' asked Francis.

'I didn't get out of the boat, so I couldn't see much,' Coleman said. 'I don't remember. I turned the boat around and headed for San Marco.'

'Where was Corrado that night?' Laura asked Inez.

Inez shrugged, not looking at Laura. 'Home? I don't know.'

Inez had asked Coleman that, too.

'I looked for him, but it was after one then, after all,' Coleman said. He glanced at the door and started, sat forward with a jerk, and looked immediately down at the table. Ray had come in the door.

'What's the matter?' Inez asked.

'Almost – almost swallowed an olive pit,' Coleman said. He saw, without actually looking or seeing, that Ray had gone out again, having seen him. 'I *did* swallow an olive pit,' Coleman said, smiling, realizing that he had no olive pit in his mouth to produce. He was glad Inez was so concerned with him, she had not noticed Ray, and that the Smith-Peters had their backs almost to the door. Ray had a beard along his jaw. He had jumped back as quickly as Coleman himself had started in his seat. 'Whew! Gave me a queasy minute. Thought it was down the windpipe,' Coleman said, laughing now.

The others talked on after that about something else. Coleman did not hear a word. Ray was still alive, and on the loose. What was he up to? He certainly wasn't trying to get the police on to him, or he would have come straight over. Or were the police collecting themselves outside now? Coleman glanced again, furtively, at the door. Two tall men were leaving, laughing and moving slowly. The door, like the windows, was of clouded grey glass, and one could not see through it. At least five minutes passed, and nothing happened.

Coleman forced himself to make conversation.

Where was Ray hiding out? Wherever he had been the past week, he would have had to change his abode today because of the newspaper picture, Coleman thought, unless he had told the truth to whomever he was with – but Coleman didn't think that likely. Or did Ray have close friends here? Coleman began to feel angry, and afraid. Ray alive was a horrible risk for him, the risk of being accused of a murder attempt – two, in fact. The second one, however, was provable: someone must have seen Ray in the water that night, someone who pulled him out, or if by some miracle he had swum to the Piazzale, someone or several people must have seen him soaking wet that night. Coleman concluded that he had better finish the job, eliminate Ray; and though he realized this thought was prompted by emotion – mainly fear – he still felt it was a valid thought, and that logic would soon provide him with a better method than those he had been using up to now.

1 O

Ray crossed San Moisè, the street of the Bauer-Gruenwald, and entered the Frezzeria. He walked quickly, as if Coleman were pursuing him, though he realized this was the last thing Coleman would dream of doing now. Coleman in the bosom of his friends again! Still with Inez, who must suspect Coleman, and yet they'd be in the same bed tonight. The world did not care really whether he was alive or dead, if he had been murdered or not. Perhaps it was the beginning of wisdom to realize this. He could have been murdered, and by Coleman only, but the world didn't seem to care.

These thoughts went through his mind very rapidly, in a matter of a second or two, then he remembered – and slowed his steps to save energy and also to avoid attention – that he had to plan what to do next. He had been out of Signora Calliuoli's house since 11 a.m. A few moments before eleven, after catching sight of his picture on the front page of the *Gazzettino* on a news stand and reading the lines under it, he had hurried back to the Largo San Sebastiano, where the door had been opened for him by the elderly woman who had said she never slept. Ray had said that he must be leaving. He had paid Signora Calliuoli through tomorrow, he said, but that did not matter. He told the woman that he had just telephoned Zurich and learned that he had to go there at once. Then Ray had gone upstairs and packed his few items before Signora Calliuoli, out marketing for the midday meal, or Elisabetta, in the bar-caffè, could notice the picture and recognize him. The elderly lady had been hovering in the hall as Ray came down with his suitcase, and he had asked her to convey his good-bye and his thanks to Signora Calliuoli. She had looked sorry to see him go.

His suitcase had not weighed much at first, but by now it did. He went into a bar and ordered a cappuccino and a straight Scotch. He thought of the gondolier who had fished him out of the lagoon, an oil-and-vegetable gondolier. Ray dreaded staying up until 3 a.m. to find him at the railway station, but he could think of nothing else to do. It was the annoying passport business, the fact that even if he faked a passport number for a while, too many people would get a close view of him in an hotel. He was in no mood to approach another girl, like Elisabetta, and he didn't know any. And if he looked for a room to rent in the *Gazzettino*, the landladies might be suspicious of a young American resembling, even with a beard, the picture on the front page of a newspaper they probably bought.

Ray went into a small restaurant, where he sat at a table near a radiator. He pulled one of his books out of his suitcase and spent as much time as possible over his dinner. Afterwards, he felt more cheerful, and took a vaporetto from the Giglio stop to the Piazzale Roma; and, as he had hoped, there was a diurnal hotel where one could have a shower and a shave and at least relax. Here no passport was demanded. He was a little worried that there might be police on the watch around the station, but he did not look at anyone, and nothing happened.

When he went out at 1 a.m., it was much colder. He asked the ticket vendor at the waterbus stop where the vegetables and oil were loaded, and was directed by a vague wave of the arm to the 'Ponte Scalzi'. Ray walked past the railroad station into the darkness. There were barges and gondolas along the canal, moored for the night. A few oil stoves burned on their decks. He saw one man.

'Excuse me,' Ray said to him. 'At what time do the boats come for the vegetables and oil?'

'Around six in the morning,' replied the man, a squat figure before a stove on a barge's deck.

'I thought some gondolieri brought their boats earlier and slept?'

'In this weather?'

Ray hesitated, then said, 'Thank you,' and walked on.

Dog dung on the pavement, in a square of light that fell from a window, looked like a deliberately vulgar display, and Ray wondered why he stared at it, until he realized it had swollen, because of the rain, to the size of human excrement. He looked away from it, and thought, 'I'm not Ray Garrett tonight, I haven't been for days. Therefore I should be in a state of freedom such as I've never known before.' For a few seconds, he recaptured his sensations of the morning after the night in the lagoon, the morning when he had awakened in the hotel room and stared out the window and thought, 'The view could be the view of a dozen Italian cities, and I could be anyone, because I'm no one.' Now he hadn't the anxiety he had felt that morning. He was no one again, without Peggy, without guilt, without inferiority (or superiority either), without a home or an address, without a passport. The feeling was easeful, like a letting up of pressure. Ray supposed many a criminal in hiding could have such a feeling, too, but it would be partly spoilt by their knowledge that they were in that state for the purpose of concealment and escape from the law. His state was a bit purer and happier. Perhaps identity, like hell, was merely other people.

He turned around. No gondolieri on the water, no one in sight.

He wondered if he should go back to the diurnal hotel for a while? He decided to approach the man on the barge again.

'May I ask you something? Do you know the gondolieri around here?'

'A few.'

'I am looking for a man who comes by way of the lagoon. He has a gondola and he carries oil and vegetables every morning from the railway station. He is about this high' – Ray indicated with his hand a stature of five feet six or less – 'with grey and black hair cut short. He speaks in dialect. Not shaven.' Ray was encouraged, because the Italian was obviously trying to think.

'About fifty?'

'I suppose.'

'Luigi? He curses about dragons in the sea?' The man laughed, then asked a bit cautiously, 'Why do you want him?'

'I owe him four thousand lire.' Ray had thought this out beforehand.

'Sounds like Luigi Lotto, I don't know. He's a man with a wife and grandchildren?'

'I don't know,' Ray said.

'If it is Luigi, he's maybe sick, maybe doesn't come tonight. Sometimes he works, sometimes not.'

'Where does he live?'

'Giudecca back of the trattoria Mi Favorita,' replied the man promptly.

'Where is that? What stop?'

The man shrugged. 'I don't know exactly. Ask anybody.' He chafed his hands at the stove.

'Grazie,' Ray said.

'Prego.'

Ray caught the next vaporetto into the Grand Canal. At Riva degli Schiavoni, he changed for a boat to Giudecca. By now it was after 1.30 a.m. He supposed it was a wild-goose chase, the hour could hardly have been less favourable, but at that moment, Luigi Lotto – who might be a total stranger, and whom he might never find anyway – seemed the only friend in Venice.

On Giudecca, he entered the first bar he saw and asked for the trattoria Mi Favorita. The man behind the bar did not know, but a customer did, and told him where it was.

'It may be too late to eat,' the man said.

'Non importa,' Ray said, going out. 'Grazie.'

Mi Favorita was set back in a court, with frigid-looking plants in front of its glass façade. Ray went in. He asked a woman who was mopping the floor if she knew of the family Lotto behind the trattoria. She said no, but there was a house just behind where fifteen families lived. Ray went there.

The house had a five-digit number followed by the letter A, and he could not see any street names anywhere. Worse, there was no name but 'Ventura' on the downstairs bells, though there were two vertical rows of bells. Ray shivered and looked at his watch. Two o'clock. It was all wrong, he thought. He was doing things all wrong. The front of the house showed no lights.

Ray started at the gritty sound of footsteps on his left. A man was approaching – Ray thought at once of Coleman, but this man, though not tall and with a rolling gait, was younger. He had even a cigar in his mouth like Coleman. Ray stepped to one side of the door, his back to the building, braced to run or to fight. The man came directly towards him, looking at him, then turned into the doorway beside which Ray stood.

'Pardon me, sir,' Ray said. 'Do you know a family Lotto living here?'

'Lotto, si,' the man answered matter-of-factly, not removing from his mouth what Ray now saw was a cigarette. 'Fourth floor.' The man opened the door with a key.

'Do you know if it is possible they are not sleeping at this hour, because—'

'Si, probably. He goes with his gondola. They are up at all hours making noise. I live below. Are you coming in?'

Ray came in, thanked the man, and climbed the stairs behind him. The halls were cracked and eaten with moisture and neglect. The interior of the building felt like a deep freeze, colder than outdoors.

'On the right at the back,' said the man, gesturing upward, and bent to unlock his own door.

Ray climbed the last flight with his heavy suitcase.

There was a light under the door, and at the sight of it, he sighed. It seemed a good omen. Ray knocked on the door, and thinking the knock had been too gentle, knocked again.

'Who is it?' called a woman's voice.

Ray stammered inwardly, and produced, 'Giovanni. Posso vedere Luigi? Sono un amico.'

'Un amico di Luigi,' the Italian echo came, reflexive, neutral. The door did not open. 'Un momento.'

Ray heard her footsteps fading in the apartment, and knew she was going to ask Luigi if he knew an American named Giovanni.

A moment later, a man opened the door, square-headed, in a grey vest and black trousers. He was the gondolier.

'Buona sera,' Ray said. 'I am the American whom you helped out of the water. You remember?'

'Ah, si! Si! Come in! Costanza!' he called to the woman, and in rapid dialect explained who Ray was.

His wife's face slowly melted, then shone with friendliness.

Ray wondered if they had seen the *Gazzettino*, and if so, had Luigi recognized him? Ray gave appropriate greetings to Luigi's wife. The sum he had given Luigi, Ray thought, was about thirty thousand lire or fifty dollars, which no doubt they had appreciated.

'My wife thought I was making up a story when I told her,' Luigi said, drawing on a sweater over his underwear. 'I am always making up stories about what I find in the water, you see. Sit down, signor. Would you like a glass of wine?'

A faint grumble from Costanza, then to Ray, 'He is sick, but he insists on going to work.' A child's cry from another room made her throw up her hands. 'While we argue, he could at least be sleeping! Permesso!' She went off, through a door at the rear of the bleak room.

'Luigi, I am sorry for the hour, but—'

'Your picture was in the *Gazzettino* this morning, *non e vero?*' Luigi interrupted him, speaking softly. 'I was not sure, but – yes?'

'Yes, I—' Ray was reluctant to blurt out his request, but better to Luigi alone than in his wife's presence. 'I came to ask if you know of a room I could rent, anywhere in Venice. You see, Luigi, I must speak to a girl here – a girl I love.' Ray hoped he was not blushing with shame. 'And I have a rival. The rival pushed me off the boat that night. You see?'

Luigi saw, and quickly. He put his head back and said, 'Ah-*ha*!'

'Does your wife know about the picture in the *Gazzettino*? I prefer that she does not know.'

'Oh, she is all right. Don't worry. One word from me! I showed her the paper today. Before that, she didn't believe I saved anyone. She thought I won the money gambling. She doesn't like me to gamble, but I don't gamble. *Some* husbands gamble! – I thought maybe you had collapsed that night! That you fell into a canal! I am happy to see you!'

Ray nodded. 'You see, I must not go to an hotel. The rival would find me. I want only to speak to the girl I love. I want a fair chance.'

'Yes, I understand,' said Luigi, glancing at the door through which his wife had disappeared. 'Where is the girl?'

'At an hotel in Venice.'

'And the rival?'

'I don't know. At another hotel, I think. He is looking for me,'

Ray added, feeling desperate, false as a corny tragedy, yet the words came.

'You should get rid of *him*.' Luigi rubbed his palms together, then blew on them. The house was cold. 'Let's have a glass of wine. Or a coffee. Which do you prefer?'

'About a room, Luigi, do you know of any?' Ray asked, because Luigi's wife was coming back.

'Luigi, you should not be up at this hour. Either you go to work or you go to bed,' his wife said.

At least, this was what Ray thought she said, and there followed a rapid conversation between them as to whether Luigi would go to work or stay home, but either way would he sleep a little now, and Luigi protested that he had slept all afternoon and so had the baby, and that was why they were both awake.

'No, I will not go to work this morning, I'll send a message via Seppi, because I have a favour to do for my American friend,' Luigi said to his wife. 'This night, you sleep here,' he said to Ray. 'After we have a wine. Pay no attention to the confusion tonight, this house is always a confusion. This baby is my son's. He has too many in his house now, his wife's parents are visiting, so we get the oldest baby.'

There were faint moans from his wife during this. Her black-bunned hair was hectic, and she was too thin.

Ray was shown into the kitchen, made to sit down, and Luigi poured three glasses of red wine.

'If my wife doesn't want hers, we'll drink it,' he said.

'You think you know of a room?' Ray asked. 'It's important for tomorrow.'

Luigi was sure he knew of a room, maybe two, maybe three.

'I must keep my name a secret,' Ray said, unwilling to mention his name, because Luigi might forget it, if he didn't mention it. 'I must have another like Giovanni – John Wilson. To everybody. In case your wife, for instance, talks to neighbours—' Ray looked hard at Luigi, trying to convey the seriousness of it to him. 'Has your wife already talked to neighbours?'

'Oh, no, I showed her the paper tonight when I came in at seven.'

'Did you talk to anyone?'

'I opened the paper here. It was in my pocket since noon. No, all right, you are Giovanni Weelson.' Luigi planted a foot in a chair, sipped his wine, and rubbed his stubbly chin thoughtfully. 'We shall win. I suppose she is a pretty girl? American?'

At least an hour later, when Ray was lying half asleep on a lumpy bed in a small cold room, which an electric stove in a corner seemed to make no warmer, he heard someone come in, and there was a short, explosive conversation between Luigi and another man. Luigi had said something about a second son who lived with him and worked in the bar of a big hotel, or maybe the Grand Hotel. This was probably the son, coming home after his night's work, and he probably had the son's room. Ray felt guilty about this, but he might be able to make it up by paying them something.

The next morning – a bright, sunny, cold morning – Luigi and Ray set out to go to a house of a friend of Luigi's a 'mezzo kilometro' away. The friend was called Paolo Ciardi, and Luigi had sent a boy on earlier to say they would be coming, he told Ray. It was 10.30 a.m. On the way to the house, they stopped, at Luigi's suggestion, for a glass of wine.

'I tell you, life is a confusion, but it is very interesting, is it not?' Luigi philosophized. His daughter was about to have her first baby, and was not sure she loved her husband, but Luigi was certain everything would work out all right. 'She is only worried about giving the light of day to the baby, but meanwhile it is a hell,' said Luigi. He insisted upon paying the bill.

Ray was concerned about getting more money. But he spent the next minutes of their walk convincing Luigi that it was best for him to have an alias at Signor Ciardi's, too. Luigi was of another mind, arguing that there was safety in telling Paolo the truth and so explaining why he wanted privacy, but Ray said that the fewer people who knew meant the fewer people who might talk, and Luigi at last gave in. Ray was to be John Wilson at Signor Ciardi's.

'If I give you a Traveller's Cheque,' Ray said, 'do you know where to cash it for me? Without a passport?' Luigi was bound to know someone, Ray thought.

'Yes, I do. He will take a little. Not much. Maybe five per cent.'

Ray had expected that. He rested his Traveller's Cheques book on the top of an ornamental stone pillar in the middle of a narrow lane, and signed two cheques for one hundred dollars each. 'Can you do this much? Two hundred? I'd be very grateful for even one hundred.'

'Two hundred.' Luigi's eyes widened, but it wasn't an astronomical figure, either, and he nodded and said with an efficient air, 'Si. Due cent' dollari, si.'

'You can get it today perhaps?' Ray asked as they walked on.

'Si. Maybe I don't deliver today. But tomorrow.'

'That would be all right. I'll give you five per cent, too, for that.'

'Ah, no,' Luigi said, pleased.

'You are doing me a favour.'

'I deliver it tomorrow at Paolo's. If I can't come in, I put it in an envelope for Giustina.'

'Who's Giustina?'

'Paolo's cook.'

Ray bought a *Gazzettino*, scanned the first page before tucking it under his arm, and was relieved to see there was nothing about him, at least not on the front page. He hoped his parents were not anxious.

'Also,' Ray said as they approached the red stone house that Luigi said was Signor Ciardi's, 'it is better if Signor Ciardi thinks I have not too much money with me.' He hated saying it, but he thought it would be safer if Signor Ciardi thought he had little.

'Sissi, d'accordo,' Luigi said.

'But I am willing to pay extra for a stove in my room – because I've just been sick. That bad cold, you know.'

'Si, capisco.'

Luigi pulled a ring in the wall, which made a bell ring inside the house, and in time the door was opened by a smiling, plump man in a sweater and an old suit.

'Ah, Luigi! Come va?' He embraced Luigi warmly.

Luigi introduced them – Signor John Wilson and Signor Paolo Ciardi – and Ray was glad to hear Luigi get down to the business of a room at once. 'For a few days, maybe a couple of weeks,' said Luigi.

Signor Ciardi graciously conducted Ray and Luigi across an untidy garden and patio into the house, which was cold but had rather fine massive furniture and a stone stairway. Ray was offered a choice of two rooms, and chose the smaller, because he thought it would be easier to heat. The room was to cost five hundred lire per day, and the wood for his fire was to be bought at Ray's expense. There was a small fireplace plus a red-tile stove. The toilet was an outdoor privy on a corner of the terrace, the bathroom a floor below Ray's room. There were flower-pots around the edge of the roof terrace, and a garden behind the house, one grapevine of which climbed up past Ray's window. Ray was quite satisfied. He paid a week in advance, and Signor Ciardi summoned a slender woman servant of about sixty and asked her to start a fire in Signor Wilson's room.

'Come and have a glass of wine with us,' Signor Ciardi said to Ray.

They descended to a large tile kitchen, and Signor Ciardi poured wine from a basketed demijohn into three glasses which he had put on the large wooden table. Luigi had said Signor Ciardi was a wholesale merchant of fishermen's gear, and had a store on the Fondamento Nuovo, but was mostly at home. Luigi, as nearly as Ray could make out, told Signor Ciardi that Signor Wilson had approached him yesterday morning near the Ponte di Rialto, where he had been delivering vegetables, and asked him about a room to be rented in 'the true Venice'. Signor Ciardi seemed satisfied and rather pleased to have a paying guest, and not at all curious about him personally, for which Ray was grateful.

'The house is empty since my wife died,' said Signor Ciardi. 'And no children.' He shrugged, a low, tragic shrug, followed by a resigned smile. 'And you, signor, children?'

'I am not married,' Ray answered. 'Maybe one day.'

'Sicuro,' said Signor Ciardi, tugging his sweater down over his paunch. He was wearing two sweaters.

Ray asked about a house key, and was given one at once from a kitchen shelf. Then Luigi and Signor Ciardi talked about things which Ray could not translate – fishing equipment – and Signor Ciardi referred several times to a stack of receipts or bills stuck through with a vertical spike on his sideboard, bringing his hand down as if he would impale it. Ray at last excused himself and said he would like to go up to his room.

'Signor Weelson has been ill with influenza,' Luigi put in thoughtfully. 'He needs much rest.'

Signor Ciardi was understanding.

Ray promised to call on Luigi or send a message tomorrow and went up to his room.

The fire had made some difference. Ray felt suddenly safe and secure, and happier than he had been for days. He looked through the rest of the *Gazzettino*. Nothing about him. He opened his suitcase, but saw nothing to hang up except his overcoat, which he put on a hook on the back of his door. Then he yielded to his tiredness, the bliss of his new-found refuge, put on pyjamas, and went to bed. The last thing he looked at before he slept was the vigorous, gnarled stem of the now leafless grapevine, as thick as his arm, beyond the glass of his window.

He slept for more than an hour. The house was silent when he awakened. Ray felt much better, but he lay for a while in bed, arms behind his head in the now warm room, and his thoughts turned again to Coleman, to the problem that was still unsolved. It was possible, Ray realized, to dispel the muddle, at least the murderous aspect of it, by simply telephoning Coleman and saying that he, Ray, was willing to tell the police he fell into a canal, one near the Seguso, for instance, and suffered amnesia for eight days. Ray smiled. Would anybody believe it? Well, suffered amnesia for *two* days, woke up to himself again, but found himself so enjoying anonymity he kept it up a few more days; but now that the police were worried – Ray laughed to himself. He could, however, at least tell Coleman he would go to the police with some innocuous story, and that would relieve Coleman of any fear that he would tell the police the truth; Coleman was bound to be anxious about that. On the other hand, Ray thought, Coleman simply *wasn't* anxious as to what he might tell the police, Coleman hadn't been anxious after his first attempt had failed in Rome. No, Coleman had been arrogant and increasingly hostile when Ray had seen him later in Venice. Still, Coleman now knew he was deliberately hiding, and that therefore he might be up to something hostile against him. Coleman just might be a little worried now, and he had certainly looked flustered when he saw him last night in Harry's Bar. Or had that fluster been purely surprise, surprise that he was still alive?

The fact remained that he could start things moving in a more pacific direction, if he said to Coleman that he was not going to tell anyone what had really happened. He could write a letter to Coleman, so there would be no chance of Inez's overhearing a telephone conversation, or possibly knowing he had telephoned.

But as soon as he thought this, Ray began to realize that Coleman's anger against him went much deeper. It was the deepest thing in Coleman's existence now. Coleman would obviously risk his own life, or life imprisonment, for it. People did that for love quite often. Coleman was doing it for hatred.

Ray could not come to any conclusion about the next thing to do, the next move to make, but he was tired of his bed, and got up. As he dressed, he felt once more, and more strongly, impelled to write Coleman a letter. He needn't post it, or at least not at once, but he had to write it. He had bought a block of writing-paper and some envelopes. He sat down at the wicker table, on which he had to spread his newspaper to get a flat enough surface even for the pad.

19 November 19—

Dear Ed,

[Ray began uneasily, hating calling Coleman by this name, but it seemed the best of three possibilities]

I thought it might relieve you, if only a little, if I tell you that I have no intention of telling the police or anyone else what happened that Thursday night. That is one reason for my writing this letter.

The second is Peggy. I have not yet made you understand, though I have tried often enough. I feel that I have failed somehow in everything I tried to put into words to you about her. I would like to say first of all that Peggy was unusually young for her age – and the word immature doesn't convey the whole thing. I think it was because she was so sheltered as a child and in her adolescence (I know I have said this before) and this of course entered into all her relationships – with me and with her painting also, for instance. She had not begun to realize the long and often slow progress every artist has to make before he becomes 'mature' or achieves any kind of mastery. Her education – finished a short while before I met her – by not concentrating on art (a pity this wasn't arranged, as she said she had always wanted to be a painter like you, that by sixteen she had been quite determined about it, but she may have exaggerated) deprived her of beginning this

129

knowledge, which is a knowledge of progress and also of capacities and limitations. Most people who are going to be painters know a great deal about these things by the time they are eighteen or twenty. I think Peggy was bewildered and frightened by the world she saw opening before her. I know she was frightened by her pleasure in sex (whatever you may think, I am in a better position than you to know) and also she expected more from it than is actually there – with anyone. But far from being frightened of sex itself, she was more enthusiastic than I was, which is saying a lot, as I loved her.

He wanted to finish that sentence with 'both tenderly and passionately', but could not bear to imagine Coleman sneering at this, not believing it, and even labelling it crude.

It seems too obvious to say that we are both still in a state of trauma from her death, but it is all too evident in our respective behaviour. Can you not realize that I loved her too and would have done anything to prevent this and would give anything to turn back time a few weeks so it would not have happened?

Ray felt he was becoming vague, and that he had said enough. He put the letter into an envelope and addressed it to Edward Coleman at the Bauer-Gruenwald, but he did not seal it, because he thought he might want to add something. He put the envelope in the pocket of his suitcase lid.

A few moments later, Ray went out to walk about Giudecca. It was called 'the garden island', he remembered, and he saw lots of trees, but the gardens were apparently behind the houses and not for public view. The day seemed warmer than yesterday. He loved the feeling of being on the large island, so close to the mainland of Venice, yet separated from it by the wide Giudecca Canal which now seemed protective to him. The Ciardi house was on the south side of Giudecca, and almost on the water (only one row of houses intervened) and from that bank there was a faint view of the marshy islands, where Ray had never been, which clustered near the mainland of Italy, and in the other direction a fuzzy view of the Lido. Ray walked across the island until he could see the mainland of Venice with its point of land on which della Salute stood, and beyond, across the Grand Canal, the heart of the city where the campanile of San Marco raised its pointed, gold-glinting tower. A handsome white ship, the *San Giorgio*, was moving to the right, towards the Adriatic, a blue-and-gold winged lion of Venice on its smokestack. And one of the ramp-nosed car ferries, which plied between the Lido and the mainland, churned the water going in the opposite direction, so close Ray could read its name, *Amminiara*. He remembered the *Marianna II*. He should keep an eye out for that boat, too, he thought, in his walks about Venice. Five or six people – Coleman, Inez, the Smith-Peters, Antonio (if he was still here), the woman on the Lido whose name he had forgotten, Elisabetta, and now the *Marianna II*.

Ray lunched at a trattoria on Giudecca (not Mi Favorita) for an incredibly small sum, but neither was the bistecca very tender. Then he took a boat to San Marco and spent the latter part of the afternoon visiting the Palace of the Doges. The huge, formal council halls, the ornate emptiness of the place made him feel more calm and in command of himself. It was, somehow, the shattering purposelessness of the Palace that now made him feel so, he realized.

When he went out into the Piazzetta, the day seemed warmer, perhaps because he had expected a contrast between the temperature of the Ducal Palace (frigid) and the outdoors. He walked slowly, smoking a cigarette, down the arcade on the south side of the Piazza. He realized he could hardly be in a more conspicuous place for Coleman's group or for the police, assuming they were actively looking for him, but just then Ray was reconciled to being found. He also realized he had felt this way before, at moments in the past week, and that the sensation had not lasted long. He was passing a tobacconist's shop on his left, when Coleman stepped briskly out of it and saw him.

Coleman stopped. They were only some eight feet apart.

Ray blinked, but did not move, and Ray had not the shocked surprise of last evening, though last evening he had more than half anticipated seeing Coleman in Harry's Bar. In a split second, Ray thought: *there is a chance now for us to speak to each other, for me to tell him I'm not going to say anything to the police.* And he made the start, a step towards Coleman, but before the step was finished, Coleman had turned himself away with a jerk of his heavy shoulders and was walking on.

Ray looked ahead of him, and saw Inez and Antonio just turning from a shop window twenty yards away, Inez looking in Coleman's direction. They had obviously been waiting while Coleman went off for cigars. For a moment, Ray felt too stunned to move, then at last he turned and walked in the direction he had come from, walked quickly so as to get away from them. He did not think Inez had seen him. He crossed the Piazzetta, bearing right, crossed the bridge paralleling the Bridge of Sighs, wanting only to go in a direction in which they would probably not go. Ray had seen the twitch of Coleman's lip, the hardening of his eyes, a look that said, 'That bastard again!' It was awful, somehow so devastating to Ray that he did not know how to take it, how he should take it.

Ray had tarried for a possible word, and it was evident Coleman did not care for one. Coleman could have beckoned him behind a pillar, Inez need not have seen him. Coleman might have said, 'All right, so you're alive. I think you're a louse, but I've had enough. Just keep out of my sight.' But Coleman did not want to come to any settlement. Ray began to walk more slowly on the Riva degli Schiavoni, but his fear, which had been almost panic as he fled the Piazza, was still with him. He had to go into a bar in order to use the toilet. Then he ordered a caffè, and deliberately tried not to think about the situation, about Coleman, because he was making no progress at all. He stood at the bar, sipping the coffee, and an image came to his mind: himself walking in a dark alley of Venice, over a small curved bridge that spanned a canal, under a street-lamp that projected from a house corner – and from the shadow of the house across from the light, Coleman stepped and hit him a fatal blow on the back of the head. Was that what he wanted? A blow with a rock in hand, with an iron pipe? Or was the image, like a dream, preparing him for something that was going to happen, most likely going to happen, anyway?

Ray lifted his eyes and saw the teen-aged boy behind the counter staring at him. He finished his coffee.

'Altro, signor?' asked the boy.

'No, grazie.' Ray had paid for the coffee, and now he fished a ten-lire piece from his overcoat pocket and dropped it into the saucer for a tip.

I 2

It was on the afternoon of 19 November, a Friday, that Coleman saw Ray Garrett in the arcade of the Piazza. That Ray walked about in the most conspicuous place in Venice – apart, perhaps, from Harry's Bar, into which he had stuck his nose the night before – that Ray arrogantly assumed Coleman would be afraid to speak to him, or to tell anyone he'd seen Ray, put Coleman into a bad temper which he tried to conceal from Inez. He could not conceal all of it. That evening, she asked him what was the matter, and since he could give her no reason, she told him that he looked as if he were suffering from a nervous disorder. This piqued Coleman further.

That night, Inez was very cool and rejected even his touch on her shoulder, his attempted kiss on her cheek. Coleman, resentful, slept in his own bed for the first time.

Then the next morning, Saturday, there came a telephone call from the police while Coleman and Inez were breakfasting. Would Signor Coleman be so kind as to come to the office of police at Piazzale Roma that afternoon at four o'clock? Coleman had to say that he would. It would be a long, nasty ride as it was a rainy day. Gusts of wind hurled the rain at their windows in the Bauer-Gruenwald, and it sounded like buckshot when it hit.

Coleman told Inez what he had to do. Then he said, 'Let's get out of this hotel today. Change it, I mean.'

'To what?' Inez asked in a tone of rhetorical indifference.

'The Gritti Palace, for instance. That's a nice place. I've stayed there.' Coleman had not; he had only eaten there once with friends, he recalled. But no matter, it *was* a good place. It irked him that Ray knew where he was based, and that he did not know where Ray was.

'If you wish,' Inez said, as if she were humouring a child.

Coleman was glad, at least, that she didn't propose leaving Venice. He was not at all sure he would be allowed to leave Venice now, anyway, and perhaps Inez realized this, too. 'We can get out by twelve easily, I should think. That's probably checking-out time.'

'You had better see first if they have rooms there.'

'This time of year? Sure.' But Coleman went to the telephone. He booked two rooms, each with a separate bath, as there was no two rooms with one bath available. Inez wanted a room of her own, even if they spent all their time in his or hers.

A few minutes later, a boy brought a letter on a tray. Coleman saw that it was for him. He gave the boy a hundred-lire coin.

'From Rome,' Coleman said.

Inez was across the room and did not see the black ink writing – angular and mostly printed – which Coleman recognized as Ray's.

He strolled slowly into his room as he opened the letter, then said, 'Yep, from Dick Purcell,' in a casual tone. Coleman had introduced Inez to Dick Purcell in Rome. Purcell was an American architect and a neighbour of his.

Coleman stood by his reading-lamp on the other side of the bed from the bathroom door, and stood sideways so he would know if Inez came in. He read the letter, and his heart beat a trifle faster at every paragraph. ' ... whatever you may think ... ' Ha! Not all the excuses and explanations in the world could explain away Ray's guilt, not even to Ray himself. The paragraph beginning, 'It seems too obvious to say that we are both still in a state of trauma from her death' made Coleman sneer. It sounded like something from an etiquette book on how to write a letter of condolence. Ray picked up a little in the last paragraph:

Another attempt by you to kill me might succeed. Though it's evident you want this, you must realize I could – now – tell someone or several people that you may try to do this. In which case you would suffer later, if anything happens to me. It is an absurd game, Ed. I am willing to see you and try to talk again, if you are willing. You may write to me Posta Restante, San Marco post office.

Yours,

Ray Garrett

Coleman chuckled loudly, partly because he felt like it, partly for Inez's benefit, since Dick Purcell was witty. Ray grovelling in the first paragraph, saying he wouldn't tell the police anything, then coming out with what amounted to a threat at the end! Coleman tore the letter into small pieces. He stuffed the pieces into a pocket with a view to disposing of them somewhere outside. He tore up the envelope, too.

'Is my red dressing-gown in there?' Inez called to him.

Coleman found it on the back of the door. Coleman was thinking that it would be amusing to see Ray calling daily, maybe twice a day, at the post office at the west end of the Piazza, and being disappointed. But Coleman had no intention of wasting time in watching him. And a fresh resentment went through him, painfully tangled with grief, at the memory of Peggy, of her soft young flesh, his flesh, her bright young eyes, her long dark hair. She had not begun to live before she died. If she had not married Garrett, she would be alive now. That was a fact, and no one in the world could dispute it. His grief frightened him, and he felt he was spinning in a whirlpool, being sucked down. Gone now the hope of seeing Peggy mature into a happy woman, dreams of taking her and a couple of small grandchildren to St Moritz or Ascona for a holiday, or playing with them all in the Jardin du Luxembourg. *Ray Garrett's* children? Well, never, thank God!

Coleman made a great effort to get himself in hand again. It took him some thirty seconds. He straightened up, squeezed his eyes shut, and tried to think of the next thing he had to do in the present. He had to pack.

By twelve-thirty they were installed in the Gritti Palace with a much nicer view from their fourth-floor windows of the hotel's lovely terrace, which ended in steps down to the Grand Canal. Two motor-boats like the *Marianna II* bobbed in the water in front of the steps, snug under canvas in the lashing rain. Because of the bad weather, they lunched in the hotel and drank a good claret with their meal. Coleman was uneasy, especially in regard to what Inez was thinking, and tried to conceal it by joviality. It also occurred to him that Ray might have spoken to the police this morning, after he posted the letter, and that the police might be ready to arrest him, or deport him, or whatever they did with an American under such circumstances. But Coleman did not really believe this. This would end Ray's guilt feelings, and in his way, Ray knew he deserved to suffer those feelings, and he was not going to end them so soon, Coleman thought.

'The police have probably heard something more from Ray's parents,' Coleman said to Inez, 'and they want to talk to me about that.'

'You said you met them?'

'Oh, yes. They were vacationing in Rome the spring Ray met Peggy. Nice people, a little stuffy. She's less stuffy than he is.'

'Don't be late for the police. That will annoy them.'

Coleman chuckled, and clipped the end of a cigar. 'They annoy me, dragging me out on a day like this.'

Coleman set out at three-thirty. The journey, or voyage, once he was on a boat, took only fifteen or twenty minutes.

The Capitano Dell' Isola was at the police station in the Piazzale Roma. He introduced Coleman to a small, thin man with grey hair who he said was the Public Prosecutor of Venice. He was a tiny man in a loose grey suit, but Coleman felt a proper awe for the unknown powers that he might be able to wield.

'It is his duty,' Capitano Dell' Isola said, 'to determine if there is a foundation for your detainment.'

So the questions began again about the night of the Lido. If Dell' Isola or anyone else had questioned the Smith-Peters or Mrs Perry, Coleman thought, they evidently had not said anything about his dislike of Ray Garrett. He knew they had not questioned Inez. Coleman was not asked his feelings. It was all cold fact, or rather cold lying, which Coleman thought he did with customary assurance.

In a pause in the Public Prosecutor's questioning, Dell' Isola said, 'We have spoken with Corrado Mancini, owner of the *Marianna Due*, and we have also examined the boat.'

'Oh? And what did you learn?' asked Coleman.

'He corroborates your story, that he was asleep at one o'clock when you left the Lido.' Dell' Isola's tone seemed more courteous in the presence of the Public Prosecutor.

Coleman waited for a remark about the boat – a dent, a new scratch? – but none was forthcoming.

'It may be necessary,' the Public Prosecutor said in his slow, grating voice, speaking in Italian, 'to issue a . . . [Coleman took this phrase to mean a legal order for detainment] but I think that is not required at the moment, if we know where to find you and you do not leave Venice. You are at the Hotel Bauer-Gruenwald?'

'I am at the Gritti Palace now,' Coleman answered. 'I was going to inform you that I moved this morning.'

This was taken down by a clerk.

The Public Prosecutor murmured something to Dell' Isola about informing the American Consulate. Dell' Isola assured him that this had been done.

'The father of Signor Garrett has telephoned,' Dell' Isola said to Coleman, 'to say that you were in Venice and might be of help. I told him we knew this and had spoken to you. I told them you were the last person we have been able to find who saw their son. I recounted the story of that night on the Lido as you told it to me, and they asked me to ask you again for anything – anything you can remember that Signor Garrett said about travelling, going anywhere. Anything about what he might have done. Because I must cable an answer to them.'

Coleman took his time, sat very coolly in his chair, and said, 'If I knew a single thing, I would have told you before.' He mixed his subjunctives, perhaps, but the idea was clear enough. 'Perhaps he went back to Mallorca.'

'No, we have inquired of the police in Palma and Xanaunx,' said the Capitano, mispronouncing the town name. 'He is not there. Signor Garrett's father also asked me to ask you if you know anyone in Mallorca who might know what Signor Garrett planned to do next. The father has also cabled to one of his son's friends in Mallorca, but there is not yet time for an answer. You have just been in Mallorca with Signor Garrett, have you not?'

'Sorry, I can't remember any names of the friends of Garrett in Mallorca. I met a few, but – I was there only a few days. For the funeral of my daughter, you know.'

'Yes, I understand,' the Capitano murmured. 'Do you think Signor Garrett was a suicide, Signor Col-e-man?'

'I think it is possible,' Coleman said. 'Where could he have gone without a passport?'

Coleman was glad to make the trip by vaporetto back to the Gritti, and stood outdoors on the deck despite the rain. The police had also asked Garrett Senior if he thought his son could have committed suicide. (Dell' Isola had not said what Garrett Senior's reply to this had been.) Ray must have written several days ago that he, Coleman, was in Venice also. Obviously the Garretts had no suspicions about him, which meant that Ray had not told his parents that his former father-in-law detested him. Ray wouldn't. People who deserved detesting seldom announced that they were detested. Coleman wished Ray would leave Venice, and he thought if he kept a cold silence Ray would finally skulk away, maybe in two or three days. But it was funny about his abandoning his things at the Seguso. Neurotic, Coleman thought. He couldn't really work it out, though he supposed he was on the right track when he explained it as Ray's wanting to put the blame on him for possibly having killed him, and also Ray's wanting to *feel* dead.

To Coleman's disappointment, Inez was not in when he got back to the Gritti, and it crossed Coleman's mind at once that she was keeping an appointment with the police, too. But there was a note for him at the desk, in one of the boxes where their two keys hung.

Went out to do some shopping for Charlotte. Back between 6–7. I.

Charlotte was her sixteen-year-old daughter, now going to school in France. A ghastly day for shopping, Coleman thought, but Inez was probably preparing for Christmas. He went up to his room, made sure the radiators in bedroom and bath were turned as high as possible (the room was quite comfortable, however), then lost himself in another pencil drawing of his figures seen from above. One of the figures had a face upturned, a hand held out – for alms or for rain, people could think what they wished.

He had a Scotch at six, and tried his composition in pastels on a larger piece of drawing-paper.

Inez knocked and came in just before seven. By now it had stopped raining, and was dark and gloomy beyond the windows.

'Well,' she said, smiling. 'How was it at the police?'

Coleman took a deep breath. 'Oh, they'd spoken to Ray's father. Just wanted to know if I had any new ideas as to where Ray might be. Told them I hadn't.' Coleman was sitting on the edge of his bed. He preferred beds to tables for drawing, 'Like a Scotch, dear?'

'Yes, I will, thank you.' She slipped off her high-heeled shoes, which were now covered in transparent rain boots. 'What a day! I like to think that the weather was better in the days when Venice had her glory, otherwise I cannot see how life could have been so glamorous here.'

'A truer word was never spoke. But it wasn't any better,' Coleman said, pouring her drink into a tumbler. He added exactly twice the amount in water from the tap in the bathroom. 'Did you find anything for Charlotte?'

'A most beautiful sweater I found, of a yellow like a Cézanne, and for her desk a leather case to hold paper and stamps. It is green morocco. Very pretty. And I wanted to say to her it is from Venice, you know.'

Coleman gave her her drink, and picked up his own. 'Salute.'

Inez drank some, sat down on the other side of Coleman's bed, and asked, 'What do the parents of Ray say?' She sat upright, her body turned, as if she rode side-saddle.

Coleman saw she was worried. 'They're interested in whether anyone in Mallorca knows anything. His friends there. I can't remember any of their names, but that village isn't big, if they want to send someone down there. He's not in Mallorca. They've looked – or asked.'

'And what do they say about you?'

'About me?'

141

'Do they think you might have done him any harm?'

The question was spoken in a calm and clinical tone, not at all like Inez. 'They didn't give me a hint of that.'

'What did you do, Edward? Did you tell me the truth?'

He didn't give a damn, Coleman reminded himself, what Inez thought, or if she knew the truth. 'I did what I told you.'

Inez only looked at him.

Coleman said carelessly, pulling a handkerchief from his hip pocket and blowing his nose, 'You look as if you don't believe me.'

'I don't know what to believe. I saw the Smith-Peters for a while this—'

'I sometimes think there're eight of them – instead of simply two. The biggest bores I've ever met, and they're underfoot all the time.'

'You know, Edward,' Inez said in a softer voice, 'they think you might have killed Ray – pushed him overboard unconscious or something like that.'

Stupidity! Coleman thought at once of the *Marianna II*, her varnished brown hull, and of the fact that they hadn't used her after that night. Their four-day rental period had run out. 'Well, I can't help what *they* think, can I? What are they going to do about it?'

'Oh, I don't think they're going to do anything about it. Or rather, I don't know,' she said quickly, shrugging in a nervous way.

She must know, Coleman thought. That was an important point. Coleman smoked a little, then started putting his pastels back in their wooden box. 'Well, what did they say? Just said out of the blue they thought I killed him?'

'Oh, no, my goodness!' Her French accent was stronger now, which Coleman knew meant she was under a strain. 'They asked me if I thought you could have done him harm, and then they said they thought you might have. They saw so well, you know, that you hate him.'

142

'And what if I do?'

'Hate him?'

'Yes.'

Inez hesitated. 'But did you kill him?'

'And what if I did?' Coleman asked in a quieter tone.

'Did you, Edward?'

Coleman walked across the room with his empty glass, walked on springy feet, and turned towards her. 'Yes, I did. But who's going to prove it, and who's going to do anything about it?' He felt he had thrown down a gauntlet – and yet, unfortunately, his adversaries did not seem important or even aroused enough to make the contest very exciting.

'You did, really, Edward? You are not joking with me?' she asked almost in a whisper.

'I am not joking. I pushed him off the boat. The motor-boat. After fighting with him. He wasn't unconscious, but he probably drowned. We were a long way from land.' He said it bitterly, but defiantly, and without regret. He said it with all the power of wishing it were true. And Inez believed him, he saw that, too. He said more calmly, 'You probably want to tell the police. Go ahead. You probably want to leave – leave me now, too.' He gestured with both arms. 'Go ahead and tell the Smith-Peters, too. Get on the telephone now and tell them.'

'Oh, Edward, as if I would say a thing like that over the telephone!' Inez said in a shuddering voice. 'As if I would tell them at all!' Now she was shrill with tears. She bit her underlip, then said, 'You *did*.'

Coleman slowly poured himself another drink, one not too big.

'The body will surely be washed up. It will surely be found,' Inez said.

'Yes. Surely,' Coleman said from the bathroom.

'Why do you stay in Venice then? It's not very safe.'

Coleman was pleased at her concern, evident in the words and

143

the tone. 'If they want to attach it to me, they'll do so, whether I'm in Venice or New York or Rome.' He walked back into his bedroom, stood with his feet apart, looking down at Inez who still sat in her erect, side-saddle position on his bed. 'I am not worried,' Coleman said flatly, and walked towards his dark window. He turned around and said, 'I detested him, yes. He caused the death of my daughter. And I consider him – considered him – utterly worthless. There are people and people. Souls! Souls, they say. Some souls are worth more than others. And my daughter's was worth a million like his. I wouldn't even compare them, wouldn't even assume they're made of the same stuff. Do you see what I mean? I took justice in my own hands; yes, and if I pay for it, I pay for it. So what?' Coleman set down his untouched drink on the night-table. He took a cigar from his case and lit it, his lips loose around it as he held it between his teeth.

Inez was still watching him.

'I don't know if you understand what I'm talking about, but it doesn't matter if you do or not. That's the way it *is*.'

'I understand what you are talking about,' Inez said.

'And I don't expect your approval,' he added.

'It's as if you stay here – just defying his body to wash up somewhere.'

'Maybe,' said Coleman. He was looking into space.

There was a yell and a *splash* from beyond the window, beyond the hotel's terrace, but the splashing sound had not been a large one, and the yell might have been one of surprise, maybe even a laugh. Only Inez had jumped at it slightly. In the distance, a large ship sounded its deep horn, which vibrated like an organ note in the wet air. Coleman thought of the water that surrounded them, the deep water into which the whole city might one day slide.

When he looked at Inez again, she had a different expression, as if her thoughts were far away, though she still looked at him. She looked, Coleman thought, content. He frowned, trying to assess this. Was it relief? He waited for her to say the next words, strolled over to the ashtray and rolled his cigar in it. Was she going to say she was leaving tomorrow? Or stay and stand by him?

He walked once more to the window, cigar between his teeth, and rested his hands on the sill. He looked out into foggy, yellowish lights on the canal, at the inevitable vaporetto passing, windows all tight shut against the weather. 'I thought tomorrow,' he said, 'I'd take a boat – maybe hire one and go over Chioggia way. Just to take a look again. Maybe you can see the Smith-Peters, do something with them.' He did not want Inez on the Chioggia trip, because he wanted to rough it, pay a fisherman to take him out on his boat for the day, something like that. 'I'll be back late evening.'

'All right, Edward,' Inez said docilely.

Coleman went over and pressed her shoulders, bent and kissed her on the cheek. She did not resist him now. 'Finish your drink and have another. You ought to have a hot bath, if you've been out in this weather all afternoon. Rest a little bit, and I'll knock on your door about eight and we'll think of a nice place for dinner. I'd like to see the things you bought for Charlotte, unless they're all wrapped.'

'They're not wrapped,' Inez said, getting up. She did not take another drink, but she went off to her room, to take a hot bath as he had suggested, Coleman was sure.

13

Coleman spent his Sunday in Chioggia, arriving back in Venice at
11 p.m. to an hotel empty of Inez. She hadn't checked out, but had
left no message for him. Coleman didn't care. He was tired, and he
had bruised his knee, falling on it when he slipped in a fishing-boat
around five o'clock. The knee was swelling. He did not feel like
looking for Inez in the Monaco, or even in the hotel dining-room
downstairs. He had a bath, and went to bed with a nightcap and a
London *Observer* which he had bought at Piazzale Roma.

His telephone rang just before midnight.

''Allo, Edward,' Inez said. 'Were you awake?'

'Yes. I got in a few minutes ago. You're in your room?'

'Mm-m. I'll come in to see you.'

'Very good.' Coleman put the telephone down.

Inez came in smiling, still in her short fur jacket and a hat. 'You
had a good day?'

'Great,' Coleman said. 'Except I didn't bring back any fish.
And I banged my knee.'

Inez had to see his knee. She recommended a cold towel, and
brought one from the bathroom, with a second towel to put under
it so his bed would not become wet. She told him there had been

a celebration at della Salute, the anniversary of the saving of Venice from the plague in the sixteen hundreds, for which occasion Santa Maria della Salute had been built. Coleman stared down imperturbably at his ugly, hairy leg, his knotty knee, now much bigger than normal, which Inez was tending so carefully with her slender, pink-nailed hands. His knee was grotesque, Coleman thought without amusement, without even concern for its swelling. It was like something drawn by Hieronymus Bosch.

'I suppose you saw those bores today,' Coleman said.

'Yes, and I saw Antonio, too. I have sent him on his way.' Inez gave the wet towel a final gentle pat, and pulled the sheet over it.

'And where is his way?'

'Positano now. He's going tomorrow morning. I made the reservation for him on the plane to Naples.'

And no doubt paid for the ticket, Coleman thought, but he was glad Inez had taken the initiative and urged him off. Coleman felt Inez was protecting him. 'You didn't have a quarrel?'

'No, but he is nosy, you know. We ran into him around five o'clock. He stayed with us until seven and would have had dinner with us, but I just didn't want him. He was asking all kinds of questions.'

'About Ray?'

'Yes. The Smith-Peters too thought he was a little rude. And silly – you know? I think he was nervous. But there is nothing to worry about from Laura and Francis.'

'How do you mean?' Coleman was only mildly interested, but still interested.

'They're not going to say anything. No matter what they think. And they do think' – she nodded slowly, looking at his pillow – 'that you pushed Ray off the boat.' She laughed nervously. 'I think they are also shy about approaching the police with their bad Italian. It is really *affreux*! After a year they can barely order a coffee!'

He had nothing to say. People like the Smith-Peters would of course keep their mouths shut, probably would never say anything to their friends in Florence, either. He thought of Mrs Perry, but he did not want to bring her name up. Anyway, she might have left Venice by now. 'So Antonio's off tomorrow?'

'Yes, a noon plane.'

'What was he talking about this afternoon?'

'He was asking questions. Where was Ray, what had we heard about him, all that. And somehow – he managed to ask if we did not think Signor Coleman could have – put him away somewhere, he said. He was speaking in English, because he was really asking Francis and Laura more than me. Trying to be funny. They didn't think he was funny and neither did I.'

Coleman was becoming sleepy. If Antonio went to Rome or Positano and talked, what did it matter? Another dramatic story, probably without foundation, from a young Italian of no consequence. Garrett was missing, yes, but that another American, his father-in-law, had killed him sounded like other dramatic stories Italians made up.

'But Edward—' Inez reached for his hand.

Coleman lifted his sagging lids.

'I did not admit a thing to Francis and Laura. I would not to anyone. To Antonio, I said he was mad to think such a thing. And so it is up to you now, if you want to do the right thing for yourself and me, to be perfectly natural with the Smith-Peters. Let them think what they wish, the proof of it is another matter. They may suspect, but they don't know.'

'Thank you, my dear. But I hope not to see them again.'

Inez shook her head quickly. 'If you avoid them, it will look strange. You can see that, Edward.'

Yes, he saw that. 'Darling, I'm getting awfully sleepy.'

'Yes, I know. Let me attend to your knee once more. Then I will go.'

She wet the towel again and applied it, covered Coleman with sheet and blanket, blew him a kiss and turned out his light.

Coleman was asleep almost as soon as she shut his door.

The weather took a turn for the better the next day. There was sunshine once more, and it was consequently a trifle warmer, though restaurants with terraces did not put their chairs and tables out. In the afternoon, Coleman and Inez went as guests of the Smith-Peters to a mediocre string quartet recital in a chilly palazzo on the canal, and afterwards made for Florian's and Irish coffee. Francis was treating everyone that afternoon.

Coleman was amused at their behaviour with him. They fairly bent over backwards to show their friendship, their loyalty, their solidarity. Not that a word was said about Ray. But their omission made their joviality more striking, reminding Coleman of the behaviour of some whites, determined to be liberal minded, with Negroes. Coleman remained pleasant and placid. The fact the Smith-Peters now believed he had killed Ray, however, made them a little less dull for Coleman.

'Have you decided yet how long you're staying?' Francis asked Coleman.

'Another week, I dunno. I dunno if Inez said anything to her caretaker at the Ste Maxime house.'

'You'll be going to the South of France?' asked Laura.

He had been indefinite about it before, Coleman remembered. He stated the truth. 'I enjoy Inez's company very much, but I'm longing to get back to my own place in Rome.'

And Coleman could see, in the glance the Smith-Peters exchanged, that they were thinking what a bold, reckless soul he was to linger on in a town, to announce where he might be next, when the body of a man he had killed might be washed up any day – even if on the coast of Yugoslavia. Francis seemed to be studying Coleman's hands, listening to the tone of his voice, with respectful attention. Laura gazed at him as on someone unique, the like of which she might never see again in her lifetime. Inez, Coleman saw, was not as relaxed as usual, and was careful not to miss a word anyone said. But nothing, he thought, from Inez's point of view could be said to have gone wrong that afternoon.

The Smith-Peters were hoping to leave on Friday for Florence. The workmen in their house had at last got the right-sized pipes for the upstairs bath, they thought.

When Coleman and Inez got back to their hotel, there was a message for Coleman. A Mr Zordyi had called at 4 p.m. and would call again. Coleman did not like the look of the name; there was an ominous sound about it.

'He was here twice,' the man at the desk told Coleman. 'He will call in again.'

'Oh, he came here?' Coleman asked.

'Yes, sir. Oh, here he is, sir.'

A big man with light brown hair walked towards Coleman smiling slightly. An American plain clothes man, Coleman thought.

'Mr Coleman?' he said. 'Good afternoon.'

'Good afternoon.'

'My name is Sam Zordyi. I'm here on behalf of Mr Thomas Garrett of St Louis. Mulholland Investigation Bureau.' He glanced with a smile at Inez, too.

'How do you do?' said Coleman. 'This is Mme Schneider.'

'How do you do?' said Inez.

Zordyi bowed slightly to her. 'Could I speak to you for a few minutes, Mr Coleman – or is now not convenient for you?'

'Now's perfectly all right,' Coleman said. 'I'll be up in a few minutes, dear,' he said to Inez. 'Got your key?'

Inez had. She went off towards the elevators.

Zordyi watched her as she moved away.

'Shall we sit somewhere in the lobby?' Coleman asked,

gesturing towards a quiet corner where two arm-chairs stood with a small table between them.

Zordyi glanced over the lobby, and the corner evidently met with his approval. 'All right, over here.'

They took the two arm-chairs.

'How long are you staying in Venice?' Zordyi asked.

'I don't know. Perhaps another week. Depends how the weather is. It hasn't been good lately.'

'And then where do you go?'

'I think back to my apartment in Rome.'

'I take it you haven't a clue as to Ray Garrett's whereabouts since that Thursday night, November eleventh,' Zordyi asked.

'Not a clue.'

'I spoke with the police here this afternoon. My Italian's not native, but it serves,' he added with his healthy smile. 'Would you tell me in your own words what happened that night?'

Coleman began to tell it again, patiently, saying also that Ray had seemed depressed, but not what Coleman would call desperately depressed. He had not been drinking. He had spoken to Coleman in a very regretful way about Peggy's suicide, said he had no idea of her mental state and was sorry he hadn't noticed any signs that would have warned him she was about to do something like that.

'What did you say to him?' Zordyi asked.

'I said, "It's done. What can we do about it?"'

'You weren't angry with him? You like him?'

'He's all right. Decent enough. Or I wouldn't have let my daughter marry him. He's weak in my opinion. Peggy needed a firmer hand.'

'Did you try to cheer him up that night?'

Coleman would have liked to say, 'Yes', but he foresaw that the man was going to speak to the Smith-Peters. 'I said, "It's done. It's been a shock to both of us", something like that.'

'Was there any particular reason he wanted to speak to you that night? The police said the others had left the table. Just you and Garrett were left.'

'He said he wanted to make something clearer to me. What it was, I gathered, was that he'd done his best with Peggy, tried to get her to go to a psychiatrist in Palma – she refused – and Ray wanted me to know it wasn't his fault.' Coleman sensed that Zordyi wasn't all that interested in why Peggy had killed herself. What he said was fitting pretty well into place, Coleman thought, the kind of statement a young man might have made before killing himself.

'How long did you talk?'

'About fifteen minutes.'

Zordyi was not taking notes. 'I looked over his things today at the Pensione Seguso. His suitcase. There's a couple of bullet-holes in the sleeve of one of his jackets. A left sleeve. Made by one bullet going in and out.' He added with a smile, 'The girl who packed up his things hadn't noticed the bullet-holes. I found them also in a shirt which still had some bloodstains. He'd tried to wash the shirt – maybe just a few days ago.'

Coleman was listening with attention.

'He didn't say anything to you about being shot in the arm?'

'No. Not a thing.'

'It's a funny place to shoot if you're trying to kill yourself. I think he was shot at.'

Coleman appeared to ponder that. 'In Venice?'

'Or in Rome, or Mallorca. I don't know.' Zordyi waited. 'Has he any enemies?'

'I have no idea.'

The only things Zordyi wrote down were the names of the Smith-Peters and their hotel and of Mrs Perry at the Excelsior, Lido. Coleman thought Mrs Perry might have left, and said so.

'What kind of person is Ray Garrett?' asked Zordyi.

Coleman thought Zordyi must have had detailed information from Ray's parents about him. 'Oh, reasonably intelligent, I suppose. Rather calm, introverted – a little bit shy.'

'Shy how?'

'Modest.'

'Melancholic?'

'I don't know him that well. Introverted, yes. He likes to spend time by himself.'

'What do you think of his gallery plans? Are they going through all right?'

'The last I heard, he was trying to get space in New York. He wants to handle European painters who paint in Europe. He has a lot of taste and knowledge about paintings, and he has money, so I suppose he can afford a failure, if it fails.'

'You think he's practical? Not flighty?'

Coleman shrugged good-naturedly. 'With money, you don't have to be practical, do you? I've never seen him undertake anything before. When I met him in Rome, he was taking a course in fine arts somewhere, painting a little himself.'

'You're a painter, too, I understand, Mr Coleman. Rome is a beautiful city for a painter to live in.'

'Magnificent. I used to be a civil engineer. I got tired of the New York life.'

'You live by yourself in Rome?'

'Yes. A small flat in Trastevere. Five-storey walk-up, but it's nice and quiet. If I have any guests, they have to sleep on the sofa in the living-room.'

'You can make enough to live on, painting?'

'Not really. But I manage. I do framing in Rome; that's what provides a steady income. Lots of painters do framing. More money in frames than canvases for most painters.'

Zordyi smiled at this, then stood up and thanked Coleman.

Coleman went upstairs and told Inez about the interview.

Coleman felt quite unruffled. After all, Ray wasn't dead. If Ray ever told the truth, they could charge him with attempted murder. A week ago, it had seemed a serious thing. Now it didn't. And Coleman faced the fact Ray would be found. He didn't know the exact odds on a man's being able to hide for ever, but he thought they were not too good for Ray. More important, he didn't think Ray wanted to hide for ever. What it came down to was whether Ray wanted to tell the truth eventually or not.

'It'd be interesting,' Coleman said to Inez with a chuckle, 'to hear what the Smith-Peters say when he talks to them.'

'Oh, Edward, don't joke!'

'They're on my side, you said.'

There was no telephone call from the Smith-Peters that evening, which Coleman thought odd, as he'd had the feeling Zordyi was going straight over to the Monaco to see them. But perhaps they didn't want to say anything, good or bad, over the telephone.

Laura Smith-Peters did ring the following morning at nine. Coleman was in Inez's room, though he had not spent the night there, and he answered the telephone. Laura asked if he and Inez wanted to meet them for a drink or coffee at eleven at Harry's.

'I *would* like to *see* you both this morning,' Laura added, almost pleading.

Of course. Coleman made the appointment.

In Harry's, Inez and Coleman had coffee, and the Smith-Peters bloody Marys.

It seemed that Francis had first spoken with the private detective alone, downstairs in the hotel lobby, because Laura had been taking her bath. But he had wanted to see her, too, so she had dressed and come down. Zordyi had been interested in what they thought was Ray's state of mind.

'I said and Francis said, too, that Ray hadn't been very cheerful, naturally, but he hadn't looked *hor-rribly* depressed.' Her hard

154

'r' made the word a glottal *cauchemar*, illustrative of what Ray had not been, and she gulped on the last word, or perhaps on her drink.

All of them listened, leaning forward, like a table of conspirators, Coleman thought, or prisoners planning a break. Francis's dry lips were pursed, his small eyes wide, innocent and neutral as he listened to his wife. Now and again, however, Francis looked towards the door, if it opened. Coleman no longer looked at the door.

'I'm really very sorry to put you through this,' Coleman said. He really was sorry.

'Oh, it's not *your-r* fault,' said Laura, so earnestly it was a moment before Coleman saw the wild humour in it.

Coleman smiled nervously, a smile which only Inez saw. Laura had come to believe the story she had told the 'authorities', Coleman felt.

'He asked about your attitude to Ray,' Laura went on in her subdued tone to Coleman. 'I said I didn't think you ever knew him very well. Isn't that true?'

'True,' Coleman said.

'I know you – don't like him much,' Laura said, 'but I didn't tell him that, because it would just stir up trouble, I thought.'

It would, Coleman thought. It seemed to be the end of Laura's story. She sat quietly, looking down at her hands in her lap, like a little girl who has performed, modestly but adequately, a part in a school play. Coleman wanted to ask if Zordyi had said or asked anything else, but he refrained. Zordyi evidently hadn't mentioned the bullet-holes, but Coleman supposed that he had told the Italian police about them.

'I am sure you said the right thing, Laura,' Inez said. 'Let us not worry.'

'That'll get us no place!' Francis agreed with a smile.

Coleman glanced up just as the door opened again. A woman

155

entered, and Coleman recognized her as Mrs Perry, swathed in a loose grey cape with a hood. 'Looks like Mrs Perry,' Coleman said, and raised a hand to her.

She saw him, smiled, and came towards the table. Another chair was found.

'I thought you were leaving on Friday,' said Laura. 'We'd have called you up if we'd known you were still here.'

'Well, the Lido weather got so bad,' Mrs Perry explained in her slow melancholic way, 'or at least it looks so much worse over there, I decided to give Venice a better chance and move to the Danieli, which I did.'

They ordered from the waiter. Coleman switched to Cinzano. Mrs Perry wanted a sherry. Then after a few moments' chatter about shopping, Mrs Perry asked Coleman:

'Have you heard anything about your son-in-law?'

'No. His father's sent a private detective over, so that ought to help.'

'Really?' said Mrs Perry with breathless interest, fluttering her thin eyelids. 'Then they haven't found him?'

'No,' said Francis and Coleman together.

'I thought since the paper said nothing, that they had. You know – clearing up a mystery isn't as interesting as starting one, so they don't print it. But still missing!'

'Nobody knows what to think,' said Coleman.

Mrs Perry looked at the Smith-Peters and at Inez, as if trying to divine what they were thinking. 'Did anyone see him after you, Mr Coleman?'

'If so, they haven't come up to say so,' Coleman replied.

'And you let him off at the Zattere quay, you said?'

'Yes, I did,' said Coleman. 'I was visited yesterday by the private detective. A Mr Zordyi.'

'I thought probably he'd seen you,' Laura said with a glance at Inez. 'What did he say?'

'He asked questions.' Coleman produced a cigar. 'I hope nobody minds this.'

Everybody but Inez said no.

'Asked me the same questions as the police.' Except, Coleman remembered, Zordyi had asked him if he had tried to comfort Ray that evening. 'There's not much else he can do.'

'You don't think a young man in his state – would've wandered off just on foot,' said Mrs Perry hesitantly. 'Not with any objective, but just to get away from himself?'

Her voice sounded as if she did not believe what she said, and the silence that followed suggested her words hadn't even been heard. There was also something impossible about wandering off from Venice on foot. Ray had not been in 'a state', Coleman thought, and they all knew this.

Mrs Perry seemed embarrassed by her own question, or the silence. 'I'm sorry. I realize that you –' she was addressing Coleman – 'that it's especially hard on you. Being questioned by the police and a private detective. But I can understand that they— It's because you were the last person who saw him, of course.' Her slender fingers trembled as she lifted her sherry.

There was another silence in which Coleman sensed the effort of everyone to think of something to say. Mrs Perry thought he had killed Ray, Coleman felt. She wouldn't be quite so rattled now unless she did. 'Well, I'll certainly stay on in case I can be of any help,' Coleman said finally. 'But at this point I don't see how I can tell them a thing more than I have.'

'Well, Ed, dear, you know where to find us till Friday, if you need any moral support,' Laura said with her slightly bucktoothed smile, the first smile from her that morning.

'And I'm not so sure we can take off Friday,' her husband said to her. 'I'm going to make sure those pipes are in and working before I budge from here. I'll call 'em again Thursday afternoon. Not a move before then.'

Coleman gathered himself and said to Mrs Perry, 'It's really nice of you, Ethel, to take such an interest.' It was the first time Coleman had called her by her first name, but he felt she would like him to now. 'It is upsetting, because one doesn't know if he's alive or dead.' Coleman spoke solemnly.

'Oh, but anyone would be interested. Anyone,' said Mrs Perry.

'You're awfully quiet, Inez,' Francis said.

'I don't know what to say,' Inez said, opening her hands quickly.

Her voice trembled slightly, but Coleman thought he was the only one who noticed. Then Francis reached out, smiling, gripped Inez's wrist, shook it gently, and said:

'Don't you worry. We'll all stick together.'

There was another round of drinks, then the Smith-Peters proposed that they have lunch somewhere. The lunch was good, and the atmosphere even jolly. Coleman felt secure among them. He began to feel, when his coffee arrived, a sense of invulnerability. It was then that he decided to have another try at Ray, this time more casual even than pushing him off a boat. An attack in a street, for instance. He imagined himself following Ray through dark narrow streets in Venice, taking up a convenient rock, and simply smashing Ray on the head with it. If there were time, he might dump the body into a canal, but if he did not – what matter? If no one saw him, what could be proved?

Coleman thought he would take more walks in Venice, trail Ray carefully, if he saw him again, and find out where he was spending his nights. That would give him a neighbourhood. And once he knew the neighbourhood, it was a matter of choosing the right time of night. Or it might be possible to do it by day, if the lanes around were quiet enough. Of course, he would have to see that the private detective wasn't on his own trail.

14

Ray discovered that Signor Ciardi gave wine parties nearly every night – not exactly parties, but five or six of his men friends could sound like fifty in the tile kitchen, and they stayed from nine o'clock till midnight. Ray had joined them, at Signor Ciardi's invitation, the first night, but only for half an hour. He did not want to show his face to many people. The other evenings, he politely declined to join them, saying he had some work to do: he had told Signor Ciardi he was interested in architecture. The curious thing was that after a few moments that first night – the night he had spent half an hour in the kitchen – Ray did not mind the din, whole sentences of which boomed up to his second-storey room, though ordinarily such noise irritated him.

It was true that he was interested in architecture, and he had bought a book (very like one he owned, but the one he owned wasn't with him) on the architecture of Venice in the fifteenth century. With this, he had wandered about the town on two occasions, comparing the originals with the photographs in the books, very much tempted to make sketches of some of the churches he looked at, but drawing on the street would have attracted attention, whereas with an art book and a bent neck, he looked like a tourist, and in fact the art book was a slight protection against the inquiring eye. Ray had started out in life intending to become a painter, but at twenty-four had abandoned painting as a career, believing he would never be good enough.

Ray stayed away from the San Marco district, except for his two quick trips on Monday afternoon and this morning, Tuesday, to see if there was a letter from Coleman. 'Garrett,' Ray had said, taking a chance that the clerk would not be aware that a man named Garrett was 'missing', and the clerk had calmly searched for a letter for Garrett, and had found none. Ray had left the place immediately on both days, via the Frezzeria. Ray strongly suspected that his parents had sent over a detective or two to look for him, and they would be equipped with photographs. He would go tomorrow for the last time, he thought, to see if Coleman had written, but Ray doubted very much that Coleman would, unless he felt inspired to send an insulting blast. If Coleman hadn't written by tomorrow, Wednesday, he would give the whole thing up. This he swore to himself, as if it were something he was not sure he could stick to; but he did see the logic in giving it up, and saw Inez's logic in so advising him. There was also the possibility that Coleman would leave Venice, or even had left, if the police permitted him to, and that therefore there was no purpose in all the dramatics. The police were probably not grilling Coleman, therefore Coleman wouldn't admit to anything. Ray doubted if he would admit anything under grilling. There was grilling and grilling, of course, but Ray could imagine that, if Coleman put his mind to it, he would die of torture before admitting anything he didn't want to admit, and certainly he was not going to be tortured by the Italian police or even the American. Ray had found out two things: that people – even people as apparently sensitive as Inez – didn't much care if a man had committed murder or not; and secondly, that it was hopeless to try to placate Coleman's wrath. Ray saw himself, by tomorrow afternoon, going to the police, telling them a story which would be no credit to himself, that he had wanted to disappear for a while, even at the expense of worrying his family, that he was sorry and ashamed of it, but had been in a bad state of mind. He would say he had seen the item about himself in the paper days ago, but nothing since, and he hoped his disappearing had not caused undue trouble. Ray did not want to tell the police about Coleman's attempt in the motor-boat. Just let that, he thought, go by the board.

Late that afternoon, when Ray was walking in the San Trovaso section, not far from the Pensione Seguso but beside and behind it, he came face to face with Antonio in a narrow street.

Both of them stopped short and looked at each other, Antonio open-mouthed. Then Antonio broke into a smile.

'Signor Garrett! It *is*! You are all right?'

'Yes.' Ray felt frozen. Antonio was wringing his hand.

'*Dio mio*, everybody thinks you're dead!'

'Sh-h,' Ray said, conscious of Antonio's fuchsia-coloured tie, the scent of his hair tonic. 'I'm glad to see you, too.'

'Where were you? What happened to you?'

'Nothing,' Ray said. The Italian, as tall as he, still clung to his hand. Ray extricated it. 'No, I'm all right, Antonio.'

'You should tell the police!' Antonio said, still looking at Ray as if he couldn't believe him. He said more quietly, 'You know, everybody thinks Edward *keeled* you?' He rocked back on his heels and laughed, perhaps with relief, and nearly lost his balance. 'Let's take a caffè.'

Ray hesitated. This young man could muck up everything. On the other hand, over a coffee, he might be able to persuade him not to tell anyone he'd seen him. 'All right, let's.'

They found a small bar-caffè around a corner, a place with one table in it, and that only a couple of feet from the counter. Antonio bought two caffès and brought them to the table. The proprietor, after making the coffee, returned to his newspaper.

'So,' said Antonio, 'you have just been – somewhere else?'

'Just in a room. Near here,' Ray said. 'You mustn't question me too much, Antonio. I wanted to get away from everyone – and even forget who I was for a while. Can you understand that?'

'Sure, I *can*,' Antonio replied earnestly, his bright eyes fixed on Ray. 'But that night – that night on the Lido, what happened?'

'Nothing. He put me off at San Marco and – I just walked. I went to another hotel that night.'

Antonio frowned. 'San Marco? Edward said the Zattere.'

'Or maybe it was the Zattere, I don't know. Yes, I think it was.' He saw doubt in Antonio's very readable face. 'At the Zattere. I owe a bill at the Seguso, but I'll pay it.'

Antonio waved a hand airily, as if to say, 'Bills!' He frowned harder and pulled at his full underlip. 'You know, Inez think Edward keeled you. She is very worried. She didn't say it, but I know. She asked me to leave Venezia.' He smiled. 'But leave Venezia so soon? No. I know she would be displeased if she thought I was still here, so I move myself yesterday to a little place in vicinity here.' He gestured vaguely. 'Venezia is too beautiful to leave! And besides I was interested in what happens to you. But you see' – he hunched forward, glancing at the proprietor, though they were speaking in English – 'she ask me to leave because she think I may say something against Edward.'

'Oh? Say what against him?'

'I dunno. I dunno anything – except he hates you.' Antonio smiled gently, a little mischievously. 'But Inez is worried. Edward maybe told her he keel you. Or maybe she just suspect. You see?' Antonio was almost whispering. 'You maybe don' unnerstand, but I unnerstand. Today – I see them all going together down a street, the Smith-Peters, Edward, Inez, all friends together. They *all* think Edward keel you. Or they suspect. But they don't want no Italian – you see what I mean? Is very usual for Italians to stay together but strange for Americans, no? But maybe we are all alike unnerneath!' He came down on his thighs with both hands, laughing as softly as he had spoken.

Ray smiled. 'I suppose it's strange.'

'They all know Edward hates you,' Antonio said in a whisper, 'but I don't think they say that to the police or they would not go out in the street with Edward to have lunch, no?' Antonio paused to let this sink in. 'I think Edward maybe *brag* to Inez that he keel you. Or why is she so worried? Is like Edward to say something like that to her. He don't give a damn. You know?'

Ray knew. He let Antonio talk on. Antonio's English was at that stage of fluency that it gave him enjoyment to rattle on.

'He say to police he let you down at Zattere, and to Inez maybe that he keel you. Or maybe he tell Inez he let you down at Zattere and she does not believe, I dunno.' Antonio turned a box of wax matches over and over on the table-top. 'What you going to do now?'

The question annoyed Ray, but he felt he had to answer it for courtesy's sake, or possibly to keep Antonio's belief in his sanity. 'I'll go to the police in a day or so and tell them I'm all right. But meanwhile, Antonio, I wish you would not tell anyone that you saw me. Not even anyone who doesn't know me. Will you promise me that?'

Antonio looked surprised and a little disappointed. 'Why?'

'I want to be by myself – incognito – just a few more days. Maybe just till tomorrow. But let me handle it.' He realized the impossibility of making Antonio understand. He could make him understand by saying, 'I'm hiding in order to put the blame for my death on Coleman, but you see that doesn't work, because nobody cares, and anyway I'm not dead,' but his motive was not so simple and, what was more important, he did not care to explain his motives to Antonio. 'It'll all be straightened out,' Ray said. 'I've—' He started to say that he had had a grief, but he did not want to mention Peggy. 'Let's leave, shall we?'

163

Antonio got up. 'Can I walk with you a little? I am free until seven.'

'All right,' Ray said, not really caring.

They walked along the San Trovaso canal towards the Zattere quay. Neither was leading the other; it was just the way the turnings took them, the jogging lanes narrower and more crooked here in this neighbourhood, which seemed older, simpler and poorer than most of Venice.

'You have a room in vicinity now?' asked Antonio.

'Yes,' Ray replied. Giudecca was in view as he spoke, that huge island across an expanse of water, his refuge that he was not going to betray.

'Edward let you down here?' Antonio asked as they entered the Fondamento delle Zattere, gesturing vaguely to the left, towards the Pensione Seguso.

'Yes, somewhere along here.'

They turned to the right. The Fondamento was broad, its house fronts straight and unornamented. It was growing dark, and the street-lamps had come on.

'We run into Stazione Marittima there and we can't pass,' Antonio said, nodding ahead. 'Let's go here.'

They walked into a narrow street going right, and after a moment, crossed a bridge over a canal. Ray realized he would have to go back the same way in order to catch a boat for Giudecca. He wanted to be free of Antonio, but did not want to appear as though he did. He would walk five minutes more and leave him, Ray thought, and he would also make sure Antonio didn't follow him when they separated.

'Maybe the police make Edward stay in Venezia,' Antonio mused. 'I know Inez wants to go to France.'

'I don't know,' Ray answered as vaguely. He turned up the collar of his overcoat.

'Why you grow a beard? To hide yourself?'

'Just for a change. I don't think it hides me much, do you?'

'You know, I thought too Edward keel you,' Antonio said, as if it were a deep confidence. 'I thought, what a strange man, walking around – an American – and – nobody do anything.'

Not even you, Ray thought, but quite without judgement on him. 'People don't want to make an accusation like that, I'm sure.'

'But even Inez, she still stays with him in the—'

Ray had started suddenly, but he had stopped walking. In the shadows ahead, emerging from a triangular shadow that clung to a small church like a dark pyramid, he saw Coleman, looking over both shoulders, obviously looking for something, someone.

'What is it?' Antonio asked.

'Nothing. I thought I saw someone,' Ray replied.

Antonio looked around quickly. 'Who?'

Coleman was still in sight. Then in another second, he wasn't. He had vanished in the slit of an alley on the left of the church square. 'I thought I saw Inez,' Ray said. 'It doesn't matter. I should be leaving you now. I'm glad I saw you, Antonio. But remember what I said. Don't tell anyone you saw me. Leave that to me, will you?'

'But – I won't be seeing any of them. Honest,' Antonio said. 'Ray, I am very glad you are alive!' He held out his hand.

Ray shook it. 'Arrivederci, Antonio.'

'Arrivederci, Ray!'

Ray went off to the right, in the opposite direction from Coleman's, not caring where it led him. After a few moments, he looked back, and did not see Antonio. Then his street bent, and he could no longer see any distance behind him. At another corner, he paused and looked back and waited. No sign of Antonio. He breathed a little more easily, and went on towards the Zattere quay – at least, he thought he was going in the right general direction for it, and he glanced around for one of the helpful arrows that were sometimes painted on house sides to show the way to the nearest vaporetto or traghetta stop. Tonight he found none. At the Zattere quay, he gave a convulsive sigh. His shoulders ached. He glanced behind him – for Coleman now, not Antonio – and not seeing him, walked on more slowly. He supposed he could trust Antonio not to say anything, and it was a little to his advantage that Antonio was apparently not going to see Inez again. And it was quite true that, in two days, he would go to the police himself. Meanwhile, he must take up the pieces of his life again. He could make a list of four or five:

Write to Bruce Main in New York; cable his parents (tomorrow, perhaps); go to Paris and take care of business there; write and see how Mac was handling the sale of the boat and some furniture in Mallorca; and in Paris, post would probably be awaiting him at the Pont Royal from Bruce, possibly also the lease for the Lexington Avenue gallery space. The question in New York was, was the building going to be torn down or not? Surely Bruce would have found out by now.

On Zattere, he bought a *Corriere della Sera* at the newsstand. There had been nothing about him in the morning's *Gazzettino*. He tucked the paper under his arm without looking at it. Rain began to fall as he boarded the boat for Giudecca.

Ray leaned against the cabin, only half sheltered, watching Giudecca come closer. Was Coleman really on the prowl again for him? Or had he been trying to avoid the private detective who might have been trailing him? But why would the detective trail Coleman in a place like Venice, when he knew Coleman's hotel? Ray knew, and had known really since the first glimpse of Coleman this evening, that Coleman was looking for him. And maybe the gun was with him now, too. Coleman obviously stuck at nothing, and nothing would satisfy him but killing him. Ray began to see the advantage of showing himself to the police tomorrow, and of leaving Venice tomorrow, too.

When he arrived at the house on the south side of Giudecca, Signor Ciardi was not in, or at least Ray heard and saw no one as he crossed the court and climbed the stairs to his room. Well, his room was here still, just the same, even tidied by Giustina. Ray looked around at his few books, his new suitcase, and at the grapevine stem beside his window. It was six-ten by his watch. Tomorrow morning, he would go to the police (even if there was a letter from Coleman at the San Marco post office) and he would be a different person, the person called Ray Garrett. The name was like a label, familiar, dull, like a package's label: this box contains twelve sixteen-ounce cans – not eleven or thirteen, but exactly twelve. Rather than bother Giustina with heating bath-water, Ray removed his shirt and washed in cold water at a stone sink he had discovered in a dark alcove one floor below. He rubbed himself hard with the rough towel, shaking with cold. He leapt up the stone steps, into his room again. There was still time to buy things in Venice, and he wanted to buy a present for Elisabetta.

Before seven, Ray was back on the mainland, trotting through the passage from the Zattere quay to Accademia, leaping over the arched bridge, down again into Campo Morosino, past San Maurizio church, on towards San Marco. He bought a handbag for Elisabetta in a reliable but rather expensive shop near San Marco. The bag was black, squarish, sturdy, and beautifully lined in beige kid. He walked to the Largo San Sebastiano and pressed Elisabetta's bell. It was seven-thirty, and he hoped they were not at dinner.

He heard rapid footsteps descending a stairway, maybe Elisabetta herself. Then her voice:

'Who is it, please?'

'It's me. Filipo,' Ray answered.

The door opened. Elisabetta looked at him with her large eyes wide, her lips slightly parted. Then she smiled. 'It *is* you!'

'Yes. I have a present for you.' He extended the striped paper bag to her. 'Because I'm leaving. I wanted to say good-bye.'

'You've been in Venice all this time?' she asked in a whisper, glancing behind her, but no one was coming.

'Yes. Take this, Elisabetta. Please. Or can you come out for a few minutes? For a cup of coffee?'

'I have maybe twenty minutes. Before supper. Wait!' And she closed the door again.

He waited in the street, delighted that she had a few minutes, and also that she trusted him enough to come out with him.

She came out with her coat on. Ray still carried the paper bag.

'Where would you like to go?' he asked.

'We don't have to go anywhere.' She stared at him with round eyes. 'Where were you? I saw your picture in the paper.'

'Sh-h. I was in Venice. We should have a coffee or a drink somewhere. Get out of this chill.'

They went, at Elisabetta's suggestion, to a bar around two corners and down a little lane. Elisabetta wanted hot chocolate. Ray had a Scotch and water.

'I showed your picture to Signora Calliuoli,' Elisabetta said, whispering again, very nervous of the boy behind the counter whose attention she had already attracted. She cupped her hand beside her face. 'I said, "That's the American who was with you for a few days. You should tell the police." She kept saying she was not sure, but I know she was sure, it was that she did not want the police to know she had a tenant in her house.' Elisabetta giggled suddenly and repressed it. 'Income tax.'

Ray smiled. 'Just as well. I didn't want myself reported.' This evening, the girl's scent seemed much nicer than the evening he had taken her out to dinner, though it was the same scent. She looked altogether charming, her peachy complexion as fresh as ever, her hair light and clean.

'Why were you hiding?' She leaned across the little table, eager for his answer. 'Why don't you now tell me the truth?'

Ray put the paper bag on the table, so he could sit up closer, too. 'It is true,' he said softly, 'what I told you before. My father-in-law was trying to kill me. I had to hide – you see.' Not the whole story, but it hung together, he thought: he had been hiding for his own protection, lest Signora Calliuoli or Elisabetta herself disclose to the police, therefore to his father-in-law, where he was. 'And also,' Ray continued, 'I was feeling sad and full of guilt. It is quite true that my wife committed suicide.' His Italian was simple, even in these words perhaps not perfectly accurate, but he could see that Elisabetta understood and believed him.

'Why did she?'

'I don't know. Really I don't know.'

She looked at him steadily. 'And now –?'

'I'm going to go to the police tomorrow,' Ray whispered. He was glad that the boy, out of courtesy perhaps, had stopped looking at them, since they obviously wanted to talk in private. 'I'll tell them I'm all right, but—'

'But?'

'I shall not tell them that my father-in-law tried to kill me.'

'Why not?'

'There's no need. I don't think he'll try it again. He's a man – crazy with grief, too, you see.'

She was quiet, but he supposed she saw.

'It is so pleasant to see you,' Ray said.

She smiled a little, uncertainly. Tonight her lipstick was a curious brownish-mauve. 'Where have you been in the last days?'

'On Giudecca.'

'You look nice with a beard.'

'Thanks. You'd better take this. I don't want to forget it.'

She took the bag, smiling like a child now. 'What is it?' She pulled the handbag out of its tissue, and her mouth opened in surprise. 'But it's beautiful! Squis-s-sito!'

Ray was gratified. 'I am glad you like it. That is to thank you for all you did for me.'

'But I did nothing.'

'Yes, you did. You did a lot. I had no friend in the city but you.' He looked at his watch. 'I always have to watch the time for you.'

He paid and they left. On the street, they held hands, then locked their arms together and held hands. 'I am sorry the walk is so short,' Ray said.

She laughed happily.

'Would you give me a kiss?'

She looked around at once, unhesitating, only looking for a little privacy somewhere. They stood in a doorway. She locked one arm around his neck and gave him a long kiss. He held her body tight to his, felt the start of great desire for her, as if he had known her before, known her a long while. And some lines of poetry came to his mind. They kissed a second time, almost as long as the first.

She pushed away and said, 'I really must go home.'

They began to walk again.

'Do you know the lines—' he began. 'Well, they're in English, I don't know any Italian translation. They go:

> "The grave's a fine and private place,
> But none I think do there embrace."

They're by Andrew Marvell.'

She didn't even know of Marvell, and he translated the lines for her, grief-stricken at having to botch them by his Italian.

'I have cheated the grave,' he said. 'Not many people can do that!'

She understood that and laughed. 'Will I see you again?' she asked at her door.

'I don't know. I may leave tomorrow morning, you see, after I speak to the police.' He was whispering again, anxious about her family inside the house. 'But if I am here – I will try to see you again.' He felt suddenly vague about it, and also as if it were of no importance. Their meeting had been perfect as it was, and that seemed now to be all that mattered.

'I hope so. Good night, Filipo – or whatever your name is. And a thousand thanks for the handbag.' She went in.

Ray then walked for an hour in an agreeable mental fog – a fog as far as his own problems were concerned, because he simply was not thinking about them, but not a fog as far as Venice was concerned, because he felt that he saw the city more sharply than ever before. The night was cold and clear, and every light stood out, sharp as the stars. And every view delighted him as if it were new to him, as things seem just after falling in love, Ray thought, but he knew he was not in love with Elisabetta. The sight of children, tiny ones that should have been in bed, playing beside a church that had stood since Marco Polo's days, pleased him, and so did a trio of mangy cats hunched in an alley – which after a hundred yards turned out to be blind. He had dinner in a restaurant where he had never been before, and read one of his paperbacks that he had brought along in his pocket.

When he came out of the restaurant at half past ten, he realized he did not know in what neighbourhood he was, but he thought he was not far from the Rialto. He would walk, he thought, until he saw something recognizable, or until an arrow directed him to a vaporetto. It was when he decided to give up a certain unpromising-looking street, and turned back, that he saw Coleman some thirty feet away. Coleman was looking at him, and Ray was sure had been following him. For an instant, Ray thought of approaching Coleman and telling him what he planned to do, go to the police tomorrow. But as before, in his instant of hesitation, Coleman turned round.

Annoyed, Ray turned back in his original direction down the unpromising street, and kept going. All streets led somewhere – to water eventually – and the edges of Venice had broad fondamenti where one could walk to a waterbus stop. After a minute, Ray looked back.

Coleman was following him.

Ray felt suddenly afraid. To right and left, lanes went off, dark alleys that would make it easy to give Coleman the slip. Ray went quickly into one on his right. There had been enough people on the street for him to hope Coleman had not noticed his turning, but Ray still took a left turn next, went under a sottoporto and found himself on a narrow pavement beside a canal. He paused, reluctant to go any farther, because the canal walk seemed to lead nowhere much, and the section was dark. Ray went cautiously back the way he had come, but stopped when he saw that Coleman was advancing. Ray returned to the canal and went left on its bank, running a little. He took the next lane left. A corner street-light ahead showed a right turning thirty yards on.

Coleman was coming after him. Ray could hear his trotting footsteps. The thing to do was get back to the larger street, Ray thought. Ray took the right turn, realizing he would have to go left to reach the larger street. He saw he had run into a blind alley, and started back again, running faster now.

Coleman came into the alley before Ray reached the corner. Ray clenched his fists, thinking at least to knock Coleman out of his way, if he put up resistance. Ray was attempting to dash past, when Coleman's right arm swung in a fast arc, and something terrible hit Ray on the left side of the head; he heard a crack, then he sat down heavily on the stone ground. Coleman was trying to lift him from under the arms. And Ray, struggling not to pass out, felt that he struggled also against dying. Coleman was dragging him a long way. They were approaching the canal's edge. Ray saw Coleman's hand, with a rock in it, drawn back for another blow, and dived for Coleman's ankles, or rather lurched against them, striking them with his shoulder. Coleman's blow went wild. Ray circled Coleman's legs, and pulled. Coleman toppled, Ray had a glimpse of Coleman's hat in mid-air, then he heard Coleman's back thud, his head crack, as he struck the cement path. Ray seized the stone beside Coleman, staggered to his feet and hurled the stone at him. It hit Coleman in the neck, or the ear.

Ray stood swaying, panting, still dazed. His own breathing was the loudest thing around, and at last he closed his mouth. He became aware of a warm trickle of blood behind his left ear. Then his legs began to move by themselves, carried him staggering under the sottoporto. How quiet everything was, Ray thought. He turned left, heard a trickle of water somewhere on his right, and made out in the street-lamp's light a small fountain and basin against a house wall. Ray went over and wet his handkerchief, and applied it clumsily to the side of his head. His head both stung and felt numb. His lip was also bleeding. While he was bent over the fountain, a man entered the street, walking quickly, but went on to a door flush with the house walls in the same street. He had only glanced at Ray. Ray wrung out his handkerchief, mopped as much blood as he could, and repeated this a few times, wiping his face also.

He walked on, shakily. He had not walked five minutes before he saw an arrow directing him to a vaporetto station. Here, Ray took a boat for the Riva degli Schiavoni, whence he could catch a boat for Giudecca. There were gondoliers available at Schiavoni, and Ray thought of taking one all the way home, through one of the canals that crossed Giudecca, but he had a dread of attracting further attention to himself, and so did not, though he realized he was perhaps not thinking clearly about the situation. Several people on the boat stared at him, and two people, both men, asked him with concern if he was all right, did he not want a doctor? Ray replied that he had only had a bad fall, 'Un' caduta.'

On Giudecca at last, he crossed the island on foot towards the Ciardi house, and let himself in with his key.

A wine party was of course in progress. A card game as well,

Ray saw through the window as he approached the kitchen. He knocked, rather feebly, he felt.

Signor Ciardi opened the door, and the din subsided suddenly as the men looked at him. He sank into a chair and tried to answer the questions they were all putting to him. A cup of wine was lifted to his lips, and was replaced by a glass with brandy in it.

'Un' caduta – caduta,' Ray kept repeating.

A doctor arrived.

The doctor shaved some hair away and stuck a needle in the side of his head. He put in some stitches. Then Ray was helped up to bed by many willing hands.

'I'll send for Luigi,' Signor Ciardi assured him. 'He will visit you tomorrow.'

The doctor also gave him a large pill for sleeping. Ray was grateful, for by now his head had begun to hurt, even through the doctor's anaesthetic.

15

It was Luigi's wife who arrived the next morning at nine o'clock and with a pot of beef broth. Signor Ciardi came with her into Ray's room. Ray had been awake with the pain since 6 a.m., but since the household slept until after eight as a rule, he had not wanted to try to get an aspirin from Signor Ciardi or Giustina.

'You must take this while it is hot,' said the active Signora Lotto, uncovering a blue tin pot on a tray, pouring the broth into a wide bowl. 'Even if it is morning, this will do you more good than caffè latte. I just heated it on Giustina's stove.'

'Grazie, Signora Lotto,' Ray said. 'And thank you, Signor Ciardi, for being so kind last night. You must tell me the doctor's bill. Also, I would greatly appreciate an aspirin now.'

'Ah, si! Against pain! Subito!' He went out.

'And what happened, Signor Weelson?' Signora Lotto demanded, seating herself on a straight chair, bony hands on her knees. 'My Luigi would be here, but he went off this morning at two – my God! – and he doesn't know yet. We had the messenger from Paolo only at eight this morning. Your head! It is not broken, the bone?'

'Oh, no. I had a fall – down some stone steps.' He was glad Signora Lotto still called him John Wilson.

She looked wondering. 'Not a fight? Not robbers? –That is good. You are not hurt anywhere else?'

'I think not.' Ray's head pulsed: he imagined a demon with a hammer banging away at the same bloody spot. 'Delicious broth! A thousand thanks.'

Signor Ciardi returned with his aspirin. Ray took two.

'I cause you a lot of trouble,' Ray said, raising himself to see if he had bled on the pillow. Happily, he had not. The doctor's bandage went entirely around his head.

'Trouble, no! Bad luck, dear friend. A friend of Luigi is a friend of mine, and he says he is your friend. Isn't that true, Costanza?'

'Sissi.' She nodded in agreement, and rocked herself on the chair. 'Finish the soup! Have some more!'

She stayed twenty minutes, then went away with Signor Ciardi. Ray had said he would try to get up and dress. The kind Signor Ciardi had even offered to help him do that. Since Signor Ciardi had no telephone, he would have to go to the nearest bar that had one, Ray thought. He did not feel up to making a trip to a police station. He was weak, but by moving slowly, he thought he could manage. He thought differently by the time he was downstairs and the scene began turning. He sat down on a chair in the living-room, and eventually Signor Ciardi saw him and came over.

'You see, Signor Weelson, Costanza was right. You should stay in bed today.'

'It is important that I make a telephone call,' Ray said. 'I wonder if you have time to go with me to the next place that has a telephone?'

'Ah, si, to my friends the Zanaros here on the left!'

'Thanks, but I had better make a call from a booth. A private call – you see.' It was somehow already eleven o'clock. 'I'd like to do it now, if you would be so kind.'

Signor Ciardi got his coat. They walked slowly towards a bar-caffè on the fondamento. Ray consulted the directory, then stood in front of the telephone which was unsheltered, fixed on a wall. Signor Ciardi strolled out of the door discreetly. The few others in the bar, after staring a little at his bandage, paid him no mind. And in fact, Ray supposed it didn't matter if they all listened.

'May I speak to someone in regard to the Rayburn Garrett situation,' he began, using the word *situazione*, as even his Italian was weak that morning.

'Yes? Who is speaking, please? – Who is speaking?' The Italian voice repeated patiently, 'Cui parla, per favore? ...'

Ray slowly hung up the telephone, which felt like a five-pound weight in his hand. He clung to the little shelf on which the telephone rested.

Then Signor Ciardi rushed to him, put an arm around him, and steered him to a chair. Ponderous bells were ringing in Ray's head, and he could not hear what Signor Ciardi was saying.

'Acqua! Un bicchiere d'acqua, per favore!' Signor Ciardi shouted towards the bar.

Was it better to faint for a moment, or fight it, Ray wondered. He breathed deeply. The ringing subsided. 'I am sorry. I lost blood last night, perhaps.'

'You must have a coffee! Maybe a cognac with it. Don't worry about anything!' Signor Ciardi was all concern, like Signora Lotto, leaning across the table, pressing Ray's forearm.

Ray was very grateful. He began to feel better with a cappuccino. He declined Signor Ciardi's offer of a cognac, but put a lot of sugar in the coffee.

Signor Ciardi smiled and rubbed his stubby cheek with a fore-finger. Signor Ciardi could dress almost like a tramp, go unshaven for two or three days, and still appear a man of dignity, even of importance, because he believed himself to be one.

With Ray's returning strength, he felt a growing elation because he had stood up to Coleman last evening. For the first time, he had struck a blow back. He had had enough of Coleman and Coleman knew it now. Coleman himself would have a few aches this morning. And Ray suddenly realized that Coleman might be very badly off indeed, if that stone had caught him in the side of the head while he was lying down. What had happened after that? He remembered throwing the stone, the same stone Coleman had hit him with, at Coleman while he lay on the ground. Then had he kicked him? Struck him with his fist? It didn't seem likely that he would have hit a man on the ground – but Coleman had been lying on the ground when Ray threw the stone. Ray realized he could have blacked out. He'd been terrified, and furious. Yes, he couldn't quite ascribe his actions to sheer courage, but at least he'd stood up to Coleman. This made him feel quite different, quite a different person from the one he had felt himself to be this time yesterday.

'I'll have another cappuccino, I think,' Ray said, and gestured to the boy behind the counter. 'And what will you have, Signor Ciardi? A caffè? A glass of wine?'

'A glass of wine, si,' said Signor Ciardi, beaming at the return of strength to his patient.

Ray ordered it.

Signor Ciardi frowned suddenly. 'Exactly where did you fall?'

'Some little steps – not far from the Ponte di Rialto. The street was dark, or it would not have happened.' Ray suddenly wondered if Coleman could be dead. His body found by now, perhaps found even last night. Ray could not decide what was logical to believe, that he was dead or not, and was more inclined to believe that it was his own guilt feelings – at having struck Coleman with a rock – that made him fear he might be dead.

'And no one was around? To help you?' asked Signor Ciardi.

'No. I found a small fountain and washed myself. It's not so bad, you see, only the blood.' Ray began to feel weak again. He downed his coffee as rapidly as Signor Ciardi finished his wine.

'We will go back to the house,' Signor Ciardi said firmly.

'Yes.' Ray pulled a five-hundred-lire piece from his pocket for the bill, insisted, over Signor Ciardi's protest, on paying. He was remembering, with some satisfaction, how last night he had won out over unconsciousness by sheer will-power, it seemed to him. Surely a blow such as he had received would have knocked out most people. He walked back home with Signor Ciardi with his head higher than usual, walked as erectly as he could, even though Signor Ciardi's hand gripping his arm was an important, maybe even a necessary, support.

In his room he slept for several hours. Then he was awakened at 4 p.m., as Signor Ciardi had said he would be, by Giustina bringing a tray of tea, toast and a brace of boiled eggs.

He enjoyed a state of bliss that he knew was temporary. And it was not actually bliss, whatever that was, he realized, only a considerable improvement over his state since just before Peggy's suicide, or even weeks before. It had been a curious and horrible thing to realize, when Peggy was alive, that their marriage was not working, not succeeding in making either of them happy, despite all the ingredients that were supposed to make a marriage go: time, money, a pretty place to live, objectives. His objective had been the New York art gallery, which Peggy had been interested in, too. She had known some painters for him to get in touch with from Mallorca, and three of them were on his list for the gallery now. Their idea had been to gather young European painters who still lived in Europe, since New York had enough European painters who were New York based. At openings, the painter would not be present unless he wanted to come over, but there would be photographs and well-displayed biographies of him or her at the gallery. New York was full of exhibitionist painters who turned up at their openings in purple velvet suits, diapers, or anything at all to get attention, and after that, success was a matter of whom the painter knew. Ray's idea was a gallery without the circus atmosphere, without even background music, just a good deep carpet underfoot, plenty of ashtrays, proper lighting. The gallery need not have tied him and Peggy to New York, if they hadn't wished to be tied there, as they could have left it in Bruce's hands. Or, it could have provided an interest for them in New York, if they had chosen. It seemed to Ray that they had had everything, except hardship.

And then Peggy's death and the Coleman onslaught – like a sea of log-laden water that had rushed over him. He had not only bowed to it, he had been knocked out by it. But he had finally stood up against it. Ray liked to imagine that it was the first time anyone had stood up to Coleman. He recalled Coleman's stories in Rome, shortly after they had met (Coleman wasted no time in boasting). Coleman, the self-made man, blustering his way into moneyed society in America, carrying off one of the prizes as a wife, forging to the top of his engineering firm, forming a company of his own soon after, and then quitting the business cold. Onward to new glories, more with women than by painting, it seemed. *I like them big. The bigger the challenge, the bigger the win,* Coleman had said in Rome not two years ago. Had Coleman been talking about women, men, painting, jobs? It didn't matter. It was Coleman's attitude that mattered. And Coleman must now be furious, Ray thought.

Ray summoned Giustina with the aid of a long-handled bell that stood outside his door, returned the tray with thanks, and asked if she would prepare a bath. The doctor was coming at six. Ray had his bath, and received the doctor and Signor Ciardi. The doctor found no fever, and did not look at the wound. The stitches could come out in four days. He prescribed rest. Ray had thought to go out that evening to ring the police, but he could see that Signor Ciardi was rather keeping a watch on him. Ray supposed the matter could wait one more day.

'Luigi is coming,' Signor Ciardi told Ray, and repeated it at two-minute intervals, until at last they heard the bell.

Giustina hurried down to open the door, and then Luigi came up, grizzle-cheeked as usual, beret in hand, his gondolier's striped shirt showing in the V-neck of his black blouse.

'Ciao, Luigi,' Ray said. 'Tutto va bene, never fear. Have a seat.'

'Dear Signor Weelson – Giovanni! Costanza told me . . .' Once more his words were lost to Ray, as they were in dialect.

'Your kind wife brought me broth,' Ray informed him, he was sure unnecessarily.

The conversation was not exactly smooth, but the oil of affection was there. Luigi had saved his life once. He was helping, through his friends, to preserve it now. Ray managed to convey this, much to the delight of Signor Ciardi and Giustina, who appreciated a flowery sentiment, but perhaps did not grasp the first part about Luigi's having saved his life, and took it to mean that Luigi had found him a place to stay.

Signor Ciardi had Giustina fetch wine. Everyone except Giustina had one of Ray's American cigarettes. The atmosphere was gay in the room. Luigi produced two fine oranges from his blouse, and they were put on Ray's night table. He questioned Ray about the street where he had fallen, and deplored the lack of light in some streets. The party might have gone on longer, but the doctor had said that Signor Weelson should have some rest, so they all filed out.

Giustina brought Ray a supper of fettucini and salad and some of Signor Ciardi's fortifying wine. Ray gathered his energy for the next day.

He had asked Giustina to buy a *Gazzettino*, and it arrived on his breakfast tray. Since he had braced himself, Ray was not too surprised – yet surprised with the solid impact of having anticipation confirmed – to see Coleman's straightforward passport photograph on the front page. Edward Venner Coleman, fifty-two, American painter and resident of Rome, was reported missing since the evening of 23 November. His friend Mme Inez Schneider, forty-eight, of Paris, staying at the Gritti Palace Hotel, had notified the police at noon on 24 November, when Coleman had not returned to the hotel the preceding evening. The paper added that Coleman was the father-in-law of Rayburn Cook Garrett, twenty-seven, who had been missing since 11 November. If anyone had seen Coleman on the evening of 23 November after 9.30 p.m. or since, would he please inform the police.

Ray had a brief sense of alarm: Coleman could be dead. But he didn't believe Coleman was dead, or that he had blacked out and pushed Coleman into a canal. Coleman was probably hiding out, turning the tables on him, in a way. Ray realized he would be answerable when he spoke to the police. He would have to tell them about the fight.

Ray got out of bed and shaved with the hot water Giustina had brought in a jug on his tray. He put on a fresh shirt. It was still only a quarter to nine. He felt much stronger than he had been yesterday, but he descended the stairs slowly instead of running as he wished to do. He met Giustina.

'I am going out for perhaps half an hour,' Ray said. 'Thank you for the good breakfast, Giustina.'

'Un mezz' ora,' she repeated.

'Si. O forse un ora. Arrivederla.'

Ray prudently slowed his steps on the fondamento, and made his way to the same bar-caffè at which he had started the telephone call to the police yesterday. Again he looked up the six-digit number which he had forgotten. The same voice answered.

'May I speak to someone in regard to the Rayburn Garrett – history,' Ray began.

'Si, Signor. Cui parla, per favore?'

'Rayburn Garrett is speaking,' Ray said.

'Ah, Signor Garrett! Benissimo. Wait one moment. We are very pleased to hear from you, sir.'

Ray waited.

He was asked by another voice if he could come as soon as possible to the station at Piazzale Roma. Ray said he would.

16

Ray braced himself, during the boat ride to the Piazzale Roma, to tell his not very proud story. His only consolation, a rotten one perhaps, was that many other men before him had had a worse story to tell – a confession of murder or theft, for instance – and that he was going to leave out Coleman's two attempts on his life, thereby putting himself in a category that might be called 'noble' with a stretch of the imagination. At any rate, he was not in a mood to hang his head. He thought a better word than noble might be simply charitable or generous.

With bandage tidy and bloodless, head up, then, Ray walked through the doorway of the questura at Piazzale Roma, which he had found after making only one inquiry. He gave his name to a clerk, and was shown farther into the building and presented to a Capitano Dell' Isola.

'Signor Garrett! And what has happened to you?' Dell' Isola – a short, intelligent-looking man – opened his eyes wide.

Ray realized that he referred to the bandage. 'I had an encounter. The evening before last. An encounter with Signor Coleman.'

'We must take this down.' The Capitano gestured to a clerk.

Pen and paper were produced. The clerk sat at the side of Dell' Isola's desk.

'We must cable your parents at once. You have no objection, I trust, Signor Garrett?'

'No,' Ray said.

'And we shall also inform the private investigator, Signor Zordzi – Zord-yi. We were unable to reach him after you telephoned, but we have left a message at his hotel that you are here, and I hope he will come at once. You should stay to speak with him. Allora.' The Capitano stood behind his desk, hands behind his hips, smiling at Ray. 'Where have you been for the past –' he referred to a paper on his desk – 'fourteen days?'

'I have been in Venice. I stayed in rooms that I rented. I am sorry for the trouble I have caused, but – I was full of grief and I wanted to disappear for a while.'

'You certainly did that. Now tell me – about the encounter the evening before last. November twenty-third. First, where did it take place?'

'In a street near the Ponte di Rialto. I was aware that Signor Coleman was following me. I tried to run from him. This was about ten-thirty at night. I was suddenly in a street with no exit. Signor Coleman had a stone in his hand. He hit me in the side of the head. But I also hit him. I think he must have been unconscious when I left him.'

'And do you know exactly what street this was?' asked Dell' Isola, glancing at the clerk to see if it was being taken down.

'No, I don't. It was beside a canal. I could perhaps find it again. The Ponte di Rialto vaporetto was about a hundred and fifty metres distant.'

'With what did you say you hit Signor Col-e-man?'

'I threw the stone at him. The same stone. I had pushed him down to the ground, I think. I was – almost not conscious myself.'

'You know that Signor Col-e-man is missing?'

185

'Yes, I read that this morning.'

'In what condition was he when you left him?'

Ray glanced at the clerk, who was looking at him now. 'He was lying on the ground. On his back.'

'No one saw you?' asked the Capitano.

'No. It happened very quickly. It was beside a small canal, a narrow—' Ray suddenly could not think of the word for walk or pavement. He passed his hand quickly across his forehead, and encountered the bandage. 'I do not think anyone saw us.'

A knock sounded at the door.

'Enter,' said the Capitano.

A tall American in a brown topcoat came in. He smiled in an astonishing way at Ray. 'Good morning. Good morning,' he repeated to Dell' Isola. 'Mr Garrett?'

'Yes,' Ray said.

'My name is Sam Zordyi. Your parents sent me to find you. Well – where have you been? In a hospital?'

'No. This happened night before last. As I was saying to the Capitano,' Ray began, embarrassed at having to repeat the story, 'I've been staying in a rented room. I wanted to be alone for a while, and – Tuesday night I ran into Coleman and had a fight with him.' Ray noticed that the Capitano was listening attentively, and perhaps he understood English.

Dell' Isola spoke to Zordyi in Italian, offering him a chair. Zordyi sat down and looked at Ray in a puzzled, speculative way. Zordyi had large blue eyes. He looked powerful and energetic.

'I better cable your parents right away,' Zordyi said. 'Or have you done that?'

'No, I haven't,' Ray answered.

'Or you, sir?' he asked Dell' Isola. Then in Italian, 'Have you told his parents – he has appeared?'

'No, signor,' Dell' Isola took a deep breath and said, 'I am wondering – Signor Garrett says he was almost unconscious from the

186

blow that Signor Col-e-man struck him on the head. He remembers that Signor Col-e-man was lying on the ground, perhaps unconscious also. I am wondering if Signor Garrett – in his anger which I understand, since Signor Col-e-man attacked him first – if he could have done him more damage than he thinks?' Dell' Isola looked at Ray.

'I hit him once with the stone. In the neck, I think.' Ray shrugged nervously, and felt he looked guilty. 'Before that, he simply fell to the ground because I pulled his legs. Unless he fractured his skull when he fell to the ground—'

'Just what happened?' Zordyi asked Ray.

Ray told him in English about Coleman following him, about the stone in his hand – he made an oval with his fingers to show its size, the size of a large avocado – and about his getting the worst of it at first, but coming back at Coleman and leaving him on the ground.

'Where was this?' asked Zordyi.

Ray again explained as best he could.

Zordyi was frowning. 'Was this the first time you'd seen Coleman? In the past two weeks?' He said to Dell' Isola in stiff but correct Italian, 'I hope that you can follow what we are saying, Signor Capitano.'

'Sissi,' said Dell' Isola.

Ray foresaw a pit that would grow deeper and deeper before him. He said cautiously, 'I saw him once in a restaurant. I don't think he saw me.'

'Were you avoiding him? Well, obviously. Why?'

'I was avoiding everyone, I'm afraid.'

'But,' Zordyi continued, 'when you arrived in Venice, you saw Coleman. Mme Schneider – I just spoke with her – said you saw Coleman a couple of times. What happened then?'

Ray hesitated, was about to say they had discussed Peggy, when Zordyi said:

'What happened the night Coleman brought you back from the Lido? On the motor-boat?'

'Nothing, we – talked a little. He dropped me on the Zattere quay. I was depressed that night, so I just kept walking around. I slept in a small hotel, and the next day looked for a room to rent for a few days. I hadn't my passport with me.'

'Where was this room?' Dell' Isola asked in Italian.

'Is it important?' Ray asked. 'I don't want to get innocent people into trouble. The income tax—'

A smile from Dell' Isola. 'All right. We shall return to that later.'

'Did you quarrel with Coleman that night on the Lido?' Zordyi asked.

'No.' Ray realized it was not making sense. 'I only failed to make him understand why – why his daughter killed herself. Maybe because I don't understand either.'

'Coleman blamed you for it – did he?' Zordyi asked.

Ray doubted if Inez had told Zordyi that, but perhaps Zordyi assumed it, or had picked it up from the Smith-Peters. 'I don't know if he so much blamed me as wanted to find out if I were to blame. I don't know if he came to any conclusions.'

'Was he angry? – When did he become angry?' Zordyi asked.

'He couldn't understand her death,' Ray said rather miserably. He felt tired, the tiredness of futility.

'I've spoken to Coleman and a few other people about your wife. Everyone thinks she was a – an unworldly kind of girl. Unrealistic. I'm sure you felt awful about the suicide. That you suffered.'

Did that matter? Ray could feel Zordyi prodding round in a circle, trying to find the soft spot in the centre that he would strike with a single question. 'I suppose I felt stupid for not foreseeing the suicide.'

'Did Coleman ever make any threats to you?' Zordyi asked briskly.

'No.'

'No statements like, "I'll get back at you?"'

'No.'

Zordyi shifted his athletic bulk in the chair. 'You came to Venice especially to see your father-in-law, didn't you?'

Ray was now on guard against Zordyi. Zordyi's job, for his parents, was finished. Why all the questions? 'I had some business here in Venice also in connection with an art gallery. But I wanted to see him again, yes.'

'Why exactly?'

'Because he didn't seem satisfied with my explanations about his daughter's suicide – such as they were.'

'He was angry with you. Or he wouldn't have attacked you in a street with a rock.' Zordyi smiled suddenly, a flash of healthy teeth.

'He had angry moments. He adored his daughter.'

'Not the night of the Lido? That went smoothly?'

'That went all right,' Ray said, with a calmness he felt was unnatural to him.

'Mr Garrett, where'd you get the bullet holes in your jacket? The jacket in the Pensione Seguso?'

Ray noticed that the Italian captain showed no surprise at the question. 'If you don't mind – I don't see that they have anything to do with what we're talking about. I'd—'

'That's for you to tell me, I admit,' Zordyi interrupted, smiling again. 'Maybe you can tell me *where* you got them. Here? In Venice?'

'No. They – that happened weeks ago.'

'Someone shot at you,' Zordyi said. 'Was it possibly Coleman?'

'No, it was not.'

'They have nothing to do with Coleman?' Zordyi said.

'No.'

'Well – have you any enemies, Mr Garrett?' Zordyi asked with

189

a slight smile, as if Ray's reticence amused him. 'I'm interested in protecting you, not accusing you – or suspecting you.'

'No enemies,' Ray murmured, shaking his head.

Silence for a few seconds.

Capitano Dell' Isola asked, 'Mr Garrett, what do you think could have happened to Signor Col-e-man?'

Ray hesitated. 'I don't know. I suppose – he could have suffered loss of memory – for a short time. Or he could have been robbed by someone who pushed his body – killed him, I mean, and pushed his body into the canal.' Ray shied away from saying the obvious, the most likely, that Coleman might want to hide in order to put a suspicion of murder on him. If they couldn't think of that, why should he tell them? For an instant, Ray felt emotionally finished with Coleman. But he realized the feeling might be deceptive, or temporary, like others he had had before about Coleman.

'You hit him with the stone, you said?' Dell' Isola went on.

'I threw it at him. I think it hit him on the neck or the ear.'

The clerk was still writing.

'He was on the ground then. Unconscious?'

'I don't know. He had just fallen.' Ray had to force the words out.

Zordyi stood up. 'If I may, Signor Capitano, I would like to send a cable. Or I can telephone collect.'

'Please, yes, there is a telephone in the next room,' said Dell' Isola.

Ray stood up, too, tired of the straight chair.

'Like to speak to your parents, Mr Garrett? It'll be about four in the morning there,' Zordyi said with a smile.

'Not just now, thank you,' Ray said. 'Please tell them I'm well.'

'That head wound—'

'It's only a cut.'

When Zordyi went out, Dell' Isola said, 'For our report, Signor

Garrett, we must know the places at which you have been staying. I promise you that people concerned will not be troubled.'

Ray reluctantly gave him the name of Signora Calliuoli, whose house number he did not know, but he said it was in the Largo San Sebastiano. Dell' Isola wanted to know the dates at which he had been there, and Ray gave them, 12–17 November.

'And at present where are you?'

'I assure you I shall keep in contact, Signor Capitano—'

'But it is necessary,' the Capitano said emphatically, his patience beginning to collapse under the weight of officialism, and under that weight Ray knew there was no hope. If he refused to tell, they would follow him home.

'He is Signor Ciardi,' Ray said. 'Calle Montesino, Giudecca. Again I'm not sure of the number.'

'Thank you,' said Dell' Isola, watching the clerk write it down. 'Signor Garrett, you know the Signora Perry, an American lady?'

Ray dredged her up from memory. The Lido. The hostess the night of the eleventh. 'I met her once.'

'I spoke with her. So did the American.' He gestured towards the room where Zordyi had gone. 'Yesterday afternoon. Signora Perry – well, we at last learned from her that Signor Col-e-man held a resentment against you.'

The word was heavy and solid in Italian – *risentimento*.

'It was Signor Zordyi who discovered that, I confess. She did not tell us. You know, there was a suspicion in all our minds that Signor Col-e-man had killed you.'

'Yes, I know.'

'You know? – You perhaps wanted us to think that?'

Ray frowned. 'No. I wanted to be by myself. To forget the past weeks by getting away from my possessions – my passport.'

Dell' Isola seemed puzzled, or dubious. 'I can imagine, if Signor Col-e-man had a resentment against you, you did not like him either? You did not like him?'

'I neither like nor dislike him,' Ray said.

Zordyi came into the room then. 'Excuse me. The telephone takes so long, I sent a cable. I'll try a call later,' he said to Ray.

'We were discussing,' Capitano Dell' Isola said, 'what Signora Perry said yesterday about the resentment of Signor Col-e-man against Signor Garrett.'

'Oh. Yes.' Zordyi glanced at Ray. 'It wasn't exactly the first thing she came out with. And Mme Schneider, she also had to admit Coleman wasn't fond of you. She'll be glad to hear you're all right, Mr Garrett.' He turned to Dell' Isola and said, 'Well, your next work is to find Signor Coleman.'

Dell' Isola nodded. He asked Ray, 'Has Signor Ciardi a telephone?'

'No, he has not.'

'I would like when you return to his house for you to telephone me at once and tell me the number of the house. Of course it would be on our records here,' with a gesture at his filing cabinets, 'but buried under mountains of . . .' He trailed off vaguely.

'I can telephone you within the hour,' said Ray.

'Mr Garrett, I have a paper I'd like you to sign,' said Zordyi, pulling some papers from an overcoat pocket. 'This is sort of an affidavit that you are really you.'

It was a paper from Zordyi's company relating to missing persons, and Ray's signature was reproduced at the bottom of the page in a box marked SAMPLE. Ray was to sign in a box underneath this, and he did. Zordyi dated the paper and signed it also.

'Are you leaving Venice at once, Signor Zordyi?' asked the Capitano.

'No, not today, anyway,' said Zordyi. 'If I learn anything about Coleman, I shall tell you immediately.'

They parted, Zordyi going out with Ray. On the street, Zordyi said, 'Why don't we have lunch together, Mr Garrett? Have you time?'

Ray did not want to lunch with Zordyi, yet he realized it was rather rude to refuse. 'I did promise my host, Signor Ciardi, to lunch with him today. Sorry.'

'I'm sorry, too.' Zordyi stood two or three inches taller than Ray. 'Listen, you haven't any idea where Coleman might be? Honestly?'

'I really haven't,' Ray said.

Zordyi glanced behind him at the police station thirty yards away. 'You don't think you might have finished him off in that fight?' he asked in a low voice. 'I'm asking for your own good. I'm trying to protect you. You can talk to me freely.'

'I don't think – I really don't think I finished him off,' Ray said, but the words stuck in his throat as if they were a lie.

Zordyi studied him a moment, then smiled. 'Since you got the best of him in that fight, maybe he snuck off in a sulk, eh? He's an arrogant type, I understand. Used to being top dog?'

Ray smiled slightly also. 'Very true.'

'I'm at the Hotel Luna at least till tomorrow, maybe longer. And you, Mr Garrett, are where?'

'Calle Montesino, Giudecca. The house of a Signor Ciardi. As I said to the Capitano, I don't even know the house number and there's no telephone.'

Zordyi nodded, and Ray could feel him committing the name and street to memory. 'I wish you'd call me at the Luna and tell me the house number. If I'm not in, could you leave a message?'

Ray said he would.

'I'll tell the American Consulate you're here,' Zordyi said absently, looking into space, 'in case the Italians don't think of it. And what are your plans now?'

'I'll be going on to Paris.'

'When?'

Did Zordyi think he was going to disappear again, Ray wondered. He supposed Zordyi might. 'In a day or so.'

'You'll get in touch with your parents today?'

Ray said he would cable or telephone. They said good-bye then, Zordyi walking on past the railroad station, Ray catching a vaporetto for the Riva degli Schiavoni. He got off instead at San Marco and went to the post-telegraph office to which Coleman had never sent a letter. He cabled to his parents in St Louis:

AM ALL RIGHT. LETTER FOLLOWS. LOVE TO YOU BOTH.

RAY

Then he went on, across the Giudecca canal. At least he could tell Signor Ciardi the truth before he saw it in the newspapers. Ray found his mind again drifting to the possibility that Coleman could be dead. He felt sick and weak for a moment, as if his own strength were ebbing, then the sensation ended, confidence began to come back, and with it a certain happiness. If he had killed Coleman, he had done it in self-defence. He'd done it after Coleman had fired a gun at him, and after Coleman had tried to drown him in the lagoon, after all. If there came a showdown, Ray thought, if Coleman's body were found with a fractured skull in a canal, he had two stories in his defence to come up with, and there would be no need for further unappreciated gallantry in concealing them. His overcoat might be mended from the bullet-holes, but the graze still showed on his arm. The jacket with the unmended holes was at the Pensione Seguso. Luigi was his witness for the evening in the lagoon. Ray felt rather confident as he stepped ashore on Giudecca.

17

Edward Coleman, who gave out casually to the Chioggi fisherman only that his name was Ralph – Ralfo, he called him – spent 25 November, Thursday, in the house of Mario and Filomena Martucci. It was Mario with whom Coleman had gone fishing some ten days before on a Sunday. On the 25th there was a nasty wet wind, and Coleman stayed indoors drinking Filomena's homemade red wine and writing a few letters. He wrote to Dick Purcell in Rome, asking him to check with his landlord and make sure his apartment was all right and hadn't been broken into, and said that he would be coming to Rome very shortly. But Coleman did not post this letter yet, nor any of the others.

He had a purple bruise under his right ear, and also a black eye that was turning yellow. Coleman told Mario that he had been attacked in a dark street by a man who had tried to rob him, but that he had put up a fight and kept his billfold. Unfortunately, Coleman had only twenty thousand lire, about thirty dollars, with him now. He had given five thousand to Mario as a kind of thank you for taking him in. Coleman had arrived at Mario's in mid-morning of the 24th, having made his way from Venice to Mestre late Tuesday night, a bedless night for him in various

Mestre coffee-bars. He said, by way of explanation, that he wanted to avoid for a few days the husband of his girl friend, and that the husband had just come to Venice. Mario no doubt thought that the husband had beaten him up, but Coleman couldn't help that, and swallowed his pride about it.

What Coleman very much wanted to do was hire Mario or one of his friends to go to the police and say he had seen a man being rolled into the canal at about 11 p.m. on the 23rd. That would start the ball rolling nicely, Coleman thought, but as yet he had not dared approach Mario about it. A hundred thousand lire more in his billfold would no doubt have given him a little inspiration, but he hadn't it.

A dog barked in a backyard of a house next door. It was tied up, Coleman knew, because he had seen it from his window.

Filomena came in about five without knocking, and asked Coleman if he would like a bowl of *brodo* that she had just made. A broth of eels.

'No, thank you, dear Filomena; the lunch you gave me is still doing its work,' Coleman answered pleasantly. 'But I'll join Mario in a glass of wine when he returns. He's due at six, you said?'

'Si, Signor.' Filomena was slender, dark, and had a front tooth missing. She looked about thirty. She had had four children, but one had died. 'You are warm enough, signor?'

'Magnificent. Thank you.' Coleman was chilly, but Filomena had lavished much care on his tile stove's fire, and he did not want to complain.

Filomena left, and Coleman walked to the window and looked out. He chewed his lips and thought of Inez. He was sorry to be causing her worry, and he was sure he was. She hadn't wanted him to go off on Thursday night after dinner for his walk – the walk on which he had spotted Ray – but Coleman had felt compelled to go. He absolutely could not have gone quietly back with Inez to their hotel that evening. Earlier that day, trailed by Zordyi,

Coleman had given him the slip in Merceria. Well, if you couldn't give someone the slip in Venice, where could you, Coleman thought, but still, Zordyi was a professional, and it had pleased Coleman to outwit him. And if he couldn't dispose of Ray in Venice, where could he? And luck had been definitely with him in finding Ray, even in the little matter of finding just the right rock handy in the street. Coleman had envisaged a back street exactly like the one Ray had run into, a canal exactly like that canal – but he hadn't envisaged Ray standing up, anyone standing up, after the wallop he had given him with that rock. Coleman frowned and cursed his luck for the twentieth time since the fight had happened. Ray must surely not be feeling too well now, but the fact that he was probably alive galled Coleman and made him, a score of times a day, snatch something up instead of picking it up, made him set his teeth, made his heart beat faster. Coleman finished the last inch of the wine, and decided to approach Mario about speaking to the police. He'd have to think of a reason for Mario's having been in Venice that night. Or was it better to have Mario write an unsigned letter? He should put it to Mario that he thought the husband of his girl friend deserved a bit of inconvenience for his murderous attack. He could offer Mario thirty thousand lire for the favour, payable later when he could get his hands on some money.

Coleman had sent Filomena out for a *Gazzettino* this morning after Mario left the house, rightly guessing that she wouldn't glance at the paper. After Coleman had seen his picture and read the item about his being missing, he had burnt the paper in his tile stove. He hoped Mario had not seen the paper that day. He had asked Mario to bring an evening paper home with him tonight, and he hoped Mario remembered.

At last, Coleman heard the shout from Mario, and the answering cry from Filomena, that meant Mario had returned. Coleman went downstairs.

The three children were clinging to their father's legs. Mario held a fish in a basket over his head.

'I didn't catch it, I bought it,' Mario said cheerfully. 'But I caught a lot of other fish today.'

'A fortunate day?' Coleman asked. He saw the newspaper in Mario's hip pocket.

'An ugly wind, but a good day for the fish,' said Mario.

They were all in the kitchen, which served also as their living-room. What looked a little more like a living-room was the room next door, but it was smaller and had a double bed in it, in which all three children slept.

'Some wine now or a plate of brodo?' said Filomena to her husband.

'My dear wife, when will you learn I don't want soup before my wine? An hour before my dinner? When we all sit at the table, yes!' Mario gave her a kiss on the cheek, and a slap on the behind.

Coleman laughed. 'Can I see the newspaper, Mario?'

Mario pulled it from his pocket and handed it to Coleman. Then he got glasses and poured wine for himself and Coleman.

The newspaper looked like a lower-class, popular one, and Coleman had not heard of it before. Nothing on the front page. He turned the page, and started at the sight of Ray's picture in the upper corner. He read it as quickly as he could, his attention fixed. Ray had given himself up to the police today. He had said he had had a fight with his father-in-law, Edward Coleman, on the night of 23 November in a small street in Venice. 'The young American, who has been missing for fifteen days, said merely that he wanted to be by himself for a while, after the recent suicide of his wife Peggy in Mallorca. Since their encounter on the night of 23 November, Edward Coleman has not been seen, and police are making inquiries about him.'

'What are you reading? Something about you?' Mario asked.

Coleman straightened abruptly – he had been leaning over the table where he had rested the newspaper – but Mario looked down at the picture.

'You know that American? – Dica, is that the husband of your girl friend?' Mario demanded with sudden amusement and inspiration.

'No, no, you can see that,' Coleman said with a casual gesture, then picked up the wine Mario had poured for him, and wished he had picked up the newspaper instead, because Mario lifted it to read it better.

'Hm-m. A fight – strange,' Mario murmured as he read.

'Che cosa?' asked his wife.

Damn their curiosity, Coleman thought.

'Not this man – is it not this man you had the fight with, Ralfo?'

Mario didn't know Coleman's name. If he'd ever told Mario his name, Mario had probably forgotten, Coleman thought. 'No, I told you no,' Coleman said. Coleman supposed his face was white.

Filomena turned from the stove at his tone.

'It was the night you had the fight, no? Is why I ask,' Mario pursued, smiling mischievously now.

'But *not* with *him*,' Coleman said.

'What is your true name?' Mario asked.

Filomena looked worried. 'No quarrelling, Mario. You should let Signor Ralfo keep his secrets.'

Coleman slowly pulled his cigar-case from his pocket, and tried to think of something casual to say. Mario was watching him. And Coleman was getting no better control of himself. In fact, he was now trembling.

'All right, all right,' Mario said with a shrug, a glance at his wife. Mario's eyebrows twitched. He had a scar from a fishhook in his left eyebrow, a spot where the hair did not grow. 'I can see you have some troubles, Signor Ralfo. If your daughter killed herself?'

'Mario!' Filomena said in a shocked voice.

'That's not true!' Coleman said. 'Not a word of that is true! She—' He had banged his glass down on the table, splashing wine.

'Hey, watch what you do!' said Mario.

It happened in a split second, like an explosion. Coleman was conscious of reaching out for Mario's shirt front, conscious, too, of what seemed like a betrayal by Mario of all he had trusted him for – friendship, loyalty, assistance when he needed it, good-fellowship when they'd gone fishing, his very roof, whose hospitality Mario had now destroyed. The table, or a chair, was knocked over, and they were both on the floor, Coleman finding it impossible to catch the Italian's wiry, flailing arms. Children and Filomena were screaming. Then suddenly a wave of fire broke over Coleman's hips and thighs. The pain was paralysing, bringing everything to a halt except his squirming agony from the burning. Mario got to his feet. Then Coleman saw what had happened: Filomena – it must have been she – had flung the vat of hot brodo over him.

Now Filomena was in tears, cringing against a wall. Mario was cursing, not in anger now but in despair. The children still screamed in chorus, and neighbours stood at the door.

Coleman stood up and plucked at his trousers, trying to keep the steaming material from his flesh. Blood dropped like red blossoms on the kitchen floor. It was coming from his mouth.

'Filomena, for the love of God!' Mario said, or something like that. 'A fine thing to do! Help the man! Some soda!'

Soda was brought, also some yellow grease, probably fish fat, in a large jar. Coleman recovered himself before either of these two things were applied, and asked Mario and Filomena to clear the room of the neighbours and also the children.

'I've got to remove these!' he said, referring to his trousers.

The room emptied, save for Mario, who hung about for a moment, hands on hips.

Coleman did not care about him. He shoved his trousers down and rubbed soda on to his flesh, under his shorts. Mario stared at him, and Coleman detested him, though he realized he had the right to be angry. And Coleman saw the wisdom, the possible advantage, of pouring a little oil on the troubled waters.

'I'm sorry – very,' he said to Mario. 'A good pot of soup gone to waste, too.' He managed a laugh. 'I'm very nervous, Mario. And when you said that about – about my—' He could not get the word daughter out. It had enraged him to see the words 'suicide of his wife Peggy' in a newspaper for the public to stare at. 'I lost my head.' Coleman put his hands up, soda-white as they were, and made a jerking gesture of removing his own head. 'I'll recompense Filomena, I hope, at least by buying some eels. I can also clean this mess up.'

'Ah, non importa,' Mario replied, still watching him.

'I shall get some water and wash myself,' Coleman said, suiting action to the word and dipping a jug into a pot of hot water that stood on the stove. 'I'll take this up to my room.'

The children and Filomena were in the room that looked like a living-room, so Coleman did not have to run the gamut of them. He went up to his room, carrying his damp trousers, washed himself and soaked his shorts in what was left of the water in the big wash pitcher. After swabbing his trousers as best he could, he put them on again, as he had no others, not even pyjama bottoms. Then he went calmly down again, intending to try to make peace with Filomena.

He found Mario in the kitchen with a glass of wine.

Coleman sensed now that Mario was afraid of the police. 'Signor Mario, my apologies again,' Coleman said. 'Have you a cloth?'

'Oh, Filomena with a mop – Filomena! She is putting the children to bed, I think.'

'At this hour?'

'When she is worried, she puts them to bed,' Mario said with a shrug, and opened the door to the adjoining room. 'Filomena, there's no need to put them to bed. A little soup on the floor, my dear. Everything is all right.'

There was a shrill retort from Filomena, which sounded more anxious than angry. Mario closed the door and returned.

Coleman had spotted a mop, and now he got to work, using the cold water tap in the sink. If there was one thing he knew how to do, he thought, it was mop a floor. He'd had plenty of practice in Rome, still had, and in Taos, in Toulouse, in Arezzo, and all the other places where he'd lived for the last fifteen years. Mario stoked the stove with more wood.

'Please tell Filomena it looks a little better,' Coleman said.

'Thank you. Have a glass of wine, Signor Ralfo,' Mario said, pouring him one.

'I understand that I disturb you, Mario. I can leave tonight, if you wish, if you know of a place. I didn't bring my passport, you know, so it is hard to go to an hotel.'

Filomena came in on this, and heard it. Coleman's Italian was quite simple. At least she was not still crying.

'The Signor apologizes, Filomena. You see, he has cleaned the kitchen,' said Mario.

'A thousand apologies, signora,' Coleman said, 'for the loss of your brodo. I have done the best I could here. I was saying to your husband, I am grateful for your hospitality, but I should be going, provided—'

Mario gave a big and essentially rude shrug, looked at the ceiling, then said, 'I think I can find a place for you. At Donato's. If you don't mind the cold. He has just a . . . '

Coleman did not know the word, but presumed Mario meant a shack. He might try that tonight, and look for something better, he thought. He didn't relish the idea, but pride kept him from asking Mario if he could stay. And he could sense that Filomena was now against him, because he had started the fight. Coleman pulled his billfold – dampish, too – from his hip pocket, and produced a five-thousand-lire bill. 'To you and Filomena, Mario, with my thanks.'

'Ah, no, signor, enough is enough!' Mario protested.

But he was genuinely poor, or poor enough, and Coleman insisted.

Coleman became more magnanimous, and declined the offer of Donato's dwelling. He had caused Mario enough bother – *seccatura* – he said. Then Mario attempted a speech, to which Coleman listened politely. The essence was, it was dangerous in the times in which they all lived to go about the world without a card of identity. All quite predictable to Coleman. Coleman knew Mario was suspicious of the newspaper item, and that therefore, he ought to get himself a considerable distance from Chioggia. Coleman drank his wine, and Mario immediately poured more.

Filomena was busy at the stove again.

'Stay and eat dinner,' Mario said. 'You must not leave our house with an empty stomach. If I worry about the police, that's one thing. We all worry about the police. What a world we live in, eh, Filomena?'

'Si, Mario.' She dropped fat into the hot frying-pan. The fish Mario had brought lay at one side of the stove, split and cleaned.

'It's true that I'm in danger of being attacked,' Coleman said. 'You see, it happened once. That is what makes me so nervous. I have a daughter who made a bad marriage. She has said she will kill herself' – another gasp from Filomena at the thought '– but so far she has not.'

'Thank God! Poor thing!' said Filomena.

'The piece in the newspaper reminded me. But my daughter is in California, unhappy but still alive. I think of her often. My wife, her mother, died when she was four in a car accident. I raised my daughter myself.'

This brought a rush of wonder and praise from Filomena, a sympathetic nod from Mario.

'Now she is married to a man who is not faithful. But it is her choice. But me – I do not care to marry again. Only I get myself into trouble sometimes with women such as I am in now.' He smiled at Mario. 'Up with life, away, eh, Mario? Now I must be off.'

He said good-bye to Filomena, and bowed over her hand. Mario accompanied him down the street to a small restaurant, because Coleman wanted something to eat. The restaurant might have a room he could rent, Coleman thought, or someone there might know of a room. Chioggia was like Venice, but without its beauty. They crossed little canals, turned down tiny lanes, yet it was not Venice, and Ray was not anywhere near. That removed all interest in the place from Coleman's point of view. Before the restaurant door, he said good-bye to Mario and thanked him once more.

'When I'm here again, we'll go on another fishing trip,' Coleman said.

'Si, sicuro!' Mario replied, and Coleman felt he might even mean it.

Then Coleman had his dinner and pondered. He would stay in hiding another week, he thought. That shouldn't be impossible. Ray had done it. He thought he should not take the chance of writing a letter himself to the police. He might, before a week, venture back to Venice for another try at Ray. Meanwhile, he was dead, faceless to everyone, because nameless. And because he was friendless, almost. Inez, like a few others, would be in a state of suspended mourning, not knowing whether to mourn whole-heartedly or wait a bit longer. So she would probably wait a bit longer, Coleman thought with amusement. And what was mourning? A long face for an hour, a day – not much longer in Inez's case. Dick Purcell would miss him for a longer time. So would an old friend in New York, Lance Duquesne, a painter whom Coleman had known since the days when he was an engineer. But otherwise? Coleman was under no illusion that many tears would be shed for him. Mourning was for a few real friends to do, or for close families whose mourning was mainly for the rest of the living family to see.

After his meal, Coleman chatted with his young waiter on the subject of a room for the night. 'I'm staying in Venice, but it's a little late to get back tonight. Do you know of a place I might sleep for tonight? I would pay, of course, but I did not bring my passport . . . ' He explained his shyness about going to an hotel.

The young waiter did indeed know of a place, a room in his own house. He set the price. Five hundred lire. 'Very warm. The kitchen is the next room.'

Coleman accepted.

It was not even far away. The young man found five minutes between customers to show Coleman to the house and introduce him to his family. No questions – such as why an American didn't go to an hotel – were asked. Coleman chatted with the parents in the living-room over a cup of coffee. The family's name was Di Rienzo.

'I like Chioggia,' said Coleman, who had told them his name was Taylor and that he was a writer. 'Perhaps you know of a place where I might rent a room for a week? I intended to fetch my typewriter from Venice.'

The man glanced at his wife, then said, 'It is possible that I can find a room for you. Or you might stay with us, if it is agreeable to my wife. Let us see how we get along.'

Coleman smiled. He was sitting – he had arranged himself deliberately – so that his yellowish eye was not exposed to the light in the room. He exerted all his charm, complimented a wooden chest in the corner, which in fact was a lovely bit of workmanship and carving, and was told that it was a wedding present, made by the father of Signora Di Rienzo.

'At the moment, I'm writing a book on the history of wall-paper,' Coleman said.

'Of what?' asked Signor Di Rienzo.

'Of paper to put on walls.'

18

Ray, when he returned to Signor Ciardi's house, was told by Giustina that Signor Ciardi was out, and that she did not know when he would return. By now, it was a quarter to one. Ray went out again, thinking he would ring Inez Schneider, and remembered that the police and Zordyi wanted his house number. He looked at the barely readable, four-figure, stencilled number on the stone door frame, then walked to the bar-caffè that had the telephone. He rang the police first, then Zordyi who was not in, but he left his name and address. Then he dialled the number of the Gritti Palace Hotel, where the newspaper had said Mme Schneider was staying. He felt a desire to communicate with her, to put her mind at rest at least about himself, and maybe a little about Coleman, too. Ray expected to be told that Mme Schneider was out, that she had even left the hotel, but Ray was connected with her room at once, and she answered:

'Ray! How are you? Where are you?'

'I'm on Giudecca now. I wanted to say – I only wanted to say that I had a fight with Ed Tuesday night and left him more or less knocked out, I think, but I don't think he's dead.'

'Unconscious where?'

'In a little street near the Rialto. I've told the police about it. Tuesday night around eleven.'

'And – where have you been?'

'I've been by myself. On Giudecca.'

'I must see you. What are you doing now?'

Ray did not want to go to see her now, but he felt he had a moral obligation to see her. 'Yes, I can see you.'

'I am supposed to meet the Smith-Peters at one, but I will cancel that. Can you come to the Gritti? Or I can meet you anywhere.'

Ray said he would come to her hotel in about forty-five minutes. Then he crossed to the mainland again, and went to the Giglio stop, the one after della Salute. It was the most beautiful bit of Venice, the Schiavoni quay, the della Salute stop where the great church seemed to expand to even greater size over the suddenly small vaporetto – mundane transport backgrounded by the Ducal Palace and the Campanile of San Marco so close across the water. Then the Gritti Palace Hotel. Coleman was alive, Ray thought, and he was himself again, Ray or Rayburn Garrett, afflicted with an inferiority complex, passably attractive, fairly rich, though without any great talent. He was once more in communication with parents and friends, though fortunately his friends hadn't had time to miss him, except perhaps for Bruce who would have written a week ago to the Pont Royal in Paris and would be expecting an answer. To his parents he would explain carefully, and they would understand – maybe not at first, but after a day or so. His mother might understand at once, his father might always think his behaviour a bit weak or neurotic. But it was nothing he couldn't weather, Ray felt, so nothing really was wrong.

To Ray's annoyance, he saw the Smith-Peters standing with Inez as he entered the lobby of the Gritti. But why not face them all at once, Ray thought. It took very little more courage, or whatever it was that he was using.

'Ray! Buon' giorno! Bonjour, bonjour!' Inez said, and Ray thought she was going to extend her hand, but she didn't.

'Hello, Inez. Hello,' he said to the Smith-Peters, with a polite smile.

'Hello, Mr Garrett,' Mr Smith-Peters said firmly, with a nod, as if to nail Ray down with it. He seemed not to know whether to smile and be friendly or not.

'You were hurt, Ray?' his wife asked, with more obvious interest and concern.

'Not seriously. Just a cut,' Ray said.

'That is from Tuesday night?' Inez asked.

'Tuesday night, yes,' Ray said.

'I have told Laura and Francis that you saw Edward then,' Inez explained nervously. 'We all wanted to see you, so—' She made a helpless gesture. She looked thinner and older, and there were circles around her eyes.

'How about going into the bar here?' Mr Smith-Peters said. 'I don't think we feel like plunging into lunch, do we?'

'Oh, certainly not,' said Inez, glancing past Ray at the door. 'I keep thinking Edward will walk in at any moment.'

'I hope he will,' Ray said.

They all, except Inez, ordered vodka and tomato juice.

'Well, where have you *been*?' Laura Smith-Peters asked Ray, with a try at a smile.

'I've been mostly on Giudecca,' Ray replied. 'I wanted to be by myself for a while.'

The Smith-Peters looked at him for a moment in baffled silence.

'You certainly had everybody *wor-r-ried*,' Mrs Smith-Peters said.

'I'm sorry about that.' A throb of pain in the left side of his head at that instant put a perfunctoriness in his tone.

'And Tuesday evening?' Inez said. 'What happened?'

'I was in a section of Venice I didn't know,' Ray began, 'around

209

ten-thirty or eleven and – I saw Ed behind me. He didn't look as if he were in a friendly mood, so I tried to get away from him.' He sensed a puzzlement in the Smith-Peters, who evidently did not believe Coleman's dislike of him could take such proportions. The Smith-Peters were not an inspiring audience to address. 'I found myself in a blind alley, and when I tried to get out, Coleman hit me with a rock he'd been carrying.'

'*Really?*' said Mrs Smith-Peters, a hand at her throat.

'It nearly knocked me out, but I did hit back. In fact I got the rock and threw it back at him. He was on the ground when I left him, and I'm not sure if he was conscious or not. I've told all this to the police.'

'Then where *is* he?' Mrs Smith-Peters asked.

'I last saw him on the sidewalk by a canal,' Ray said.

'By a canal,' said Mr Smith-Peters, leaning forward over the table as Ray had seen him do before. 'He couldn't have fallen in, do you think? And drowned?'

'Francis! It's a *hor-r-rible* thought!' his wife whispered.

'I suppose it's barely possible,' Ray said, 'but I think he was moving when I left, trying to get up.' Ray wet his lips. 'Maybe I shouldn't say that, because I'm not sure.'

Mr Smith-Peters was frowning. 'Had he a lot of money on him, Inez?'

'I don't know, but I don't think so. What is a lot? It depends on who is robbing. But I know what you are thinking.'

'You just left him,' Mrs Smith-Peters said to Ray, and there was a note of accusation in it.

'Yes,' Ray said. 'I was nearly out myself, and you don't—' He gave it up. Could she expect him to be a Samaritan to Coleman?

'And there wasn't anybody around?' her husband, incredulously.

'I didn't see anyone,' Ray said.

'That is so strange, that no one—' Inez began, and stopped.

It wasn't taken up. They talked about what the police were doing now. The atmosphere grew more tense, Ray felt, stiffening against him. He felt they thought he might have blacked out and done something worse to Coleman than he had, or that he had done something worse and wasn't admitting it.

'That night we were all at the Lido ... ' Mr Smith-Peters began.

Ray was asked the old questions, and gave the old answers, that Coleman had put him down on the Zattere quay, that he had taken a walk and finally gone to a small hotel.

'I feel sure,' Inez said, 'that Edward was horrible to you that evening. I wish you would tell me the truth, Ray.'

In front of these nice friends, Ray thought. He felt he blushed like a boy caught out in a lie. But it was Inez who was deceiving him a little. As Antonio had suggested, Coleman might have bragged to Inez that he had done away with Ray Garrett that night. If so, that hadn't upset Inez seriously. She hadn't spoken to the police. Now she wanted the truth, probably because it was more 'interesting' or because she was simply curious, or because she was finished with Coleman. Ray said, 'He was rude, but he didn't *do* anything.'

Inez squirmed in her chair and said, 'Laura and Francis, I am unable to think of lunch today – if you don't mind.'

The Smith-Peters were understanding, and agreed that Inez should stay on and talk with Ray, if she wished. Francis Smith-Peters was looking for the waiter, and insisted upon paying.

'We won't be leaving tomorrow,' Laura Smith-Peters said to Inez in her high, nasal voice, a sympathetic whine. 'We're just as concerned about Ed as you are. We want you to know that, Inez.'

Inez nodded. 'Thank you, Laura.'

Laura Smith-Peters gave Ray a tentative smile. Ray felt she was at a loss what to say to him, that she was both curious about him and afraid of him.

'You're staying on a while, I suppose, Mr Garrett?' her husband asked, in a tone of certainty, perhaps because he believed the police would detain him.

'Oh, a day or so, I think,' Ray replied.

'We'll call you up later this afternoon,' Laura Smith-Peters said, patting Inez's shoulder as she got up. 'You'll be in around four?'

Inez nodded.

They said good-bye to Ray and left.

Ray sat down again. 'Another Cinzano?' he asked Inez.

'No, thank you.' She lit a cigarette. 'You know what I want to ask you, Ray. To tell me the absolute truth. I thought when I first met you, you were very truthful. Now you do not seem so.'

Again Ray felt embarrassed. 'About Tuesday night, I'm telling you the absolute truth. Maybe I shouldn't have left him lying on the ground, but after all – a man who'd come after me to crush my skull with a rock, and hit me hard with it—'

'How big was the rock?'

He told her.

'If you did kill him,' she said in a whisper, 'and if someone else found him that night – they might have been afraid to report it. Don't you think? Some people are like that. They'd rather walk away – or push the body into a canal.' Her brows trembled.

Everybody would rather walk away, Ray thought. He looked away from her distress, a distress caused by her feelings for Coleman, he realized. 'That's possible. It's also possible he's hiding out in order to get me in trouble. I suppose you've thought of that?'

Inez hadn't, to Ray's surprise. It seemed to show a lack of imagination, that she hadn't thought of it.

'Where do you think he might go, if he were hiding out?' Ray asked.

But he didn't get anywhere with this. Inez said he had left his passport in his room, and she thought he had not much money, and no Traveller's Cheques, because he never had any. 'He is so violent when he is angry,' she went on. 'One can see it bubbling in him.' She curled the fingers of one hand. 'And he can get in such trouble. I saw it in Rome.'

'What happened in Rome?'

'An argument with a police officer over a parking violation. It was my car, which is now in Venice at the garage, because I had her driven here. Edward was trying to defend me, of course. The Italian police are used to argument, but Edward was almost hitting him. I had to hold Edward's arm. We got the full fine, I assure you, and afterwards I ask Edward, "What did you accomplish? I could have got off the fine."' Inez smiled sadly. 'You are not afraid to tell me – if you think you killed him?'

Her emotion bothered him. Would he be afraid to tell her? She might not report him, just as she had not reported Coleman, when there were strong grounds for suspicion. Therefore, he decided he would not be afraid to tell her. *Murderers have nothing to fear from society* crossed his mind swiftly. 'I've told you, I don't think I did.'

Inez sighed.

Ray drank the last of his drink and watched her. Was she really so perturbed about a man like Coleman? Perhaps she was upset now, but wouldn't there be another such man in her life in a few months? Or weeks? All at once, her mystery, her attractiveness – inevitably mingled with a certain dignity like a mandate that she should be respected and highly respected – all this fell away from her, and Ray saw her as another human being like himself, just as selfish and maybe more so, since what was she doing with her life besides trying to please herself at every turn? At the same time, a certain gallantry and generosity rose in him. He sat up. 'You don't think he could have gone back to Rome?'

'Yes, he could have. But I don't think so. You know – Edward told me he pushed you into the water that night of the Lido.' Inez was not looking at him as she spoke. 'I am so glad he did not.'

And what had she done about it? Continued sleeping in the same bed with Coleman, probably, as Antonio started to say. 'Did you tell the Smith-Peters?'

'No. I was not sure whether to believe him – and yet I believed him. You had disappeared. And then – the day when Edward was in Chioggia fishing – Sunday – I look in his wardrobe to see if he has a gun anywhere. I find your scarf under all his handkerchiefs. You know, the scarf you showed me.' Now she looked at him.

'Yes.'

'So I thought – maybe Edward killed you and took that out of your coat. So that evening – this was Monday night the last – I said to him, "Edward, I saw the scarf you have under your hand-kerchiefs. Where did you get it?" He said, "It's Peggy's. I got it from Ray. Ray had no right to having it," something like that. I could see he was suddenly – crazy. So I said to him – really to calm him down, I said, "You know Ray told me about that scarf. He bought it here in Venice because it *looked* like Peggy, not because— It *never* was Peggy's scarf," I said. Then Edward got more angry and said you had lied to me, and that I knew it and wanted to annoy *him*. He put the scarf in his pocket then, as if I had somehow insulted the scarf. You know?'

'Yes,' Ray said. He could imagine it. 'He saw it the Lido night. I pulled the scarf out of my pocket by accident, and he just demanded it.' He was glad to tell Inez this. It gave him the relief of a confession, which was strange since the scarf in a way was a false prop, or object. Suddenly Ray's emotions about Peggy became unreal also, his guilt, that vast, grey, cyclonic form that he had been unable to deal with, seemed suddenly a thing of one dimension, fooling the eye, fooling the heart. Peggy was not false like the scarf, yet the emotions they both caused seemed now equally unwarranted, unwarrantable. Ray shuddered, ducked his head, then deliberately sat straighter.

'What's the matter?' Inez asked.

'The trouble the scarf caused. The trouble!' Ray smiled. 'And I only bought it on impulse one morning!'

'Now he carries it in his pocket all the time. He guards it.' Inez spoke seriously.

Ray might have smiled, but didn't. 'People carry crosses. They're not the real cross.'

'M-m. I see your point.'

'Antonio,' Ray began on a more cheerful note, 'I saw him on the street one day. He said you all thought Coleman killed me. He talked as if you discussed it.'

'Oh, we did not discuss it,' Inez said. 'But I am sure they suspected, yes.'

'But you didn't speak to the police,' Ray said.

'No. We were not sure enough.'

'Even when Coleman told you?' Ray asked.

'No.'

Inez, Ray supposed, like most people, had a departmentalized brain. Coleman she loved, or liked, so she would protect him. The Smith-Peters were 'outsiders', possible dangers, so she would throw off as much of their suspicion of Coleman as she could. He sensed this without questioning Inez any further, and it would have been hard to put into words and maybe ungallant to ask a woman about. Women were supposed not to have an abstract sense of justice, Ray had read somewhere. But was this abstract, since she knew him? Ray said, 'I think you should tell the police he went once to Chioggia. He might go there again because he has friends there. I'll look for him, too, Inez. And now I must be going.' Ray stood up. 'You should stay in the hotel here, so you'll have any news as soon as the police get it. Good-bye, Inez.'

She looked startled at his 'Good-bye'. 'Where are you staying on Giudecca? I must know where to reach you.'

Ray told her the four-figure number and street, but said the house had no telephone.

Now she looked disappointed, lost.

Ray started to offer to ring her later today, then asked himself, why should he? 'The police know where I am. Bye-bye, Inez.'

Ray walked away from the Grand Canal, into the centre of the city, to the Teatro La Fenice. From here, five narrow streets led off in varying directions. Ray looked for Coleman. He had an oppressive realization that looking, one person looking on foot, was an absurdity in Venice. This little start-of-a-maze in which he stood, at La Fenice, was duplicated two hundred, three hundred times all over the city of Venice. And behind the wall of any house, really any house he walked past – except maybe the Ca' Rezzonica or the Ca' d'Oro – Coleman could be hiding. Or in the back of scores of bars, trattorie, or in the rooms of a hundred small hotels. Ray walked on, finding no Coleman, but feeling very conspicuous himself with his head bandage. He zigzagged and walked until he was tired, and then aimed for a vaporetto stop which turned out to be the Ca' d'Oro stop, prophetic, he thought, of the utter hopelessness of finding Coleman, because he surely wasn't in the Ca' d'Oro. But just on the off chance, Ray bought a ticket to the museum and went in and walked through all the rooms looking for Coleman. He was not there.

When he came out of the Ca' d'Oro, it was darker and colder. Ray remembered he had had no lunch, but he was not hungry. He walked towards the waterbus pier.

And suppose he had killed Coleman? Suppose Coleman had been swept out to sea via some canal, and he simply was not in the city now? Ray, as he waited for the boat, looked up at the blue-and-purple sky above the rooftops of Venice, over the ancient skyline with its occasional thrust of church dome with a cross. Suppose Coleman were never to see this view again, and that he, Ray Garrett, was responsible for that? Ray felt suddenly discouraged, guilty, untouchable. He shivered, partly from the cold, partly from what he was thinking, or trying to imagine, which was himself striking a blow, or several blows, that had put a stop to someone's life. Had he struck more than one blow with that rock? Ray, when he tried to remember, was as vague on this point as on whether Coleman had been stirring, or conscious, when he left him.

The light was on in Signor Ciardi's kitchen and living-room when Ray arrived back, but he quietly used the outside stone stairs, which led into the first-floor hall. In his room, where he was glad to see that Giustina had built a fire, Ray lay down on the bed, pulled his overcoat over him, and slept like one exhausted. He had two disturbing dreams. In one, Ray had found a baby whose owner he could not find anywhere, though no one seemed to mind his keeping it. This dream woke him up. It was five thirty. Ray washed his face in cold water, and went down to speak to Signor Ciardi. It occurred to Ray that he had not bought an evening paper, and there might well be something about him or Coleman in the papers this evening.

Signor Ciardi was in the kitchen with Giustina, and he had a newspaper on the table before him.

Signor Ciardi jumped up. 'Ah, Signor Weelson! – Or Signor Garrett? Is this not you?' His smile was sly but friendly.

Ray glanced at the photograph. 'It is,' he said. He read the short item under it. There was nothing about Coleman's where-abouts.

'So it was not a fall the other evening. It was a fight, no? With the man who is your father-in-law, the Signor Coleman.'

Ray looked at Giustina, who was watching with open-mouthed fascination, yet with no alarm. 'That is true, Signor Ciardi.'

'And now Signor Col-e-man is missing.'

Ray smiled. The atmosphere was so different from that at the police station, or with the Smith-Peters! 'I think he got up and walked away. And hid himself,' Ray said. 'I gave him quite a – a blow that night, too.' Ray illustrated in pantomime. 'He was following me with a stone and he hit me first.' How simple it all sounded in his simple Italian!

'Ah, capisco! And why did you not say so, Tuesday night?'

'I – well, I didn't want you to know that I knew Signor Cole-man,' Ray replied, automatically pronouncing the name in Italian. 'I was trying to avoid him.'

Signor Ciardi frowned thoughtfully. 'It was his daughter then – who killed herself. Your wife.'

'Si.'

'Just recently?'

'About a month ago,' Ray replied.

'Some wine for the Signor, Giustina, please,' said Signor Ciardi.

Giustina hurried to pour some.

Ray wanted to make a telephone call before six. 'I mustn't stay long now,' he said, looking at his watch.

'But have a glass! So you spoke to the police today?'

'I told them who I was,' Ray said. 'I had hidden myself long enough – myself and my grief. My thanks to you, Signor Ciardi, for being such a good friend. Like Luigi.' He made this little speech in a straightforward way.

Signor Ciardi seized his hand and pumped it. 'I like you, Signor Garrett. You are a gentleman!' He handed Ray his wine, and pointed to the newspaper. 'If Luigi sees this, he will be here tonight. Providing his wife doesn't lock him in to sleep. But she will not. She *can't* do that!'

Ray gave Giustina a nod of thanks before he drank. The wine was good. 'Signor Ciardi, if you wish, I can go to an hotel now with my own passport. If you don't wish, I can stay just a day or so more—' There was something nice about not having a tele-phone at Signor Ciardi's. A certain quietude would be ended at an hotel.

Signor Ciardi spread his hands in protest. 'No question of my not wishing! Of course I wish that you stay. But we now call you Signor Garrett, yes? – You are an art dealer, Signor Garrett?'

'I intend to open a place of exposition in New York. Signor Ciardi – if I may go out to make a telephone call—'

'Ah, si, I regret that I have no telephone,' said Signor Ciardi, who probably did not regret it at all, since there were always small boys in the neighbourhood to run messages.

'I don't,' said Ray, smiling. 'I'll be back in five minutes.'

Ray ran out, without his overcoat. He wanted to ring Elisabetta. The caffè where she worked was called the Bar Dino, and he hoped it had a telephone listing. He found it after some searching, and by then it was three minutes to six.

A man answered, and then Elisabetta was summoned.

'This is Filipo,' Ray said in Italian, expecting any kind of reac-tion to that – her hanging up, or a polite statement that she had had enough of wild newspaper stories and did not want to see him again.

But she answered in a calm tone, 'Ah, Filipo! How are you?'

'Very well, thanks. I am wondering if I can see you this evening? Maybe after dinner? Or I would be very happy if you are free for dinner.'

'I should not go out for dinner, not tonight,' she replied. 'Perhaps after dinner?'

'At eight-thirty? Nine?'

They made an appointment for nine.

She had evidently not seen the paper, Ray thought. He would take a paper along with him tonight when he saw her, and if she hadn't seen one by then, she might be amused. There had been *some* truth in the stories he had told her, anyway!

An orologia shop window caught Ray's eye as he walked homeward. An electric clock for the kitchen would make a nice present for Signor Ciardi and Giustina, he thought. Giustina had complained more than once about the old alarm clock on the kitchen sideboard which ran too slowly, and which Signor Ciardi frequently carried to some other room of the house. Ray bought a fancy cream-coloured clock with a gold-and-black face for eight thousand three hundred lire. It was pleasant to be able to use Traveller's Cheques again, and Ray remembered also that he was due to send two cheques for a hundred dollars each to his painter friends in New York. He usually sent the cheques on the fifteenth of the month. The painters, a young man named Usher in the village, and an old man, who lived on the edge of Harlem, preferred the cheques by the month instead of in one lump for the year, as it helped them to economize.

Ray presented the box to Giustina when he returned to the kitchen of the Ciardi house. 'A present for the house,' Ray said.

Giustina was enchanted with the clock. Signor Ciardi pronounced it magnifico. A place on the wall was decided upon. But they must wait for Guglielmo, one of Signor Ciardi's friends who was a carpenter, to put it up, as it had to be fixed to the wall properly.

'Signor Ciardi,' Ray said, 'may I invite you to dinner tonight? It would give me great pleasure.'

'Ah—' Signor Ciardi thought, looked at Giustina, then said, 'Si, why not? With much pleasure, I accept. Giustina, I know you have veal cutlets, but cutlets can wait. Or have two yourself. If you allow me, Signor Garrett, to touch my face,' he added, gesturing to the two- or three-day beard. 'Have another glass. I'll just be a moment. Giustina, if anyone comes, I am back a little after nine, maybe. Va bene, Signor Garrett?'

Ray made a gesture as if that, or anything else, were quite all right with him, and went off to get his overcoat.

Signor Ciardi was ready in a very short time, and even had on a shirt and tie.

'One thing,' Ray said as they walked out, 'let us not discuss problems tonight. Life, maybe, but not problems.'

Signor Ciardi seemed cheerfully of accord. 'And later we will see Luigi. I feel sure he will come.'

'Much later. I have an appointment at nine with a young lady.'

'Ah, si? Benone. Later then.'

In the Italian ambience of that evening, everything seemed possible to Ray.

19

Elisabetta, coming out of her house door, gasped at the sight of his bandage.

'It is not as serious as it looks,' said Ray, who had prepared this sentence beforehand.

She looked right and left before she closed the door and came out. They walked quickly to the right, the direction Elisabetta had always taken with him. 'I have just seen your picture in the paper,' she said. 'Just now, after dinner. I didn't say anything to my parents and they didn't notice the picture. They would not have let me see you tonight. Or the last time either, I think. But a fight with your father-in-law!'

'Where are we going? Let's go somewhere beautiful.'

'Beautiful?' she asked, as if nothing in Venice was.

Ray smiled. 'Maybe on the Piazza? Quadri's?'

She nodded, smiling, too. 'All right. The police are not look-ing for you?'

He laughed. 'I've made a complete statement to the police. This morning. You have read that. The police know where to find me. On Giudecca.'

'Ah, you have been on Giudecca!'

'Yes. And maybe we can talk about other things tonight.' Ray tried, by asking her how was Alfonso, the young man in the Bar Dino. But she did not want to talk about Alfonso.

'It is true, your wife was a suicide?' she asked, whispering, with a kind of awe, or horror.

'Yes,' Ray replied.

'And it's true, that your father-in-law pushed you into the lagoon?'

'Yes. And it is true that I am an art dealer. Or at least starting to be one. You see, some of the things I told you are quite true.'

She said nothing, but he felt that she believed him.

'But – and this is very important – I did not tell the police anything about the lagoon. You are one of only – two people who know. So if by any chance you have to speak to the police—' He immediately regretted that. 'You will not have to. There is no reason why you should have to. But I do not want you to tell anyone that my father-in-law pushed me into the lagoon.'

'Why not?'

'Because he is a very angry man, and he cannot help it.'

'He tried to kill you.'

'Oh, yes.'

'He is angry because of his daughter?'

They were in the Piazza now.

'That is exactly right. But I could not help what his daughter – what she did. And if you will, Elisabetta, I cannot talk about that tonight. I wanted to see you, because with you I do not have to think about any of that. I can just remember the early morning I first saw you – and remember the way you smiled when you were showing me the way to Signora Calliuoli's house.'

That pleased her, and it was so easy to say, because it was true.

They sat indoors at Quadri's. Elisabetta did not want champagne, so Ray suggested a pousse-café. He had a brandy. And for nearly half an hour, mostly thanks to Elisabetta, they managed to

223

talk pleasantly about things of no importance. Elisabetta asked him what kind of house he was staying in on Giudecca, and Ray was able to tell her a great deal about it and about Giustina and his red tile stove without mentioning Signor Ciardi's name, which Elisabetta was not curious about. She pronounced her pousse-café 'Strong', then said:

'You are the strangest man I've ever met.'

'I? I'm extremely ordinary. You are the strangest girl I've ever met.'

Now she laughed, leaning back in her chair. 'I know what a dull life I lead!'

That didn't make her dull to be with, Ray thought now. It was the freshness, the generosity of her face that he liked so much. And perhaps she would be delightful to go to bed with, and then perhaps not. It was a little strange to feel such joy in being with her, and yet to think it was really a matter of indifference to him whether they ever made love or not, and that he would certainly never want to marry Elisabetta. But he was as happy now with her as if he meant to propose to her, or as if she had said 'Yes' when he had. He wanted the pleasure to last a long while. 'What time must you be back tonight?'

'You see?' She smiled at him. 'No one else in the world asks me questions like that – eleven, I think. I told my mother I was going to see my friend Natalie.' Elisabetta giggled.

The pousse-café was indeed strong, Ray thought. 'You are very safe, because I have to be home a little before.' It pleased him to say 'home', and to be expected there, too.

'You have another appointment?' she asked.

'Yes,' Ray said, still feasting on her with his eyes, though now and again he looked away at the ornate decor of the old coffee-house, at the upholstered benches, so that the Venetian Elisabetta would have a proper setting in his memory.

She did not want another pousse-café.

They walked slowly back towards her house, as if neither of them wanted to arrive there. Ray thought of asking her to join him tonight with Signor Ciardi and Luigi, if he came, but it was not the lateness that made it impossible, it was that he did not want to share her with anyone. He would have to explain how he met her, or she might mention Signora Calliuoli. It was all too complicated. Ray wanted Elisabetta like a small enamel portrait that he carried in his pocket and showed to no one. And he felt that after tonight, he would never see her again, although there was no reason to feel that if he was going to be in Venice two or three days more.

'Good night, Elisabetta,' he said at her door.

She looked at him a little sadly. 'Good night – Rayburn,' she said, pronouncing it 'Rye burn,' and gave him a kiss on the lips, a kiss that he barely had time to reciprocate, then turned to her door.

Ray walked away, glanced back to see if she had gone in, and saw the disappearing tail of her coat, heard faintly the solid door closing. Not as stirring a kiss as the other two, he thought, and yet somehow much more real. At least, Rayburn Garrett had received it. She had called him Filipo the last time he had seen her. Ray walked slowly, as he had with Elisabetta, in a pleasant trance, heedless now of the people who looked at his bandage. Suddenly it seemed to him that love – erotic and romantic love – was nothing but a form or various forms of ego. Therefore the right thing to do was to direct one's ego to recipients other than people, or to people from whom one expected nothing. Love could be pure, but pure only if it was unselfish.

He stopped walking for a moment, and tried to think more precisely. It was an idea from the age of chivalry.

It was important that the objects of love be nothing but recipients, he thought again. Love was an outgoing thing, a gift that one should not expect to be returned. Stendhal must have said that, Proust certainly, using other words: a piece of wisdom his eyes had passed over in reading, yet which he had not applied to Peggy, he felt. Not that a specific had arisen with Peggy to which this might have been applied, but Ray thought he would have been wiser, even omniscient, if he had only thought of this abstract recipient-object when he had been with Peggy.

He went on, still in the beatific trance, towards Signor Ciardi's house.

It was ten past eleven when he got there. Luigi had not arrived, but was expected. And Signor Ciardi had a message for Ray which had been delivered by a police officer. It was a piece of folded yellow paper with an illegible signature:

Would you please telephone office of police 759651.

He hated doing it at that moment. 'I must telephone the police,' he said to Signor Ciardi.

Ray walked again to the bar-caffè.

Capitano Dell' Isola was not there, and Ray was passed on to another man. 'The Signora Schneider is very worried. She wants us to make sure you are still where you said. You are at the house of Ciardi?'

'Yes.'

'She spoke about a Signor Antonio Santini. You know him?'

'Yes,' Ray answered, somewhat reluctantly.

'She has spoken with him,' the voice said enigmatically. 'The Signora Schneider is worried that you did harm to her friend Signor Col-e-man.' The voice gave this information as impersonally as if it were a weather bulletin. 'She wishes us to report back where you are. That is all, Signor Garrett. Thank you.'

Ray hung up as the police officer did. Antonio adding his bit now? That was a sour note. Or Inez might be simply 'worried'. But it seemed that Antonio had done nothing to calm her. Ray walked back to Signor Ciardi's, wishing he had not to make the call. He tried to think of Elisabetta, as he had thought of her after leaving her, but the magic was gone.

'Rye-burn!' cried a voice behind him. 'A-oul! Ho!'

It was Luigi, trotting towards him.

'Hello, Luigi!' Ray answered. 'How goes it?'

'I saw your bandage a kilometre away!' Luigi said, banging Ray on the shoulder. 'How are you feeling?'

'Very well, thank you. I hope the doctor will remove this bandage tomorrow. To put on a smaller one, at least. People look at me as if I were Lazarus!' Ray said, in sudden good spirits. 'Like Lazarus of the grave!'

Luigi roared companionably. He pulled from under his arm a newspaper-wrapped bottle. 'A good Valpolicella for us.'

They rang Signor Ciardi's bell, or Luigi did, though Ray had his key. Giustina admitted them.

'Hey, I hope you gave that Col-e-man a good . . .' Luigi said as they crossed the courtyard.

Ray was glad of Luigi's happy acceptance of story, fact, counter-story, counter-fact. 'I did. He was almost unconscious.'

'Good. Where is he?' Luigi asked, as if Ray were certain to know.

'I don't know. He's hiding somewhere.'

In the kitchen all was merry and rather celebratory for five or ten minutes. Luigi's daughter's baby was due within a week. They had to drink to that in advance. But Luigi had not finished his questioning of Ray. How had the fight started? Why did Col-e-man hate Ray so much? Luigi sympathized with Ray over the suicide of his young wife, crossed himself, and made a wish, or prayed, that the Virgin Mary might forgive her, and that her soul might rest in peace. Just where was the fight, exactly? How big a man was Col-e-man? Was he crazy?

And with a cautious glance at Signor Ciardi, who was listening as attentively as if the story were all new to him, Luigi asked, 'And the night we encountered each other, you had not been with Col-e-man?'

Ray slowly shook his head, with a slight frown at Luigi, which he hoped conveyed that he did not want to talk about that. 'I'd been with friends,' Ray said, and drank from his glass.

'Friends!' Luigi said with a smile, and his short body bent suddenly at the waist, as it did a thousand times a day at his rowing, and he seized his green packet of Nazionale cigarettes on the scrubbed wooden table. His fingers looked huge, extracting a cigarette from the packet. His blunt head and utilitarian features suggested the ruggedness of a tree-stump. But his eyes twinkled warmly at Ray, and Ray remembered that this man had saved his life. Ray had asked Luigi not to tell anyone the lagoon story, and had even paid him not to tell, in a way. He had given Luigi fifteen thousand lire of the money Luigi changed for him. But Ray knew that Luigi would not keep the story much longer, maybe not even all of tonight, after a few more glasses, because what was the purpose now of keeping it?

'Why did you want to hide, dear Rye-burn?' asked Luigi Lotto through a cloud of smoke.

'I needed to be alone. To forget who I was. And I did – almost.'

'You were not afraid of Col-e-man?'

Luigi was convinced, Ray realized, that Coleman had pushed him off a boat into the lagoon. And indeed why shouldn't Luigi think he had? 'I was not afraid of him,' Ray answered.

Signor Ciardi, back in his comfortable sweater again, watched Ray as he spoke.

Luigi looked puzzled, but what might have been a sense of courtesy or a respect for Ray's privacy kept him from saying anything else. 'Life is a confusion, is it not, Paolo?'

Signor Ciardi ignored this, which he must have heard from Luigi many times before. He lifted a finger to Ray. 'The police. What did they want?' An automatic resistance to police, and strength like a fortress, showed in his heavy frown.

'They just wanted to know if I came back here,' Ray said.

Luigi was drinking his Valpolicella with relish. 'Dica, Rye-burn, you didn't give Signor Col-e-man too good a . . . did you?'

Again the word Ray didn't know. 'Certainly I didn't kill him,' Ray said, smiling. He looked at Signor Ciardi then and saw, in his lifted eyebrows, in his teeth that bit his underlip, a hint of doubt at this, though no unfriendliness at all towards Ray. 'But of course the police may think so until he is found. Tomorrow I shall go to Chioggia to look for him,' Ray said.

'Chioggia?' Luigi asked.

Ray explained why he was going, because Coleman had gone fishing there once.

'Who is the Signora who is the friend of Col-e-man?' Luigi asked. From his black blouse, he pulled a bent newspaper and looked for the item.

'Inez,' Ray said. 'Inez Schneider.'

'You know her?'

'Slightly.' Ray wished they would get off the subject. He sensed that they could never completely understand; with their different temperaments, they would have done things quite differently from the way he had. He sensed also that because he did not talk at great length, they thought he was concealing something. He was, of course. The lagoon story. Ray debated. Luigi was studying him, smiling a little, and Ray looked away from his eyes. If Luigi told it, if Signor Ciardi heard it, it might get at once to the police. The police might very likely pay a visit to Signor Ciardi, and perhaps they had this afternoon. 'Signor Ciardi, I hope the police did not disturb you today. With the message for me. Did they ask you any questions?'

'No, no. It was only one policeman. He asked me if I was Signor Ciardi and if you were staying here.' Signor Ciardi shrugged and smiled. 'Drink, Signor Garrett! Sit down!'

Ray sat down uneasily on a straight chair beside the table. He was thinking that Inez must have been told the lagoon story by

Coleman absolutely as it had happened, if Coleman had told her he had killed him. Of course, Inez wouldn't ever tell that to the police. Ray suddenly thought that Coleman had probably told Inez this *after* he had seen him, Ray, in the doorway of Harry's Bar. It would be like Coleman to boast about a thing like that which wasn't true. There was a kind of wild Colemanian humour about it. Ray smiled a little.

'That is better! He smiles!' Luigi said, watching him. 'Dica, Rye-burn – why do you protect Signor Col-e-man?' Luigi looked at him with an intense curiosity, his head tilted. 'You say you go to Chioggia tomorrow to find him. You should find him and kill him!' he finished with a laugh.

'Oh, no, no. Too dangerous. Do you think this is Sicily?' said Signor Ciardi, making the conversation even funnier to Ray, because Signor Ciardi took Luigi seriously.

'You're right, Luigi. Why do I protect him? Luigi, have you told Signor Ciardi about the night you found me in the lagoon?'

'Ah, no, signor! You asked me to keep that a secret!' Luigi clutched his shirt-front with emotion. 'Did you want me to tell him?'

'I don't care now if you tell him,' Ray said. 'I just don't want the police to know. I thank you for not telling anyone until now, Luigi.'

His word of thanks was lost on Luigi, who was gathering himself for a splendid dramatic effort. He narrated the story in the swiftest Italian, with gestures, in his dialect which Signor Ciardi understood perfectly, though Ray caught only a quarter of it.

Signor Ciardi nodded, laughed, sobered, became anxious, then gave a chuckle and a wondering headshake as Luigi's story poured forth.

'Then three or four nights later,' Luigi went on, and he told now of the nocturnal visit of Ray to his house on Giudecca. 'The miracle of this! To see him suddenly stand before me again – at my house! He stayed with us that night … My daughter's baby to come … We sent a messenger to you, dear Paolo …'

Luigi managed to talk for another two or three minutes.

Signor Ciardi's mouth hung appropriately open with wondering attention.

'And now this man,' Luigi wound up, extending an arm in Ray's direction, 'persecuted by the same Col-e-man— Were you *alone* with him on the lagoon that night?' he asked Ray.

'Yes. In a motor-boat,' Ray said.

'You see? Now this man' – with another fling of the arm – 'defends this man who twice tried to kill him! Why? Just because he is your father-in-law?' Luigi demanded of Ray.

And Ray thought of the gunshot in Rome, too, but he wasn't going to bring that up. 'No, no. He is angry because his daughter killed herself. He is like a man insane,' Ray said, with a feeling of futility, yet he felt he owed it to Luigi and Signor Ciardi to explain as best he could. 'And I myself was full of grief because of the death of my wife. Maybe too much grief to feel hate against Coleman. Yes, perhaps that was it.' He was staring at the scrubbed wood of the table as he spoke, then he looked up. It was easy to say it in Italian, the simple words that did not sound emotional or false, only like the simple truth. But his audience did not completely understand. 'Anyway, it's all understood now, all known—' His Italian suddenly slipped away from him. 'I am sorry. I am not speaking clearly.'

'No, no, no,' Signor Ciardi assured him, patting the table gently near Ray's forearm. 'I understand you.'

'I'll help you look for Signor Col-e-man tomorrow,' Luigi said.

Ray smiled. 'Thank you, Luigi, but you have your own work to do.'

Luigi came forward, holding out his square right hand, though not for a handshake. 'We're friends, no? If you have a job, I help you. At what time tomorrow do you want to go?'

Ray saw there would be no putting him off. And maybe it was not so much because Luigi was devoted to him as because the job fascinated him. 'At nine? Ten?'

'Nine o'clock. You come to my house. It's on the way. I know a boat.'

'What boat?' Ray asked.

'It doesn't matter. I know one. A friend.' Luigi smiled at Paolo. 'We Venetians have to help each other, eh, Paolo? You want to come, too?'

'I am too fat. I walk too slowly,' Paolo said.

'You have a picture of Col-e-man? No,' Luigi said to Ray, registering disappointment in advance.

'I can get one. It was in the newspaper two days ago. I can also describe him to you. He is fifty-two, a little taller than you, and heavier, almost without hair . . .'

20

Coleman, on Friday, 26 November, awakened unrefreshed in his scoop-shaped bed. The bed was even worse than that at Mario's and Filomena's, and the mattress seemed to be stuffed with straw which had long ago become hard-packed and now had no resilience whatsoever. His underlip was thrust out from the swelling of the cut inside his mouth, and Coleman hoped he wouldn't have to have it lanced. He pulled his lip down and looked at it in the mirror. A bright red slit it was, but without any sign of infection.

It was nine-twenty. Coleman supposed the family had been up for hours. He decided to dress and go out for a paper and a cappuccino. He was on his way to the door, when he encountered Signora Di Rienzo coming towards him with a breakfast tray on which he saw besides coffee and milk some cut pieces of bread, but no jam or butter. Of course, he had to stay and eat it, at a round dining-table with a lace square thrown over it. That was an example of the general awkwardness he found at every turn in the Di Rienzo house. His room was cold, and no one offered him any means of heating it, because it was assumed, Coleman supposed, that people were in bedrooms only to sleep, and then they were covered up. The living-room was also frigid, though a portable electric fire – which Coleman was too shy to turn on himself – was standing in it. Last evening when he wanted to use the bathroom (the toilet was there) someone had been in it, bathing. There was a fat maid who looked sixteen, and Coleman thought the Di Rienzos must be getting her free or employing her out of kindness, because she was mentally retarded. When Coleman said anything to her, she only giggled.

There was nothing in the morning papers that day about himself or Ray. He wondered what Ray was doing now, and where he was. The newspapers had not said where he was staying. Coleman wondered if the police would let Ray leave Venice, if he wanted to, or would detain him on suspicion of murder or manslaughter? Once more, Coleman wished that he had a chum who would write to the police about seeing a man rolled into a canal on Tuesday night. Then it occurred to Coleman that Ray could be looking in person for him. And if Inez had mentioned to the police that he'd been to Chioggia once fishing, the police might well come here. Or Ray might.

Coleman, on the street as these thoughts came to him, looked around quickly in the small square in which he stood, and frowned with uneasiness. The fact that there hadn't been the smallest thing in the paper, such as that the police were still looking for him, made Coleman feel they were going to look in Chioggia, and intended to surprise him. How much had Ray talked, Coleman wondered. Coleman had not before considered that Ray might have told them about being pushed into the lagoon, or about the gun in Rome, but maybe Ray had.

Mestre, Coleman thought, Mestre on the mainland. That was the place to go to. Coleman started to go into a barbershop for a shave, but thought he had better save every lira, and that he could find Signor Di Rienzo's shaving gear in the bathroom and make use of it. Coleman returned to the house numbered 43, which he had taken note of on leaving it, and pressed the Di Rienzo bell. He decided it would be wise to stay in all day today. Perhaps the Di Rienzos had some books.

Coleman managed his shave, and was lying on his bed reading – he had plucked up courage and asked Signora Di Rienzo if he could have an electric stove in his room, if he paid her a little extra – when at 11.30 a.m., the house began to fill with noisy children, at least ten, Coleman thought, and he opened the door slightly and looked out. Signora Di Rienzo was bringing trays of pastries to the dining-room table, and three children were squealing and chasing one another around her. The doorbell rang, long and loud, and Coleman felt sure more were arriving.

Somewhat angrily, he quit his room and walked towards the bathroom, knowing he would encounter Signora Di Rienzo or the fat maid, answering the door. He met the fat maid and asked:

'What is happening? A party for the children?'

The fat girl covered her pimply chin and mouth with one stupid hand and exploded, bent over, in giggles.

Coleman looked around for Signora Di Rienzo, and saw her emerging from the kitchen, this time carrying a large white cake with turquoise icing. 'Buon giorna,' Coleman said pleasantly for the second time that day. 'A birthday party?'

'Si!' she acknowledged brightly and emphatically. 'The little son of my daughter is three today.' She spoke very clearly for Coleman's benefit. 'We have a party today for twenty-two children. They are not all here yet,' she added, as if she thought Coleman could hardly wait for their arrival.

Coleman nodded. 'Very good. Benone,' he said, and resolved to get out of the house as soon as possible. Not that he disliked children, but the din! He refrained from asking the signora how long they were staying. 'I shall be going out for lunch,' he said, and Signora Di Rienzo, who had turned from him to go back to the kitchen, acknowledged this with a preoccupied nod.

Coleman went out, sat in a bar-caffè drinking an Espresso and a glass of white wine, and tried to think how he could get his hands on some money. He was wondering also if he dared write a letter himself to the police? He thought he should try. Write it now, post it from Chioggia, then go to Mestre. Coleman got a piece of paper from the barman, cheap paper with tiny blue squares, just the thing. He could buy an envelope at a tobacconist's. He had his ball-point pen. He sat at his table and printed in Italian:

26 November 19—

Sirs,
The night of Tuesday 23 November near the Ponte di Rialto I saw two men fighting. One man was on the ground. The other rolled him into a canal. I am sorry I was afraid to say anything before.
Respectfully,
Citizen of Venice

It had the right primitivity, Coleman thought, and one or two bits of bad spelling or grammar, he had no doubt.

Coleman got up. He glanced back at the table to see if he had left anything, and noticed that in the light in which the table stood, what he had written was visible on its red Formica surface. But as he stared, a boy removed Coleman's cup and glass, and wiped the table clean with one stroke of a wet cloth.

He didn't post the letter. He bought an envelope, then lost the heart to address it. He tore the letter up. It should come from Venice, first of all. His mistakes in the letter were American mistakes and not Italian, he feared. Best not to risk it.

Coleman did not want to go to the restaurant where the young Di Rienzo worked, as he did not want to get into conversation with him. Coleman supposed he had slept late this morning, as

236

he hadn't seen him in the house, and that he was probably on duty now. Coleman realized he hadn't a single possession at the Di Rienzos' and could just as well not go back, except that he had not paid them the five hundred lire for the night. Well, he might drop that into their mailbox. He needn't see any of them again. That was a nice feeling. Then he felt a pang as he thought of his drawing-pads, his sketches, his box of good pastels, his paints and brushes carefully selected in Rome for Venice, in the box at the Gritti Palace. But surely Inez would take care of them, wouldn't abandon them, if she left. He realized he didn't care if Inez left for France, even really if he never saw her again, but those five or six *drawings* – they were good drawings, and he could do at least three canvases from them. He longed to ring Inez, to see what she intended to do, to tell her to guard his drawings, but could he trust her not to tell the police he had telephoned, if he asked her not to? Coleman wasn't sure of this. Above all, Inez wouldn't do such a good job of pretending he had really vanished, if she knew he were alive.

He tried to imagine Inez believing he was dead. Would she eat the same breakfast at the Gritti, remove her stockings in the same way, standing on one foot and peeling them off inside out? Would her mouth turn a little more down at the corners, and would her eyes be puzzled, or sad? And his friends in Rome, Dick Purcell, Neddy, and Clifford at the F.A.O., would they frown for a minute, shake their heads, wonder what gesture of respect or humanity to pay, and find none, not knowing any of his family? Coleman looked up at the sky, a lovely blue-grey more blue than grey, and tried to imagine not seeing it, and, failing to do this, tried to imagine not seeing it after this instant. *My life is finished. Fifty-two years. Not a bad length of time, since many wonderful people like Mozart and Modigliani had less.* Coleman tried to imagine his loss of consciousness, not as anything taken away from the world or from space, but as a stopping of identity, and a most dreadful stopping of work and action. For one freezing instant, Coleman imagined his own flesh as dead flesh walking about, a subject for burial, apt soon to putrefy. That was closer to the truth, or what he wished to know, but the experience vanished as soon as he realized he was having it. He was, just now, devoid of ties of any kind. That was the mechanical though not the philosophical essence. A bump from someone behind him, a hurrying adolescent who murmured a '*scuzi*', made Coleman aware that he had been standing still on the street. He walked on.

He made inquiries about the boat and train to Mestre, then had a lunch of *misto mare* in a trattoria. On a scrap of paper napkin, he printed 'Grazie tanto', and wrapped this around a five-hundred-lire note. This he deposited at 2.30 p.m. in the Di Rienzos' well-polished brass letter-box. He was walking towards the fondamento to take a boat to the mainland, when he caught sight of Ray Garrett with a shorter Italian. They were walking towards Coleman, but were some distance away, and if it had not been for Ray's bandage, Coleman thought, he wouldn't have spotted him. Coleman drifted at once into a narrow street on his right.

But Coleman was not hurrying. Anger began to stir in him as he took five slow steps into the little street, and turned. His coat-tail brushed an orange off a shopkeeper's pavement display, and Coleman stooped and put it back. He saw Ray and the other man passing the opening of the street now, and Coleman followed. At least, he told himself, he could see when and if they left Chioggia today, or tonight. If they left today, they probably would not be back, Coleman thought, therefore Chioggia would be a safe place for a few more days.

But rational thoughts like these wilted before Coleman's rising anger and hatred. It was curious, Coleman thought, because since he had been in Chioggia he had felt no hatred against Ray, as if their fight had spent a certain passion. But the sight of Ray brought it all back. Coleman had even been aware of a vague reconciliation, which he never intended to admit to Ray or anyone, with Ray in the last two days. Now that equilibrium, of sorts, was gone, and Coleman knew he was going to boil over, that he would become as enraged as he had ever been, if he continued to look at Ray Garrett. Coleman felt the folded scarf in his pocket, fingers trembling nervously, clutching the silk convulsively, releasing it again. He wished he had the gun now, the gun he had thrown away in Rome that night, thinking that he had hit Ray. Coleman cursed his bad luck that night. He followed Ray and the other man slowly, because they were not walking very fast, and it was difficult for Coleman, because he had a desire to go closer and closer to Ray.

Ray and the other man parted at a street intersection, Ray making a circular gesture as he spoke to the Italian. Coleman watched only Ray. Ray was looking around in all directions, but Coleman was quite a distance away, and there were ten or twelve people between them in the small street. Ray turned left, and Coleman followed him, trotting a few steps at first, because Ray had vanished from sight. It occurred to Coleman that he, Coleman, might disappear utterly, permanently, not even collect his paintings in Rome – just hide himself for ever and make Ray live under the shadow of suspicion for all time – but Coleman realized that he not only couldn't bear to abandon his paintings, but he'd want to go on painting wherever and whoever he was; and what did the world do about people it suspected of murder, anyway? Nothing much, it seemed. To kill Ray was the only possible thing to do, his only real satisfaction. The instant he thought this, he caught sight of a length of grey pipe lying in the corner between the street and a house-front, and picked it up. It was about two feet long. Ahead of him now, Ray's head bobbed as he walked.

People glanced at Coleman, and edged a little away. Coleman carried the pipe pointing downwards, and tried to appear more relaxed. But my God, he swore in an agony of repression now, he'd swing this pipe in broad daylight for all and sundry to look at, and in just a few minutes' time.

Ray turned to the right.

Coleman approached the little street on the right very cautiously, thinking Ray might turn round and come out again, but Coleman saw that he was going on. Coleman felt a bitter but bold realization that his own life might end very shortly after Ray's, if the crowd set on him, but this fact wasn't daunting at all, and actually rather inspired him. His right hand took a harder grip on the pipe, thumb locked over fingers.

Ray turned right again, and when Coleman had made this turn he saw to his annoyance that Ray and his Italian friend had met up. Well, what the hell, Coleman thought, advancing slowly. Ray and the Italian were standing still now.

'Tonio! Don't forget the bread!' a woman's voice shrieked very near Coleman, from a first-floor window, but Coleman did not glance in that direction.

A woman stepped wildly out of Coleman's path.

'Hey, what are you doing?' asked a man's voice in Italian.

Coleman kept his eyes on the back of Ray's head.

Then Ray turned round, and immediately saw Coleman. They were only six feet apart.

Coleman lifted the bar. People ducked away from him. Ray's arms were spread, and he was half crouched. And something seemed to hold Coleman's arms in the air, something that paralysed him. He thought, *It's the Goddam people all around, the people watching!* A man shoved both his arms upwards – it was the little Italian with Ray – and, as Coleman's body was rigid, the shove took him off his feet and hurled him sideways, stiff, to the pavement. Someone was trying to wrench the pipe from his hands, but failed because Coleman's hands might have been welded to it. Coleman was aware of pain in his left elbow.

'Who is he?'

'What's the matter with him?'

'You know him?'

'*Polizia!*'

'*Nunzio! Come here!*'

A small crowd gathered, all talking, all staring.

'Ed, drop it!' That was Ray's voice.

Coleman fought against passing out. In his fall, he had hit his head, too. The pain in his elbow was horrible, and he had the feeling he wasn't breathing, or couldn't breathe. He snuffled loudly, his nose full of what he realized must be blood. Ray was tugging at the pipe in his hands, but had to give it up, because Coleman was refusing to let go. Then Coleman was lifted up by Ray and a policeman. The policeman jerked the pipe away in an instant when Coleman was holding it with only one hand.

'Edward Col-e-man,' Ray was saying to the policeman.

They began to walk. A few people trailed after them.

'He would have killed you *again*!' said the Italian walking with Ray, glancing back at Coleman.

They were in a police station. Coleman avoided looking at Ray. Coleman's overcoat was removed – they had been shouting at him to remove it, but he had ignored them – and, seeing it leave his arms, Coleman fought for it, because the scarf was in it. His jacket sleeve was soaked with blood from the elbow down.

'I want my coat!' Coleman roared in Italian, and it was handed back to him. He clutched it under his right arm.

They lifted his left arm, which Coleman now realized was limp. His jacket came off next. They sat him in a straight chair, and told him that a doctor was coming. He was asked questions, name, place of residence, age.

Ray and his Italian friend stood together on Coleman's left, the Italian staring at him, Ray's eyes touching him now and then and drifting away. Then Ray whispered something urgently to the

Italian, something negative, Ray pressing his hand down again and again in the air. The Italian frowned and nodded.

They went to Venice on a police launch, Ray and Coleman, the Italian friend and three policemen. They landed at the Piazzale Roma, and went to Dell' Isola's office. The detective Zordyi was there. Coleman's nose had stopped bleeding, but he could feel stickiness on his upper lip, and the handkerchief he was using was sodden. He was asked by Dell' Isola about the fight on Tuesday night.

'He hit me with a rock and tried to push me into a canal,' Coleman said. 'Fortunately for me, a man came along and he' – pointing to Ray – 'had to stop. He left me unconscious.'

'But did you not begin the fight, signor?' Dell' Isola asked politely. 'Signor Garrett said you followed him with a stone in your hand.'

Coleman took a breath through his mouth. 'I wouldn't know who started it. We met – and we started fighting.'

'Why, signor?' asked Dell' Isola.

'Why is my affair,' said Coleman, after the briefest hesitation.

Dell' Isola looked at Ray and Zordyi, then back at Coleman. 'The stone, signor. You found the stone, did you not?'

'And struck the first blow?' Zordyi put it in English, and said it in Italian for Dell' Isola.

The interrogation was irksome to Coleman. He felt a confusion of emotions – insult, abuse, injustice, boredom too, and they were weakening him physically with all this drivel. His arm tortured him now, although the doctor in the station at Chioggia had given him a pill, presumably against pain. 'I am not admitting anything about the stone,' Coleman said to the officer.

'Or the lead pipe in Chioggia?' Zordyi asked in English.

With his right hand, Coleman groped in his coat pocket, still holding the coat with his right elbow, until he found the scarf, but the coat slipped, and he was left holding the scarf alone. It embarrassed him at first, then he shook it at Ray in a clenched hand. 'By this I swear what I'm saying!' he said in English. 'My daughter's scarf!'

Zordyi chuckled. 'That's not her scarf. I heard about that scarf from Mme Schneider.'

'What does she know about it?' Coleman said.

'She knows from Ray Garrett – who bought it here,' Zordyi said.

'You're all lying!' Coleman said. 'Every one of you!' And Coleman saw that Ray seemed to break under this.

Ray walked towards Coleman with an anxious expression on his face, as if he were going to confess something. 'Try to calm down, Ed! You need a doctor. Un dottore, per piacere, Signor Capitano!' Ray said to Dell' Isola.

'Si, d'accordo, subito. Franco, chiama il dottore,' Dell' Isola said to an officer.

As Dell' Isola spoke, Coleman gathered his saliva and spat in Ray's face, hitting his right cheek.

Ray started to lift his right hand to it, then reached for a hand-kerchief.

His Italian chum, who had seen it, shouted something at Coleman that he could not understand. Ray turned away, like the coward he was. But Coleman's strength suddenly gave out, and he allowed himself to be led to a chair rather than fall on the floor. Everyone seemed to be talking now. The party was breaking up. Ray and his chum were talking to Dell' Isola's clerk, who was writing down what they said. Zordyi hovered. A doctor arrived, and Coleman went into another room with him and Zordyi. Coleman's shirt was removed.

There were murmurs of '*frattura*'. Two policemen stood about watching.

'Tell me what really happened that night on the Lido,' Zordyi asked Coleman, bending towards him with hands on his knees.

Coleman was aware of Zordyi only as a vague, physically large presence which disbelieved him, which was an enemy. Coleman did not look at him. Ray's chum might be a gondolier who had picked Ray up, and maybe Ray had told Zordyi this. Coleman said in Italian to a near-by policeman, 'Telephone to my friend Mme Inez Schneider, please, at the Hotel Gritti Palace. I want to speak to her.'

By 11 a.m. the next morning, Ray had collected his suitcase from the Pensione Seguso on the Zattere quay, and paid his bill, which they fixed at three days at demi-pension. They were very pleasant, asked no questions, and Ray added two thousand lire as tip for the maid. He had no post, as he had not asked anyone to write to him there.

But the young woman at the desk did look at him with some astonishment, and asked, 'You were wounded?'

'Just a cut,' Ray said. They were speaking in English. 'I am sorry for the trouble I gave you. Thank you very much for your patience.'

'Not at all. We hope to see you again.'

Ray smiled. That was kind, indeed!

'You want a porter?'

'No, thanks. I'll manage.' He went out carrying his suitcase. It was fairly heavy.

Out on to the terrace before the pensione, past the Ruskin house-of-work, on to the Zattere quay – but this was really the wrong direction. He had an appointment with Inez at noon at Florian's. Should he take the suitcase to Giudecca and come back? Ray decided to hump the suitcase with him. He crossed the island, and took a vaporetto at Accademia. With his suitcase, containing his worldly effects, or some of them, he had a terrible feeling of quitting something for ever as the boat left the Accademia pier. Inez had sent a message which had reached him just as he was leaving Signor Ciardi's that morning. He was to telephone her, and he had. She said that Coleman had come to the Gritti Palace early that morning – after an operation on his elbow the night before – to collect his things. Ray assumed, though Inez had not said so, that Coleman did not want to see her again. But Inez wanted to see Ray, and was leaving Venice that afternoon. Ray got off at the San Marco stop, and walked towards the Piazza, pausing now and then to stare into shop windows, as he had time to spare. The Bar Dino was not far away; he might pass by and have a coffee there but he did not really want to. And perhaps Elisabetta didn't work on Saturdays. But it pleased him to imagine her behind the counter as usual this morning, smiling at people, chatting with old customers. It pleased him equally to think of her at home, perhaps washing her hair, giving herself a pedicure, washing a sweater, or having a mild set-to with her mother or father about the dullness of life in Venice. And it pleased him to think of her getting married in another year.

The expanse of San Marco made again the vast 'Ah-h' in his ears, made him for a few seconds feel diminished, then somehow renewed his energy. He looked behind him for Inez, who would be coming from his direction if she came from the Gritti, but she was not in sight. A pigeon with one foot missing, but giving tit for tat among the peckers, hobbling about on his stub like an old sailor, made Ray smile broadly. He would look for him, he thought, next time he came to Venice.

He was not so early after all; it was ten to twelve, and as soon as he reached Florian's and looked in the Gritti direction he saw Inez in the Piazza. Her step was a trifle slower, but her head was still high. He went forward to meet her.

'Hello, Ray, hello,' she said, pressing his outstretched hand. 'My goodness, what a morning!'

'Was it so bad? Let's have something nice to drink. A Cinzano? Champagne?'

'A hot chocolate. I need comfort.'

They sat at a table inside.

'You are leaving, too?' she asked.

'I just picked my suitcase up at the Seguso. Late enough doing it,' Ray said. He ordered from a waiter.

'What happened yesterday? I think Edward is not telling me the truth.'

That was very likely, Ray thought. 'He came after me with a length of pipe.'

'Of what?'

'Pipe. The kind of pipe water flows through.' He made a circle with his fingers to show the size. 'But he never hit me. Luigi – an Italian I was with – pushed him aside, you see – and that's how he fell and hurt his elbow.'

'This was in Chioggia.'

'Yes. He must've spent a couple of nights there.'

'He said you were looking for him. To do him some harm.'

'Ah, well,' Ray sighed. 'I was looking for him to prove he was alive. It's quite simple.'

'He is a *madman*,' Inez said intensely. 'Absolutely out of his head. On the subject of you and his daughter.'

Ray remembered that Inez had said this during their first conversation. 'What happened this morning?' Ray asked.

Inez shrugged slowly but emphatically. 'He just arrived without even telephoning. But I knew he was in a hospital last night, and I tried to telephone him last night – but the place sounded like a madhouse and it was impossible. So this morning, he said, "I have come to get my things." So he did. Then he just said, "Good-bye".'

There were tears in her eyes, but Ray thought there were not enough to fall. 'The police aren't holding him, then – I hope?'

'I don't know. He said he was leaving for Rome, but I think he would tell me that no matter where he was going.'

'Did you hear anything from Zordyi?'

'Yes, he rang me after Edward left. He said – well, he thinks Edward is to blame for everything. After all, he said, a rock first, a piece of pipe afterwards.' Inez looked into space, her eyes empty. 'He does not believe that Edward did not do something to you the night of the Lido.'

Coleman hadn't broken down then. Ray felt a slight relief at that, though without knowing why. Then suddenly he did know why: he wasn't on the defensive or angry with Coleman any longer, and he could afford to feel sorry for him, even sympathize. Also Ray felt that Coleman would never make another attempt on him. Coleman had given his all on this last one. Ray could imagine Coleman's stubbornness, like granite, under Zordyi's questioning, and there was something admirable about it. Coleman had conviction, even if the conviction was mad. Ray hoped that he himself was not due for more questioning from Zordyi, or from the Italian police who had asked him to telephone once more. 'Zordyi said he was leaving?'

'Yes, I think today. He said Edward might be given a fine. I suppose that means no prison.'

Ray could see in her eyes that she hoped there was no prison. 'I suppose so. You know, I'm not pressing any charges against Edward.'

'You are very kind, really, Ray.'

Ray sensed that she was trying to feel more emotion than she had for this situation. 'And the Smith-Peters? Are they still here?'

'Yes, but leaving this afternoon. I think they did not even want to see Edward. It's too bad. You know, they are afraid of him now.'

It amused Ray, but he didn't smile. 'What did they say?'

'Well – after I told them about the lead pipe – I was not sure *what* it was until you explained – there were witnesses to that, no?'

'Yes.'

'They said, "It is horrible. Didn't he do something to Ray the night of the Lido?" I said to them, "No, because Ray said no." They were thinking – something like a needle of something to make you sleep or forget your memory.'

'Really?' Ray put his head back and laughed. 'And you? Will you see Edward again?'

'I think not. He is a man by himself, really.'

'A very interesting painter,' Ray said politely, and felt the conversation at an end. He looked around at Florian's interior, as he had looked at Quadri's when Elisabetta had sat opposite him. He would remember this scene with Inez. Her feeling for Coleman had not been strong, not strong enough to change her life. Coleman had been just an especially difficult lover, or whatever she cared to term him. All the passion seemed to be Coleman's. Ray had a sudden desperate sense of futility, and wanted to leave – to leave Inez to her destiny, which wouldn't be a penniless one, anyway, and to struggle on with his own. Inez proposed they go.

'You should have more confidence in yourself,' Inez said in the Piazza. 'Find another girl to marry.'

Ray had no reply to that.

She shook hands with him. 'Good-bye, Ray.'

'Good-bye.' He watched her walk towards the San Moisè outlet from the Piazza. He was going in the same direction, and after a moment, he picked up his suitcase and walked, but more slowly than Inez.

He took the boat that brought him to Giudecca.

Signor Ciardi had a telegram for him. Ray read it in the kitchen.

LEAVING 6 PM FOR NEW YORK. COLEMAN FREE. CANNOT
UNDERSTAND ITALIAN LAW OR MAYBE YOU. BEST WISHES.
ZORDYI

Ray smiled as he stuffed it in his pocket.

'Nothing bad? Good,' said Signor Ciardi.

Ray had told Signor Ciardi he would probably leave today. He had to see about a plane ticket. Signor Ciardi pressed him to have a glass of wine, then to have lunch – Giustina had cooked lasagne – but Ray declined the lunch. He answered Signor Ciardi's questions about police actions mechanically, not really seeing him or the kitchen or Giustina, yet feeling that he saw them profoundly, in their essence, their kindness, their – Ray groped to make his thoughts more definite, and could only come up with their ability to forgive. They had taken him in, he had given them some trouble, yet they were willing to be his friends. Ray quit the kitchen, embarrassed by his emotions. He went up to his room, and with pleasure put on another suit, wrinkled though it was from the suitcase. He packed his newer suitcase and came down again, aware of the two toothbrushes now in the larger suitcase, the old green one, the newer blue one. They disturbed him, being together, and he wished he had thrown away the old one. He left the suitcases in the kitchen, and told Signor Ciardi that he had to make a telephone call and would be back in a few minutes.

'Then there are the stitches,' he added, remembering suddenly.

'Si, oggi!' exclaimed Signor Ciardi. 'I send a message to Dottore Rispoli immediately!'

Ray thanked him. In the Italian manner, it would get done, he knew. The doctor would arrive, maybe a little later than he promised, but he would arrive and remove the stitches, and he would also be able to catch any plane for which he had a ticket. In the bar-caffè, Ray placed his first call to Alitalia, reserving a

250

ticket on a flight taking off at 10.45 p.m. for Paris, then, after arranging to pay the proprietor of the bar, he sent a telegram to the Hotel Pont Royal for a room. Then he rang the police.

He was able to speak to Dell' Isola.

Dell' Isola said, 'We do not need to see you again, if you do not care to ...' a long phrase which Ray took to mean lay charges against '... Signor Col-e-man.'

Ray said, as he had said yesterday, that he didn't.

'We shall merely fine him then as disturber of the peace,' said Dell' Isola.

Disturbatore della quiete pubblica. The phrase had considerable dignity, Ray thought. 'Very good, Signor Capitano.'

Back at Signor Ciardi's, Ray had some lasagne, after all. The new electric clock gleamed on the wall. Giustina looked at it every five minutes. Ray told Signor Ciardi that he was taking a late plane, but would have to arrive early to buy his ticket.

'Luigi,' Signor Ciardi said, 'he is working this afternoon. An unusual thing. He would like to see you off if you are leaving, he said. Maybe he is home by six. Shall I find out?' He was ready to dispatch a message from the street.

This could go on for ever, Ray thought, but he was pleased nevertheless, that Luigi wanted to see him again. Luigi was probably telling the lagoon story to various gondoliers. In time, Ray supposed, it would become embellished and exaggerated until it surpassed Luigi's most fearsome dragon stories. 'Thank you. Never mind, Signor Ciardi. I will write to him, I promise. That is, if you know his address, because I don't.'

Nor did Signor Ciardi know it by number. Ray at least knew Signor Ciardi's address – and he now thought a name would do in the neighbourhood, anyway – so he said he would write here, and Signor Ciardi promised to have the letter delivered. 'I must find out the news of the daughter's baby,' Ray said, and Signor Ciardi laughed.

The doctor did come around four, and the stitches were removed. A little soon, the doctor said, but there was no bleeding. Ray had an ugly patch where his scalp had been shaved, which he concealed as best he could by combing his hair over it.

At six o'clock, Signor Ciardi and an adolescent boy whom Ray had never seen before and who carried one of his suitcases, went to the Fondamento San Biagio, and Ray caught the boat for the mainland. Signor Ciardi would have accompanied him, but Ray dissuaded him. With a little encouragement he would have accompanied him to Paris, Ray thought, and when there would have sent for Luigi.

'Arrivederci!' Ray called. They had embraced three times. 'Addio, Signor Ciardi!'

'Paolo!' He looked back. 'Addio, addio, Rye-burn!'

The boat gathered speed. The lights of Venice twinkled, burned steadily, rose and fell with the boat's progress through the windblown water. Ray imagined, in the flickering lights of the San Biagio pier, Signor Ciardi and the boy waving, looking, though eyes might not see, waving their friendship on to him.